W9-ARR-700

THEY WERE BLAZING A TRAIL TO
GOLD COUNTRY . . .
BUT THEIR JOURNEY HALTED IN THE LAND
OF THE SIOUX. . . .

The man who was the leader of the band was one of the last to step into the clearing. Once in view he strode directly toward the prisoners and studied them critically. He was a tall Indian with a fiercely handsome face swatched with broad stripes of colored pigment.

Staring back at the Indian, John Bozeman noticed a glint of malice in his eyes.

"White pigs!" the brave spat in broken English. The backhanded blow he delivered to Bozeman's jaw caught the explorer completely off guard and sent him staggering backward. Next the Indian turned his attention to No Tongue Girl. Snarling some angry phrase, he caught the girl by the hair and began slapping her repeatedly with his open palm.

In an instant Bozeman's partner, Jacobs, was leaping forward in Girl's defense. "She ain't no whore!" he shouted. "She's my daughter!" He delivered a hard blow to the side of the Indian's head. Before he had a chance to strike a second time, several of the Sioux braves had him firmly and were beating him as they dragged him away from their leader.

When Bozeman saw his partner battered to the ground, he decided they all might as well go out fighting together. With a roar of anger he launched himself at the men who were beating Jacobs. . . .

JOHN BOZEMAN

MOUNTAIN JOURNEY

JOHN BOZEMAN
MOUNTAIN JOURNEY

Greg Hunt

A Dell/Banbury Book

Published by
Banbury Books, Inc.
37 West Avenue
Wayne, Pennsylvania 19087

Copyright © 1983 by Greg Hunt

All rights reserved. No part of this book may be
reproduced in any form or by any means without the
prior written permission of the Publisher,
excepting brief quotes used in connection
with reviews written specifically for inclusion
in a magazine or newspaper.

Dell ® TM 681510, Dell Publishing Co., Inc.

ISBN: 0-440-04340-9

Printed in the United States of America

First printing—July 1983

Chapter 1

April, 1863

The taste of the fresh buttermilk was like nectar to the lips of John Bozeman. It reminded him in a nostalgic sort of way of the Georgia homeland he had left behind four years before. It was then he had left to seek his fortune in the Western frontier regions.

Back home he could never have guessed what importance such little things would take on. But in the rowdy mining town of Bannack City, all sorts of values began to rearrange themselves into a new order. In Bannack City he was glad to pay up to fifty cents simply to enjoy the fleeting pleasure of a quart of buttermilk, and never mind the fact that once he could have had the same jar of milk free on the family farm back home.

Bozeman's fiery red hair and vigorous stride gave him an air of carefree self-assurance. At twenty-eight he was a man of medium height, but his husky shoulders and solid build were evidence he was no stranger to hard, physical labor. The features of his face were not excessively handsome. Yet the friendly expression usually found there indicated a man who was easy to get to know and like. He wore a pair of heavy trousers and a wool shirt that were well worn but clean. And sitting on his head at a jaunty angle was a sweat-stained felt hat.

Bozeman felt good as he strolled down the "main street" of Bannack City. In one hand he carried his Hawken rifle. In the other was his jar of buttermilk. And heavy over one shoulder he wore his pack.

After a winter of isolation and near starvation, the spring thaws had come at last. With them arrived renewed waves of wagons loaded with food, trade goods, and of course more immigrants seeking a fresh start and the chance of fortune in the gold fields.

Accompanying the arrival of the wagons was opportunity. Through a clever round of trading during the past few days, Bozeman had turned the cabin he had wintered in—along with two yoke of oxen and a Conestoga wagon badly in need of repair—into a string of four fine ponies, grub for six weeks and all the equipment he would need for an extended trip across the mountains. In addition, he had ended up with nearly fifty dollars worth of gold dust in his poke. The money wouldn't last long, but it was enough for a few necessities and a few luxuries, too.

He was strolling toward the edge of town in a crowd of about fifty men who were eager to see a scheduled bear fight. Big Jim Lafferty had come down out of the mountains the day before with a half-grown grizzly that he swore he had wrestled down and captured with his bare hands. He was offering a fifty-dollar prize to any man who would ante five dollars in gold dust and stay in a pit with the critter for ten minutes without being mauled to death.

The event promised to provide some of that season's

2

most rousing entertainment. The previous season, a crooked gambler named Mark Kershaw made his way to Bannack City and found himself being strung up from the crossbar of a half-finished cabin no more than half an hour after he had raked in his first ill-gotten poker pot.

Nestled along the banks of the Beaverhead River and east of the Beaverhead Mountain Range in the Idaho Territory, Bannack scarcely deserved the label of "city." It was really nothing more than a rough assemblage of squat log cabins and roughhewn buildings. But the founders of the place shared the universal trait of practically every person who undertook the arduous journey to this section of the wilderness. They had hopes of great prosperity. Most would not have come that far without those hopes.

As Bozeman neared the edge of the ten-foot square pit Big Jim had dug, he could hear the massive, bearded trapper taunting the onlookers to step forward and prove their manliness.

"C'mon, boys," he boomed out to the crowd. "Hellsbells, he ain't but just a little shaver! Why, I carried him half the way back slung under one arm whilst I led my string of animals with t'other, an' he slept at my feet at night like a cur pup. C'mon here! Who amongst you wants to show the rest what a man he is?"

As Bozeman crowded closer to the rim of the pit, he had good reason to doubt the accuracy of some of the things Big Jim was saying. The "cur pup" that the trader had brought back with him would weigh in at close to four hundred pounds. He snarled occasionally, and by the way he paced the dirt floor of the pit and glanced malevolently at the ring of spectators, it was obvious that he was dissatisfied with his situation.

Many in the crowd were not quite so prudent as Bozeman, who had decided immediately not to try to double his cash by fighting. The first to step forward was a tall, hulking young man whose clothes and ways labeled him as a new arrival. From his looks, Bozeman judged the newcomer to be no great shucks for brains. But he shifted his broad shoulders and thick arms powerfully and it was obvious that he considered himself an exceptional physical specimen.

He pulled out a small roll of cash from the pocket of his trousers and peeled off five crumpled greenbacks.

"Where's yer gold dust?" Big Jim scoffed, but he was not about to let his first customer get away for want of the proper currency.

The young man stripped off his homespun shirt and leaped confidently into the ten-foot-deep pit. For the first minute or so he and the bear merely circled one another cautiously, taking each other's measure and deciding on their separate strategies. The crowd was soon keyed up and watching expectantly. There was a scramble as a few of the onlookers made the last few side bets before the real action began.

Suddenly the grizzly snarled and reared up on its hind legs. In an instant he closed the distance between himself and the young man. Standing up, the bear was not quite as tall as its opponent. But what it lacked in height it more than made up for in bulk and power. The young contender ducked and dodged to avoid being locked in the animal's outstretched paws. But one paw lashed out, leaving a long row of gashes from shoulder to waist down the stranger's back.

At the sight of the first blood, the crowd began to swell with excitement. The encouragement called down into the pit seemed to be split evenly between the man and the animal, but because he was faster, the young man succeeded in getting around behind the bear. Immediately he locked one strong arm around the animal's throat, hoping to shield himself from the bear's menacing claws and teeth.

It wasn't long before both man and bear were growling ferociously at one another and soon the scene looked more like a primeval struggle than a simple contest designed to entertain. The man locked his teeth into the bear's ear. As he held on, he groped with his free hand across the animal's face, searching for his eyes.

Because his aim was poor, however, and before he realized what was happening, the bear had the bulk of the stranger's right hand gripped between its jaws. With a shriek the fighter lost his strangle hold on the animal and in another moment everyone watching knew the fight was finished.

"Enough?" Big Jim called down loudly.

The young man had wisely curled up in a ball and was desperately trying to protect his head and midsection as the bear raked his back and shoulders. But even from that position his squawking plea for help was unmistakable. Displaying a sort of calloused calm, Big Jim twirled a loop of rawhide rope down into the pit and caught the young grizzly around the throat. Then he took a couple of turns with the free end of the rope around a stout post nearby and began to pull, hauling the choking animal steadily away from its victim. When the animal was secured, Big Jim leaped down into the pit long enough to pass his bleeding customer up to safety. Then he was pulled up by a second rope.

"All right, boys," Big Jim boomed out once he had regained his footing at the edge of the pit and freed his bear, "you all saw what he done wrong, so you should know now it ain't no easy chore to outmuscle that critter. If a man's gonna whip 'im, he's gotta outsmart 'im. But I know it can be done, 'cause I done hauled that bear a sight better'n two hunnert miles, an' I'll give a half a pound in gold to any man who can find a single scratch on my hide that he made. Who's next?''

Remarkably, another man stepped forward and poured out the measure of gold dust that Big Jim required. He was somewhat shorter than his defeated predecessor, but by his buckskin outfit it seemed obvious that he was more wise to the ways of the wilderness. And his broad grin indicated that he was more in the mood to fight the bear for the fun to be had rather than for any reward he might gain.

He lasted for nearly three minutes, then was hauled up from the pit with his left arm dangling and his face raked horribly. But he was still grinning and drawling out his half-drunk admiration of the bear's fighting ability.

During the next hour, man after man tried his hand with the bear, but none could stay in the pit for the prescribed ten minutes. A few prudently called to be hauled out after only a moment in the hole, but most came out bloodied. A couple even had to be carried off to the nearby trading post for what turned out to be crude medical treatment.

Through it all, Big Jim was having a fine time watching his ''cur pup'' take on all comers. He was spending his money on whiskey nearly as fast as he took it in, but it scarcely seemed to matter to him. To a man of his sort, money was a luxury he enjoyed but could adequately do without.

The hills were full of game and there was plenty to drink because streams overflowed with fresh spring run-off. He had a hide tent to sleep in, a humble squaw to warm his bed and cook his food, a rifle for provisions and protection, and three horses for mobility. It was the only life he had known or needed for the past twenty years, but occasionally he would tip the jug with the best of them when the opportunity arose and he had the means to buy all the whiskey any man could hold.

The crowd was beginning to thin finally when it became apparent that there would be no more stout, foolish souls willing to pay for the privilege of a mauling by Big Jim's pet.

But then from the rear of the crowd one last man spoke up. Casually shedding himself of his rifle, powder horn, knife and other pieces of survival equipment he wore strapped in various places over his clothes, he stepped slowly forward. Bozeman and the others watched him with quiet surprise for a moment, unwilling to believe that he really was going to do what he appeared to be preparing for.

"Be you of mind to give him a throw, Jacobs?" Big Jim boomed out with a sarcastic grin.

"Reckon I am, Jim," the man stated calmly.

"A'right," Big Jim slurred. "But I'll warn you up front that I'm too damn drunk to dig a hole to plant you in today. When my critter gets done with you, we'll cover your carcass over with rocks an' me an' the boys will turn you under proper tomorrow. Will that suffice?"

Looking at the new challenger, Bozeman could easily imagine that Big Jim's predictions of the man's death were offered only half in jest. This man named Jacobs was neither as young nor as burly as any of the others who had gone down in the hole with the grizzly. His frame had obviously been honed lean and leathery by dozens of years of wilderness living. He appeared to be of the age when most old trappers and traders were about ready to settle down in some Indian village or settlement to pass their remaining years in peace. And yet lank though he was—a man of fifty-five or sixty winters and clad in the greasiest

7

of buckskins and leggings—he was preparing to pile down in the pit as readily as any of the young bucks who had come before him.

"I got no money, Jim," Jacobs admitted after he was ready to go down, "but I'll offer up this here rifle and fine-honed sheath knife forged of Swedish steel."

"It's a fair bargain against my fifty dollars," Big Jim conceded.

"Too fair," Jacobs put in. "If I win, I want the fifty and the bear, too."

Big Jim looked around at the other men nearby, seeing if they were enjoying the humor of the situation. "Done, you old weasel-skinner," he guffawed loudly. "Hell, if you stay down in with the critter for ten minutes, I'll even throw in my squaw to chew your boots soft on cold winter mornings!"

"Nope, I got me a squaw up to the Flathead regions," Jacobs replied. "But I will take the bear."

With the agreement made, Jacobs turned back to the pit as if to leap down inside. But then he did something that made all the other men there stare at him in puzzlement and surprise. He unstrapped one of his moccasins along with the high leather legging attached to it and cut the toe out of the moccasin. Next he strapped the whole outfit around his right arm so that only his fingers protruded from the end where the moccasin toe had been cut away. And finally he took the heavy leather pouch which he had worn on his side to carry shot and other small items, emptied it on the ground and pitched it into the hole ahead of him. The crowd was quiet and curious when at last he sat down on the edge of the hole and slid down into the pit with the bear.

There had been well over an hour of battle and the grizzly was nearly insane with rage. After the first few opponents the animal had ceased to do any circling or calculating. All of the last men before Jacobs had found themselves under immediate attack when their feet touched ground in the hole.

But unlike the others, Jacobs seemed to welcome the attack. He did nothing to avoid the animal's charge. In fact, the only thing he did do was lean down to the ground briefly to pick up a stone slightly smaller than a man's fist.

"If you're of a mind to bean 'im with a rock," Big Jim boomed, "then you'd best find you a bigger one than that!"

But Jacobs was beyond listening to anything that was being said above him. All his concentration was focused on the animal in front of him as the bear reared up and moved in for yet another attack.

Most of the other contenders had tried to best the grizzly with superior speed and agility, but Jacobs stepped right in between the animal's outstretched paws as if he were being welcomed in an embrace. It was at that moment that Bozeman and the others realized what he had in mind. As the bear opened its mouth wide and leaned its head forward to clamp down on anything that came within range, Jacobs plunged his leggings-wrapped right arm straight in the animal's mouth and forced the stone far down its throat.

By then the bear had already enveloped his opponent. But the stone lodged in its throat caused a moment of panic and rage and allowed Jacobs to slip free. For a minute the animal was frantic, as if unable to decide whether to press the attack or to clear the mysterious obstruction from its throat. With surprising agility, Jacobs snatched his leather pouch from the ground, maneuvered until he was behind the bear and jammed the pouch down over the bear's head. When the drawstrings were pulled tight, the gagging animal was successfully blinded. It was only a matter of staying out of its way until it finally choked to death.

When the contest was all finished, John Bozeman stood shaking his head in admiration. From down in the pit, Jacobs looked up with the first smile to appear on his face since the ordeal began and asked, "Will you concede my victory, Big Jim, or should I stay down here for the full ten minutes anyway?"

"I'll concede you're a rogue and a deceiving scoundrel, John Jacobs," Big Jim roared down in drunken anger, "an' I'll concede that it's going to be a damn sight harder for you to ever get back up out of that hole than it was for you to get in!"

All around Big Jim the other men grumbled disapprovingly. Most agreed that Jacobs had committed no wrong against Big Jim. He simply had used his cunning to win what others had failed to win with sheer brawn.

But Big Jim Lafferty was of a different mind entirely. Pulling two percussion pistols from the belt of his buckskins, he began to wave one in the general direction of the crowd. The other he pointed down in the pit where Jacobs stood.

"By gawd, no man bests me with connivery and lives to boast of it," he swore bitterly. "We've rode us a few trails together, John, but we've settled our debts square before and now I owe you nothing. I'm sendin' you to the devil instead, an' when you get there you can tell 'im I'll probably be along soon after."

After drawing a clumsy bead on Jacobs, Lafferty hesitated an instant too long. He never even caught a glimpse of the young Indian girl easing up behind him. She plunged her thin dagger into his back and gave him a hard shove forward toward the pit. Almost simultaneously both pistols discharged, but Big Jim's aim had been disrupted and the bullet meant for John Jacobs plowed harmlessly into the dirt bank. The round from the second gun ripped through the hand of one man in the crowd and embedded itself in the thigh of another.

No one tried to seize the Indian girl. If Big Jim was dead, they thought, it was more or less his own doing, and if he was not yet finished, he might soon be for wounding two men without just cause.

Big Jim wasn't dead, though, and after duly withdrawing his rightful fifty dollars from his fellow trapper's pouch, Jacobs even went so far as to help a couple of others haul the wounded man's unconscious body up out of the pit. Big Jim's squaw appeared from somewhere nearby and dragged him off feet first to tend to his wounds. Nobody seemed to express much concern over how seriously he was hurt or whether he would live or die. The entertainment was finished and soon the crowd dispersed.

But John Bozeman stayed on. He was intrigued by this wizened man who had done what so many others could not. And he was curious, too, about the young Indian girl who had saved his life.

Jacobs set to work immediately on his prize, drawing his pouch from over the animal's head as he called up, "Girl, fetch my skinning knife from the horses and then round me up a good long pole to lay across the top of this pit. I'll skin this critter out down here and then quarter it before I try to raise it up."

Without a word the girl moved off to obey.

In a moment, when Jacobs noticed Bozeman still nearby, he asked, "You want to buy any of this bear, young feller? The hide'll go for twenty, tanned with the hair on. You can have fat for cooking at eight cents a

11

pound and meat for fifteen. If you ain't never ate no bear, you're in for a treat.''

"Eight of us that were snowed in winter before last down in Colorado ate us a black bear,'' Bozeman told him, ''and none of us had any complaints back then. But when there's other fare available, I'll pass on the bear meat.''

"Suit yourself.''

"I *will* help you skin it out for a portion to sell, though,'' Bozeman offered, keeping his reasons for doing so to himself.

No Tongue Girl ladled another bowlful of bear stew out of the cooking pot for John Bozeman. Then she returned to her place on the far side of the campfire, where she busily repaired the moccasin that John Jacobs had damaged earlier in the day. Despite what Bozeman had said about his taste for bear meat, he admitted to himself that the stew he was eating was one of the best he had been served in quite a while.

No Tongue Girl did actually have a tongue in her mouth, but a series of ugly scars across her throat bore witness to how she had come by her name. Jacobs explained that his thirteen-year-old, half-breed Flathead daughter had been mauled by a badger at an early age. Her throat had been damaged to the point where she was never again able to speak.

Jacobs himself had lived with the Flatheads as a trader and trapper for over thirty years, much preferring that tribe to most of the others that inhabited the northwest portion of the continent.

"The only reason I didn't stay with them,'' he explained, ''was because of the wife I had. Proud Belly was such a shrew that I simply had to get away from her occasionally to keep ahold of my mind.''

Bozeman could tell that the old trapper's complaints were only half-serious. If Jacob's wife had made his life that miserable, he would have traded her off or sent her away. Probably, Bozeman figured, Jacobs' marital problems provided him with the excuse he wanted to exercise his wanderlust.

A good part of the afternoon had been spent butchering the grizzly bear and hauling the meat up out of the pit. But the work had paid off just as Jacobs had known it would.

Bear fat was prized in areas where most men had to eat their meat roasted for want of any sort of grease to fry with, and many people in the area seemed to enjoy the heavy, pungent flavor of the meat. By evening Jacobs had enlarged his fortune by nearly twenty-five dollars from the sale of meat and fat. Little remained of the animal but the skin, which Girl had already begun to prepare for tanning. Bozeman accepted two dollars, a fine supper, and Jacobs' companionship for the night as payment for his labor.

When dinner was over and the men were working on their second cup of coffee sweetened with Bozeman's sugar, the two settled contentedly around the fire for a period of peaceful conversation.

''So you say you got the gold fever, huh, boy?'' Jacobs teased with a knowing chuckle, alternating contented puffs on his pipe with swigs of the scalding coffee.

''I'm here, aren't I?'' Bozeman grinned.

''Like the rest of us damn fools,'' Jacobs answered. ''But you know the funny thing about my being here, John? I tell myself that I come down from the North to look for gold, but I don't even know what I'd do with the money if I did make a big strike. If I got a horse to ride, meat for my belly an' a woman to tend my fires, that's all I ever need or want. I guess it just has more to do with being where things is going on."

"Well, I came for the gold and I guarantee you I'd know what to do with it," Bozeman assured him. "But I guess my thinking has changed some since I lit out from Georgia four years ago headed for the Colorado gold fields. I saw down there what a miserable life prospecting is, and I learned, too, that there's a damn sight more losers in the game than even small winners.

"I guess I still have the bug some or I wouldn't have come rushing up here when word got out about the strikes they were making near here in Grasshopper Gulch. But you know one thing that's finally started soaking into my head after all this time, Jacobs? It's that the men who seem to be making good money and hanging on to it aren't the prospectors at all. It's the men they turn to for goods and services."

Jacobs cackled out loudly and exclaimed, "Why, it's always been that way, boy, clean back to the days when this wild country wasn't used for nothin' more than trappin' an' tradin' and Indian fightin'. Once a year we trappers'd have ourselves a grand big shindig that we called the Rendezvous. We'd bring in all the hides we'd collected for a whole year an' trade them for supplies an' whiskey an' the like.

"But after the two weeks of Rendezvous, most of what we'd worked for all year would be blowed on high times. It was the traders that brought the supplies in who headed back to the States with the profits. That was the way of things then an' I s'pect it ain't that much different with these here gold diggers."

"So the thing for a smart man is to figure some way to make money from the men who're digging fortunes out of the ground," Bozeman announced. "I've spent a long boring winter studying on the matter, and that's the conclusion I came up with."

"In that case," Jacobs grinned, "I wished we'd met last fall so's I coulda saved you a whole winter of head work. But all that is providin' that what a man wants out of this country is money an' such."

"It'll do for my purposes," Bozeman told him.

"An' have you got yourself a way figgered out how to get it, too?" Jacobs asked.

"Maybe," Bozeman replied. "Maybe." The fact was that he had come up with an idea over the winter that had the potential of becoming a very lucrative enterprise. But it was not something he thought he could handle by himself, and until he'd met John Jacobs, he hadn't run across anyone he felt easy enough with to discuss the matter.

Bozeman picked up a twig and poked the fire reflectively. Then he glanced up and saw that Jacobs was looking at him, too. The old man's eyes, Bozeman judged, said that somehow their destinies were soon to merge.

Chapter 2

In the early 1840s the first trickle of land-hungry immigrants headed west from the territory that was then considered the United States. Undertaking a perilous journey across the Great Plains and the Rocky Mountains, they traveled toward what rumor depicted as a prosperous West Coast region known as Oregon Country.

Those first pioneers had very little concrete information to guide them. They found their own passes between the rugged mountains and their own fords across the rushing rivers, often relying on mere scraps of information provided them by mountain trappers and an occasional friendly Indian tribe. Most reached the Oregon Country and enough thrived there to send word back that there was plenty of free land available for the taking.

As the migrations across the continent became an annual event, a set trail was established. It was known by various names, but the two most common were the Emigrant Trail and the Oregon Trail.

The Oregon Trail had various starting places along

17

the Missouri River, although Independence and Westport, Missouri, were two of the most common. The trail led northwest to the Platte River, then followed the river along to the junction of the North Platte and the South Platte. After crossing the South Platte River, it followed the North Platte to Fort Laramie and then to present-day Casper, Wyoming. It crossed the Continental Divide in the Rocky Mountains at the broad, level South Pass, then traversed a stretch of rugged country to a divide near Fort Hall on the Snake River. From there it led to Fort Boise, stretched across the Blue Mountains, and finally reached on to Fort Walla Walla and the Willamette Valley in the Columbia River region.

The Oregon Trail represented a hazardous, six-month journey from civilization into the most perilous wilderness regions. But to people who had little to lose except unceasing hard work and little hopes for a better life, it was also the road to opportunity, adventure and a new beginning.

In those early years the vast area between Missouri and the Oregon Country was nothing more than a great wilderness. Hostile Indians often blocked the way of the travelers, as did dozens of rivers and streams, steep mountain trails and passes, and a multitude of other unpredictable dangers and obstacles. But for twenty years the wagons never stopped rolling westward.

In the early 1860s, at about the same time that the Nation was plunging itself into Civil War, some unknown prospector turned up gold ''colors'' in an unfamiliar stream in the northern Rocky Mountains. It was that simple find that gave the entire region new value.

Within months, hordes of gold-hungry hopefuls began pouring into the area from the east, from Colorado to the south, and from the Oregon Country and California to the west. All were seeking the promises of wealth.

Towns and settlements sprang up quickly as word spread that a particular gulch or stream bed contained placer deposits of gold. In a matter of only a few years, an area contained within what is present-day southwest Montana, northwest Wyoming and eastern Idaho became a bustling center of growth, commerce and greed.

Roads were necessary to get to these new settlements. Soon paths began to diverge from the old established trails to accommodate the pilgrims headed in new directions. Prospectors, traders and others found ways to get to the gold fields.

To get from Fort Laramie on the South Platte to the new settlement of Bannack, for instance, a party on horseback or in wagons had to cross the Sweetwater River three separate times, then ford the Little Sandy and a fork of the Green River. At this point their journey was far from over. The Wyoming Range had to be crossed, plus five tributaries of the Snake River, the Centennial Mountains, the Tendoy Mountains, and finally the Beaverhead River, for a total of several hundred miles.

But in the spring of 1863 this route was the only southern one leading to the gold fields. And until something better came along, it had to do.

"Jes' spoutin' off without givin' the matter much thought," John Jacobs scoffed. "I'd say your scheme's as harebrained as they come an' if you tried it you'd be as crazy as a betsy bug on a hot rock."

"Wellsir," Bozeman conceded, "maybe I'd rather hear your reaction *after* you've given it some thought."

"You might or might not," Jacobs told him soberly. "In the first place, them lands you're talking about crossin' were ceded to the Crow, Blackfoot an' Sioux by treaty as their exclusive hunting grounds. An' in the second place,

I've fit all three of them tribes at one time or another in my span, an' I can tell you I'd druther jump back down in another hole an' take on another grizzly barehanded than to go out an' face 'em again. I tell you, John, them Indians out to the Bighorn regions east of here are plumb mean, especially the Sioux!''

"I've heard that," Bozeman said. "But I've also heard in the four years I've been out west that—"

"Boy, don't try to tell me about Indians!" Jacobs interrupted with marked irritation. "I been roamin' these here Rocky Mountains for nigh onto ten times your four years an' I s'pect there ain't much new you're going to spring on me about Indians at this stage! I was swappin' furs an' threats an' lies with the Sioux before you was even a twinkle in your daddy's eye. Me an' Jim Bridger are two of only a few white men who ever outstole horses from them thievin' Crow. An' back in '41 me an' Tom Fitzpatrick wintered for four months on the run from a Blackfoot war party that swore our scalps would hang on their belts before the valleys greened up for spring. When you done that kind of livin', then's the time you come back an' tell me all you know about Indians!"

For a moment Bozeman puffed on his pipe in silence. He realized he had struck a nerve and wondered if he had been wrong to bring up his idea in the first place.

He had spent the previous night with Jacobs and his Indian daughter in their camp a few hundred yards outside Bannack City. After a bear stew breakfast they had spent much of the day soaking, scraping and stretching the grizzly bear hide in preparation for tanning. By late afternoon they had attached the hide to a stretching frame Jacobs had built from green cottonwood branches. The remainder of the work had been left to No Tongue Girl.

A few minutes earlier the two men had settled in the

shade of a broad aspen tree to relax and enjoy a bowl of tobacco while Girl built up the fire and hung several strips of bear meat on a spit to roast for supper. It was then that Bozeman had decided to lay his plan out openly before Jacobs and get his reaction to it. But things were not working out exactly as he had hoped. He had not been prepared for the kind of stinging criticism he was receiving.

And yet he was convinced that Jacobs had the expertise he wanted. He needed the old man and knew he had to figure out some way to make him cooperate. He decided impulsively that this was no time for timidity. Believing that, he said, "They say that at sixty, Jim Bridger still fears no man, red or white, and that he still goes wherever he pleases and does whatever he takes a notion to. How old are you, John?"

"I've been fifty-seven summers on this earth," Jacobs answered darkly. "And though I won't say there's no man I fear, I will say there's none I won't face if the need comes. You're about to find that out, young feller."

"It's not my aim to insult you or to challenge you to any sort of fight," Bozeman commented respectfully. "I would like to challenge you with an opportunity, but you seem already to have set your mind against me. It frustrates me that you won't even permit me to speak my piece."

"In brief or in detail it's plumb crazy," Jacobs insisted. "The Sioux won't let you blaze a wagon road across their prime hunting grounds. An' that's the long and the short of the whole matter."

"But would you do me the service simply of *listening*?" Bozeman pressed. "In all your travels, surely I am not the first cracked-brain to ever warm your ear with a suicidal scheme!"

"You are not, my boy," Jacobs confessed, breaking

forth at last with an amiable grin. Pulling his pipe and tobacco from his pouch, he settled back against his saddle more comfortably, signifying that he was willing at last to let Bozeman have his say without interruption.

"The way I see it is this," Bozeman began, starting almost at once to sketch a map in the dirt between them. "The main problems that people face in getting to these new gold fields is the stretch of territory between, say, Deer Creek Crossing on the North Platte River to here at Bannack. The Oregon Trail might suffice to carry folks on over to the West Coast, but men with the scent of gold fresh in their nostrils want a faster way to get there, even if it means facing more danger along the way.

"Now I've talked to enough of the early mountain men like yourself to know that there's better land routes available from the North Platte to here than the one the Oregon Trail follows. What if a man struck out north from Deer Creek instead of heading west toward South Pass? He could hang to the east of the Bighorn Mountains, crossing the Powder River here, the Tongue here, the Bighorn here and the Yellowstone here. When he finally pushed into the edge of the Rockies he'd be right on the doorstep of the gold fields without ever having had to fight the mountains at all. And if my figuring is right, this new trail would actually be about four hundred miles shorter than the old one. That could be a savings of nearly one month's travel!"

"Aye, but at what cost?" Jacobs could not refrain from interjecting. "An extra month is a lot easier for most men to spare than the hair on their heads."

"The Indians wouldn't like it. That's a fact I don't deny," Bozeman agreed. "But if the people traveled in large, well-organized groups—if they were heavily armed and ready for a fight—what could the savages do to them?"

"A'plenty if they were of a mind," Jacobs advised.

22

"Traveling in large groups would help, but still they would have to expect to suffer losses. That's because the Indians would never permit a road to be cut through their lands without a fight. You might as well face that fact."

"All right, so we'd fight," Bozeman proclaimed with bravado. "But we'd still get through. And think of the possibilities. If we put together a train of two hundred wagons and charged four dollars per wagon for our services as guides, that would be four hundred dollars apiece clear profit at the end of the line. And it's not unthinkable that we could bring through two or even three wagon trains per season. Tell me, John, have you ever even seen twelve hundred dollars at one time, let alone had that much yourself?"

"I can't say as I have," Jacobs responded, "nor have I cared to since I was about your own age. Fifty or a hundred dollars I can understand. It will buy me powder and lead for my rifle so I can eat. It'll put a quart of whiskey in my belly an' a new calico skirt on my girl. It'll buy salt an' blankets an' suchlike things that I need for the winter. But twelve hundred dollars? I'd say a sum that size would likely only buy me an ounce of lead in the back from the first scallywag that heard I had it an' decided to wait behind a rock for my passing."

"Well, I admire your simple dreams," Bozeman sighed, scarcely concealing the disappointment in his voice, "but permit me the option of not sharing them. I've told myself that someday when I return to Georgia it will be atop the finest white stallion that money can buy. I want my saddlebags to be filled with the wealth I've earned in the wilderness. In two or three seasons of guiding travelers across my trail and perhaps bringing along a few freight wagons of my own, too, I could have that dream and return home a wealthy man.

23

"But I suppose I just chose the wrong man to share my plans with. After yesterday's piece of business with the bear, you have the money for your salt and your blankets and your calico for Girl, so I suppose now you can go back to the Flatheads a happy man."

Jacobs puffed up a rich cloud of tobacco smoke. It enveloped his face, nearly concealing the patient smile there. "Did I ever tell you straight out I wouldn't go along?" he asked.

"You might as well have said it outright," Bozeman answered. "It's clear that you consider my plan nothing more than a fool's errand."

"True," Jacobs chuckled, "but there's times that I've wondered if this frontier would have been populated at all if it wasn't for the fools of the world who just couldn't seem to stay out of it.

"I've talked your plan down, John," he went on, "because I wanted to test your resolve an' take the measure of your determination to go through with it. I'll not ride any trail with a middling sort of man. Like I said, it's life an' death out there."

"You mean you actually might consider coming with me?" Bozeman asked in surprise.

"I'll do just that," Jacobs said calmly. "In my span, I've risked my life for an ounce of strong drink or a pretty woman's favors on more than one occasion. So why not to help a young friend find out if his dreams are made of iron or smoke?"

A broad smile spread slowly across Bozeman's face. Impulsively he reached out to clasp Jacobs' hand in a firm handshake.

"It's a little late in the day to break camp," Jacobs remarked, "an' I have to admit my old bones are callin' for rest after the day we've put in. So how about if we commence tomorrow morning?''

"You mean you're ready to leave so soon?'' Bozeman queried in amazement. After all the weeks and months he had spent dreaming of his venture, it was hard to realize that he would be starting out to fulfill those dreams so quickly.

"If you can rustle up an as-is buyer for that hide while I'm over to the trading post laying in a few supplies for the trip, why not tomorrow morning?''

"Why not?'' Bozeman echoed happily. "By Jove, why the hell not?''

Chapter 3

They first spotted the five distant riders from a rolling hilltop where they had paused to let their horses blow. Jacobs noticed the men first, which was no special surprise to Bozeman.

"Indians, I'd say," Jacobs announced, staring off into the distance through eyes narrowed to thin slits against the harsh, midday sun. "Mebbe Crow, mebbe Blackfoot." Bozeman's pulse quickened. These would be the first Indians they had encountered during the first eight days of travel.

"Do you think they mean to bother with us?" Bozeman asked, trying with little success to speak as calmly as his companion.

"I'd say so, one way or t'other," Jacobs told him. "They prob'ly cut our trail a few miles back an' decided to pick it up 'cause of that shod pack team of yours. But with any luck they'll just be Crow out to steal or beg for anythin' they can get."

"And without luck . . . ?"

27

"If they're Blackfoot, then they might be out to take somethin' a little more personal from us than a slab of bacon or a couple of ponies."

Jacobs studied the distant specks a moment longer. Then he turned his horse, started down the far side of the slope they had just ascended and was out of sight temporarily. No Tongue Girl went next and Bozeman came along last, leading the string of four horses which bore provisions for the journey.

"We won't ride fast enough to make 'em think we're running away, but we won't stop an' wait neither, 'cause I don't want 'em believin' that we're all that fond of the idea of meetin' up. Up ahead a couple of miles or so there's a series of draws an' box canyons. We can hole up there to wait. If this thing comes to a fight, I want it to be on ground I choose."

Tensely Bozeman began to check over the loads in the Hawken rifle and in the two pistols he carried. Counting his three guns, Jacobs' rifle and pistol, and the small pistol Girl carried in her sash, they could get off six shots without having to reload. That knowledge gave him a measure of reassurance. Still, the thought of actually having to point his weapon at a man and letting the hammer fall made his blood rush.

Jacobs began to talk to his daughter in their curious Flathead tongue. Occasionally the girl nodded or grunted her understanding. Bozeman was curious about the conversation, but since Jacobs didn't offer any explanation, he didn't ask for one. He assumed the old man was simply giving his daughter some instructions and reassurances about the risky situation they would soon be facing.

Their small party had made good time since leaving Bannack on the first of May. Now—by the eighth—they had already crossed the Madison and Gallatin Mountain

Ranges and had left the worst of the Rocky Mountains behind them. The day before, they had forded the Yellowstone River just south of some distant peaks Jacobs had identified as the Crazy Mountains. At the present time they were traveling on a generally southeastern course deep into Indian territory.

Riding across the rolling hills and the broad valleys of the Yellowstone drainage basin, Bozeman could easily understand why the Indians would want to protect this refuge from any incursions by white men. Game was so abundant all along the route that except for staples like flour, salt and coffee, they'd scarcely needed to dip into their supplies of provisions. The ground cover alternated between thickly forested hilltops and lush, grassy valleys. In addition, fresh water was abundant in the myriad small streams they encountered. But what was good for the Indians would also be good for the wagon trains of immigrants and traders Bozeman hoped soon to be leading through this country.

As they began to near the series of draws Jacobs had mentioned, the trapper began to slow their pace as he studied the terrain ahead. The hill that rose up in front of them was scored in several places by deep ravines. The creeks coursing down them joined at the base of the hill to form a lovely stream. While Jacobs searched for the best ravine in which to make their stand, Bozeman divided his time between gazing at the terrain ahead and casting numerous glances back to mark the progress of the Indians.

At last Jacobs made his choice and led them into the mouth of the nearest ravine. There he stopped his horse a few feet into it and dismounted. On either side of him the steep walls of earth and stone rose for more than twenty feet. Bozeman noted approvingly that it would be next to

29

impossible for anyone to ride around to either side and approach them from behind.

Jacobs encouraged his horse to wander a short distance farther up the draw, then told Bozeman, ''Take the mounts an' pack team an' picket them on back out of our way. Then bring your rifle an' come back with me. We'll stand our ground here so the only way they can reach our goods an' animals is to go over us.'' Bozeman moved to comply as Girl rode a few feet farther into the draw and remained atop her horse.

By the time Bozeman returned, Jacobs had already identified the approaching visitors. ''Praise the Lord, they're just Crows,'' the old man announced, ''an' not a man of 'em sportin' war paint. But still be on your guard. They'll take their coups where they find them, warpath or not.'' Just as Jacobs was doing, Bozeman raised the muzzle of his Hawken in the general direction of the Indians and held it there.

When the Indians got to within about ten yards of the white men, they all stopped, stepped down from their barebacked ponies and ground-reined the animals. Then one of them, the leader of the group, started over toward Jacobs and Bozeman. On his face he sported a broad, conciliatory smile. He did not seem in the slightest offended by the two rifles pointed at him and carried his own weapon in one hand, pointing it down at the ground. Bozeman was relieved to note that though all the Indians were armed with bows and arrows, only one other carried a firearm.

The Crow leader was dressed in buckskin leggings and a light vest, both decorated with a variety of beads, bones and eagle claws. He was a fairly short man, probably standing no more than five feet four or five. But his body was thick, compact and muscular. His thick black hair hung down his back and across his shoulders in greasy disarray and was kept back out of his face with a wide cloth headband. A small totem of fur, feathers and animal claws dangled from his neck on a piece of rawhide.

Despite the Indian's smile, Bozeman thought he could clearly read threat and deception on the man's features. The Indian appeared to be the kind of man who could speak of friendship and never lose his grin, even as he was drawing his knife to slit your belly open. His nose was bulbous and his eyes were cold and steady. Heritage and the elements had given his flesh a deep, reddish-brown glaze, and the leathery skin of his face was deeply creased with wrinkles, though he looked no more than thirty-five years of age.

The Indian said something in his own language and Jacobs responded to him in the same tongue. "He asks if we're lost, or if we're out lookin' for the yellow metal," Jacobs translated. "I told him neither. I said we're just passing through and want to take nothing from the land."

Again the Indian spoke. This time he began to gesture toward the string of pack animals and then toward the horses the Indians had ridden up on, all of which looked gaunt and overworked. Jacobs no longer bothered to translate. But Bozeman could tell that the Crow leader either wanted to trade horses or was demanding some sort of tribute because they were on Indian land.

For the few moments that the Indian and the old trader negotiated, at times the conversation became rather heated. Meanwhile Bozeman kept his eye and the muzzle of his rifle on the four other Indians. They had spread out on either side and were looking past him and Jacobs at the treasures they had brought along.

When the conversation finally ended, Jacobs turned to Bozeman and told him, "This feller has kindly offered to camp here with us tonight to help us guard our horses an' supplies from thieves, an' in return he says we should give him food an' his pick of the mounts. I turned him down, but I did say we'd give him some food. He'd lose face with the others if he didn't wheedle us out of something an' then all hell would surely come crashin' in on us.''

"We can spare the food," Bozeman agreed. "Game is plentiful enough in these parts."

"Okay, go back an' fill 'em up three or four flour sacks with some staples—sugar, bacon an' truck like that. But no coffee. After a full winter without none, they're goin' to have to fight me toe-to-toe if they aim to take any of that.''

Bozeman moved back to get the food while Jacobs and the head Indian began to talk again. When Jacobs returned, he announced, "They say they still aim to sleep nearby and help guard the camp of their new white friends."

"That'll mean a sleepless night for us guarding our guards, won't it?" Bozeman asked. "Can't you talk them out of it?"

"I might be able to convince 'em elsewise," Jacobs reflected. "I think I'll try givin' No Tongue Girl to 'em an' see if that doesn't convince 'em to move along."

"You what?" Bozeman asked.

"Jus' watch, boy," Jacobs returned, trying to keep the conspiratorial smirk from showing on his face.

The Indian looked apprehensive when Jacobs made his offer. But as he gazed over at the girl, still astride her horse a few yards away, he couldn't find anything wrong with her. No Tongue Girl was a fine, strong young woman. A girl like her would be a useful addition to any camp, and she might bring as many as three fine horses during a shrewd bargaining session. At last the Crow grunted and nodded that he would accept the gift.

"Go get Girl an' bring her over," Jacobs told Bozeman.

"Just a minute!" Bozeman protested. "Think of what you're doing! She's your own daughter. . . ."

"Jus' get her," Jacobs ordered more sternly.

Bozeman moved hesitantly back to Girl. He looked up at her, trying to communicate his sympathy to the mute child. To see a father give away his own flesh and blood simply for the sake of safety was nearly more than he could take. He reached up and touched No Tongue Girl's arm, indicating that he would help her down off the horse.

But Girl didn't accept his offer. Instead, her eyes rolled back in her head, her mouth sagged open and she began to weave unsteadily in the saddle as if about to fall into a swoon. A jagged, choking wail issued from her fractured throat and she started to wave her arms wildly in front of her, as if trying to ward off the assault of a host of invisible demons. Without warning she tumbled off the side of the horse. Bozeman caught her, but soon wished he had let her fall. In an instant he found himself holding eighty pounds of clawing, biting, kicking fury. It was a moment before he was able to shove Girl away and scramble from her reach.

Displaying little concern, Jacobs marched over and popped Girl on the back of the head with the butt of his pistol. Bozeman could see from where he stood that it was a light, glancing blow, but Girl immediately slumped to the ground in a lifeless heap. There she lay until Jacobs pitched her across the back of the nearby horse, took the reins and led the animal over to the Indians.

The Crow leader backed his horse away. He was not about to touch the reins, the horse or anything else that had anything to do with this strange, bewitched creature. The grin melted from his face. Jacobs' offer to include the horse in the arrangement could not stop his retreat. In another moment all five Indians were mounted up and thundering away.

Cackling with delight, Jacobs lifted his daughter off the horse. Before Girl's feet touched ground, her eyes were open and she, too, was smiling.

"By jingles," the old man snorted, "this here gal's about the best I ever did see! Did you catch that arm-wavin' an' eye-rollin' stuff, Bozeman? I swear she does it better every time, an' she's pulled our hides out of more scrapes than I ever could with just this here rifle!"

"I don't get it," Bozeman exclaimed. "You mean all of it was an act?"

"Why, hell yes!" Jacobs replied. "You don't think I'd really jus' hand this gal over to them cutthroats, do you? But, see, if you ever want to scare an Indian better'n any gun or knife could, then jus' wave some sort of spirit in front of his nose. He can't take it. It sets 'em off every time!"

Bozeman grinned in appreciation of the trick and glanced over to where No Tongue Girl stood, rubbing the slight lump her father had raised on the back of her head with the pistol butt. Entering into this project, he had thought that his four years of frontier experience had prepared him adequately for the kinds of things he would face along the trail, but he was beginning to see how much more he would be able to learn from Jacobs over the coming weeks.

Their trail led them in a generally eastern direction until they passed the northern foothills of the Bighorn Mountains. Then they cut back southeast, skirting the eastern fringes of the Bighorns and heading in nearly a straight line toward their ultimate objective, the spot where the Oregon Trail met the North Platte River at Deer Creek Crossing.

Some of the route was unknown to even Jacobs, but both he and Bozeman delighted in what they found along every new mile they traveled. As far as the terrain and the availability of water, wood and grass were concerned, this trail was infinitely preferable to the standard roads west and north into the gold fields. All of Bozeman's grand dreams of cutting miles off the route into the mountains and finding a way that was much more easy and convenient to travel seemed to unreel before them day by day. And during the times when they rode for scores of miles without sighting another human being, it was easy to believe that somehow even the presence of hostile Indians in the area could be dealt with easily.

During the long hours in the saddle and evenings in the quiet of the camp, Bozeman found himself opening up to Jacobs more than he had to any man he had met since he came west. In many ways, Bozeman's past had been a tragic one, though he seldom permitted himself to dwell on it. His eye was toward the future and his reveries were aimed toward what might someday be, rather than what was dead and done.

For months and years he and his mother had struggled along on their Georgia farm, always hoping to receive some word from the West Coast, where John's father had headed to make his fortune in gold. Never hearing a word, at last they admitted to themselves that he must have perished.

Only three years later, Bozeman had married at the age of seventeen, and he and his young wife Sarah had settled down to raise a family of their own. Their three daughters came along at two-year intervals, and by the mid-1850s his future seemed set. But in 1858 the lure of wealth began to call to him from the West just as it had called to his father nearly ten years before.

Men were sluicing and panning the yellow metal out of the streams and gullies in a place called the Pike's Peak Country. And rumors were rampant of prospectors who gathered more wealth in a single day than any hard-luck Georgia dirt farmer like Bozeman could earn in a year of dawn-to-dusk toil. The temptation was just too great.

Against the wishes of his wife and the desperate pleas of his mother, John Bozeman headed out on the family mule in the spring of 1859 to seek his fortunes on the frontier. Despite his eager vows to return in a year with enough gold to buy them the best farm in the valley, Sarah Bozeman made no promises to her husband that she would wait for him. She and the children couldn't eat dreams, she told him scornfully, even for just one year.

Though his letters were seldom answered, for the first two years he wrote home faithfully. Over and over he promised Sarah he was close to the big strike. When he made it, he wrote, then he would come home again with his pockets filled with loot and they would all live in grand style for the rest of their lives. But that day never came.

A three-month-old letter, the last he ever received from his wife, caught up with him in early March, 1861, in a tiny cabin deep in the mountains west of Denver. In it Sarah explained that she needed to live with a flesh and blood man again, a man who was there to be a father to the girls and a supportive husband to her. With the aid of a lawyer and a local county official, she said, she was obtaining a divorce. And after a respectable time had passed, she planned to betroth herself to D.L. Simpson, a hard-working and successful farmer who lived a few miles from the Bozeman farm.

The news was a crushing blow to Bozeman, but he

knew there would be no way for him to return home in time to stop it all from happening. For a while he began to doubt the potential of his dreams and considered himself a fool for having left his family in the first place. His doubts deepened into depression. They plagued him for months and at times he considered suicide as the only possible escape from the burden of his own failures.

But in late summer, word began to filter south along the Rockies of new gold finds hundreds of miles away. He was working a small placer claim at the time and chose not to leave it. But a year later, when the tiny deposit played out, he became a part of a new rush to the north. His grand dreams and schemes had taken root again. And someday, with the fortune he would gather, he would have no trouble finding himself a sweet young wife to share a new start with him.

John Jacobs smiled knowingly when he heard Bozeman's story. He had heard it many times over the years, told by many different tongues. Decades before, it had been a story that he told about himself. The treasure had been furs back then, the state had been Pennsylvania and the girl was named Priscilla, but those details were all simply variations on the same theme.

Now Jacobs was also delighted to discover he had a fresh captive audience to open up to. He had forty years of accumulated tall tales to tell and Bozeman made a good, if often skeptical, listener for hours each day.

Eventually Bozeman developed a game for himself, trying each time Jacobs began another of his stories to judge how much of it was truth and how much was exaggeration. He could believe the story about the huge geyser Jacobs had once witnessed in the jumbled mountain terrain to the northwest, but he doubted the parts about it shooting as high as two hundred feet into the air, as well as the part about it erupting so faithfully that a man could nearly set his watch by it. It was a little harder to put any credence in the old man's tales of pools of water so hot a man could boil his dinner in them, or a gigantic hunk of stone, called the Devil's Rock by the Indians, which rose straight up a thousand feet above the rolling plains to the northeast.

And yet as he traveled deeper into the vast, incredible West, each day it became easier to believe even the most far-fetched yarns and legends. Who was to truly say that somewhere out here there was not a critter that, half man, half beast, stood twelve feet tall and could whip a full-grown grizzly ten throws out of ten? Who could be sure that somewhere there wasn't a place where white stone flowed out of a mountain top and froze on its sides like icy waterfalls?

Somehow in this amazing land it all seemed possible, just as it seemed possible at times for any man to realize his most fantastic dreams of wealth and success.

John Bozeman awoke from a deep sleep and stared up at the dense darkness around him. Instinctively he fought an unexplainable sensation of panic which gripped him from the moment he opened his eyes. He had no idea how long he had been asleep, but a few feet away, the evening campfire had burned down to a dim bed of coals.

What sound or movement it was that had startled him awake, he didn't know. But now his heart was thudding like a smithy's hammer and his whole body was keyed and tense. The oppressive weight of impending danger hung ominously in the air around him. His hand snaked tentatively out from under his blanket, searching for the reassuring feel of his Hawken rifle.

It was John Jacobs' turn at watch. Somewhere out there he was supposed to be alert as he always was while on nighttime guard duty. Surely he would have sounded the alarm if any intruders were approaching the camp, Bozeman thought. But what if they had already done away with Jacobs? he wondered. What if the noise which had alerted him was the sound of his partner being killed? Again the faceless panic seized him.

Camp had been pitched the previous evening in a cottonwood grove along Crazy Woman Creek, which was a tributary of the Powder River. At the time, Bozeman had complimented Jacobs on an excellent choice of campsites. The surrounding trees provided them with privacy from any chance intrusion and there was good grass close at hand for the stock. But now the dense foliage seemed imprisoning rather than protecting. It blocked out even the barest illumination that a starlit sky might have given off and provided cover for attackers as well as for defenders of the grove.

They were just beginning their fourth week on the trail and their destination, Deer Creek Crossing on the North Platte River, was tantalizingly close. Jacobs had estimated that it lay only about a hundred and fifty miles to the southeast. At the pace they had been moving along, that meant scarcely more than four days' travel time.

During the past few days Bozeman had been enthralled by the grassy, rolling hills of the Powder River Country. Jacobs was, too. He had never traveled this particular area. The old mountain man had called it "a fine chunk of the Almighty's handiwork," and Bozeman had enthusiastically agreed. To the west, the forested slopes of the southern foothills of the Bighorn Mountains would provide all the wood any wagon train would need. Cattle and horses would thrive on the thick prairie grasses. It was obvious that the hills in the region were gentle enough for even the heaviest of wagons. And available fords across rivers and streams were abundant.

The previous evening Bozeman had gone to sleep with visions in his head of a long, winding chain of wagons threading its way across this lovely country. The image had been so real that he could almost taste the dust rolling up from the iron-rimmed wagon wheels. He could almost hear the bawling protests of dozens of teams of laboring oxen.

"John!"

The urgent whisper came from no more than a dozen feet away across the camp. It was Jacobs' voice. Bozeman was sure of it. Relief flooded through him and he sat up in his blankets.

"I'm awake," he whispered hoarsely.

Jacobs eased over silently. "We got ourselves some comp'ny out there," he grated. "I was over to the edge of the grove an' when I spotted 'em goin' for the horses I come back here to wake up you an' Girl."

"You mean they're taking our horses and you haven't tried to stop them yet?" Bozeman asked.

"I seen at least ten redskins creepin' through the grass toward our animals," Jacobs explained, "and if I *seen* that many, you can pretty well figure that there's twice as many close about that I didn't get to yet. We can't take on a group that size. The only thing to do is jus' let 'em have the horses an' hope that's enough to satisfy 'em."

"You mean we're going to end up on foot out here with a hundred fifty miles yet to travel to our destination?" Bozeman asked.

"Only if we're lucky," Jacobs told him. He moved

off to wake No Tongue Girl and warn her of the danger while Bozeman began fumbling around in the darkness. Locating his boots and shirt, he pulled them on.

The horse thieves were probably Sioux, Bozeman realized. Jacobs had announced days before that they were well into the territory which that tribe claimed. The thought was not a comforting one. Even when an experienced old mountain man like Jacobs spoke of the Sioux, he did so with a greater degree of respect and caution than he did about such peoples as the Crow, the Blackfoot and the Nez Perce.

Surprisingly to Bozeman, now that the enemy was known and most of the uncertainty had been removed from the situation, his nerves were calming and he felt more ready to accept whatever their fate might be.

It took the Indians a while to locate the camp. But after a time Bozeman began to hear occasional, almost inaudible, noises indicating the Sioux warriors were approaching from several directions at once. Using still another Indian dialect, at last Jacobs spoke up.

"I told them there wasn't but the three of us," Jacobs translated. "Two men and a girl. We might as well let 'em take us without a fight 'cause as soon as we fire the first shot, we're goners for sure."

On orders from an anonymous voice in the brush, Jacobs pitched a few twigs and dry branches on the fire. The flames began to lick up and the Indians began emerging from the trees.

Bozeman noted immediately what a fierce and haughty lot the Sioux were that approached them. They appeared secure both because of their fighting ability and their vastly superior numbers. Some of the braves took immediate possession of their firearms. Bozeman and Jacobs surrendered them without protest. The others started rifling

41

through the packs and provisions, seizing what they wanted and pitching other items carelessly aside.

The man who was the leader of the band was one of the last to step into the clearing. Once in view he strode directly toward the prisoners and studied them critically. He was a tall Indian with a fiercely handsome face swatched with broad stripes of colored pigment.

Staring back at the Indian, Bozeman noticed a glint of malice in his eyes.

"White pigs!" the brave spat in broken English. And the backhanded blow he delivered to Bozeman's jaw caught the explorer completely off guard and sent him staggering backward. Next the Indian turned his attention to No Tongue Girl. Snarling some angry phrase, he caught the girl by the hair and began slapping her repeatedly with his open palm.

In an instant Jacobs was leaping forward in Girl's defense.

"She ain't no whore!" Jacobs shouted. "She's my daughter!" He delivered a hard blow with his fist to the side of the Indian's head. But before he had the chance to strike a second time, several of the Sioux braves had him firmly and were beating him as they dragged him away from their leader.

When Bozeman saw his partner battered to the ground by a throng of flailing fists and kicking feet, he decided they all might as well go out fighting together. With a roar of anger he launched himself at the men who were beating Jacobs. Catching the two Indians from behind, he yanked their hair and bashed their skulls together. Then he spun just in time to deliver a powerful kick to the groin of another who was rushing toward him.

The attack was short-lived. A blow from behind by some hard object, probably a rifle butt, staggered him and he dropped weakly to his knees. For an instant he remained like that, reeling drunkenly as he struggled to keep hold of his consciousness.

Through blurred vision he saw moccasined feet approach him, but he did not have enough strength remaining to look up. Almost as if in slow motion, he saw the knee begin to rise toward him. The blow caught him on the corner of his chin, snapping his head backward. At once a rush of shimmering yellow stars flooded his vision. And then the blackness claimed him.

Bozeman could see a face in front of him, but it seemed to float in a pale, murky pool and he could only hold his eyes open for a second or two at a time to gaze at it. At first, as consciousness slowly returned to him, he was only aware of great pain. But in stages the pains began to become more distinct and associate themselves with specific areas—the left side of his face and chin, the base of his skull, his lower abdomen and back.

"Is he startin' to come around, Girl? Wash his face with that rag again an' see if he won't come to."

The damp cloth stung as No Tongue Girl applied it to his face, but the coolness was refreshing. Gradually he began to see Girl's features more clearly and noticed the deep welts and scratches on her face and arms. They obviously had come from the beating she had taken. But Girl was smiling now, looking pleased that he was awakening.

"Boy, we'd about gave up on you," Jacobs exclaimed. "I about figured they'd dimmed your lamp for good." The simple effort that it took to roll his head to the side to see Jacobs sent a pain shooting down Bozeman's spine. As he tried to shift around slightly, he felt as if every inch of his body had been flogged.

"Once he caught his wind, I thought that Indian you popped in the seeds never was goin' to let up on beatin' you. But finally their head man—I found out his name is Blue Eagle—made 'im stop."

"Where are we now?" Bozeman managed to rasp. He recognized the hide shelter around them as that of an Indian tepee, but he could not understand why they were in it, or even why they were all still alive and together.

"After they worked us over out there for a spell," Jacobs explained, "then they brung us back here to their camp in the foothills. I s'pose it's so the whole bunch, women an' kids an' all, could have the fun of watchin' us tortured."

"I wished to hell they'd have just killed us out there at Crazy Woman Creek," Bozeman grimaced.

"Well, these red-skinned peoples got their own ways of doin' things, hard though they may be, jus' like everybody else," Jacobs replied with infuriating composure. "An' sometimes there's good reason for it, too. I remember once when my wife's people caught a young Cayuse brave who'd just raped an' scalped a Flathead girl. Wellsir, the first thing they done to him was take their skinning knives, an'—"

"Damn it, John!" Bozeman complained. "Do you really think this is the best time to be telling a story like that?"

"Mebbe you're right," Jacobs agreed. "It's jus' that after a spell you get so you don't think nothin' of such things, an' you tend to forget that other more civilized folks still do."

"Well, what I'd really like to hear is what you think might happen to us now," Bozeman told him.

"It's plumb hard to tell," Jacobs answered. "They brung us back here to their camp 'bout dawn, an' for the past three hours we been in this tepee with no word of what's goin' on. Like I said before, likely as not they plan to torture us, but nothin' ain't sure when you go to dealin' with redskins. By all rights we should already be dead after the way we jumped them out there. But here we are. There jus' ain't no figurin' it.''

The wait lasted for at least another hour. After he had recovered somewhat, Bozeman passed the time by observing what was happening in sight of the open flap of the tepee. Jacobs had mentioned that they were prisoners in some sort of large hunting camp that included about forty braves and twice that many women and children. Bozeman could see two women dressing down a large deer that hung by its back legs from a tree branch. Farther away, a couple of hides were curing in the sun on large stretching frames similar to the one Jacobs had built for the bearskin back in Bannack City.

At last three braves came to the tepee. They gestured with their rifles that Bozeman, Jacobs and No Tongue Girl were to go with them. As the three prisoners started out, the women and children of the Indian camp began to harass them with stones and switches, laughing gaily as they shouted out taunts and insults at their victims.

The three were taken to a large tepee that towered several feet higher than any other in the camp. Jacobs explained quietly to Bozeman as they were led inside that this was the council lodge.

Eight men were inside the council lodge. All sat cross-legged around a smoldering ceremonial fire whose smoke filled the air with a peculiar, aromatic fragrance. Their captor, Blue Eagle, presided over the group. On one side of him was a stern, leathery-faced old man whom Bozeman took to be the medicine man. The others were elders and subchiefs.

45

Bozeman and Jacobs were left standing alone before the council as No Tongue Girl was shoved off to the side by one of the guards. The proceedings were very formal and, following Jacobs' cue, Bozeman remained silent, making no show of defiance as Blue Eagle began to speak. As the Indian talked, Jacobs quietly translated for his companion.

"You are one of the old ones who came here long ago, not to take our land, but simply to trade with us," the chief began, addressing Jacobs directly. "Sometimes you fought against us, as brave men sometimes will, and sometimes you gave us iron tools and rifles and blankets for the furs we brought to you. But always you respected our land and our ways. You recognized that you were the visitor here and that this was our territory, not yours."

"True enough," Jacobs agreed.

"But now a new kind of white man comes," the chief continued, "and he tells us that we must give our land to him because he is many and we are few. He wants to dig holes in the ground for the yellow metal and scrape his plow in the dirt to plant his seed.

"But we Sioux are not a nation of feeble old women. We will fight for what is ours. We will defend the land where the game which we live on roam. We will not give it up to the greedy white men who say on paper that this land is ours and then try to take it from us.

"I brought you here to kill you but in council the elders tell me that because you are one of the old ones I should respect you. They tell me that I should let you live, you and your young friend and your daughter, and I have listened to their words. You may go. But listen well and carry with you this message. We Sioux are still a strong nation. Our gods live in secret places in the mountains and our food roams the prairies below. Without them we are

46

nothing, and without the land we are nothing, so we will fight. Tell your people that.''

''I will,'' Jacobs promised, and by the look on his face, Bozeman could tell that the old man was not simply making empty vows in order to survive.

A part of John Jacobs' heart would always want to see the Indians remain forever as they were now, a savage people freely roaming the boundless mountains and vast prairies of the great wilderness.

Chapter 4

Jeremiah Pendleton exhibited the weary, resigned features of a man who had worked himself to exhaustion six days a week during his entire adult life. His build was solid and bullish. The dulled expression in his eyes revealed that he was a man who plodded through each day. And the patched and tattered shirt and trousers he wore looked as if they could have been the same ones he had put on back in his Ohio home three months before.

Here was no bright-eyed adventurer chasing hopes of an easy fortune in the gold fields. John Bozeman knew that. Men of Pendleton's ilk came west in search of land to farm. More than likely it would be his breed that would stay behind and eventually bring stability and a civilized way of life to the wilderness regions.

"I tell you, Brother Pendleton," Bozeman remarked with a bright, confident smile, "this new road will cut weeks off your travel time! Just think of it. Instead of reaching Bannack City in late August, you could be there by the end of July! That would give you a whole extra month to stake out your homestead and start building a home for this fine family of yours."

Pendleton was standing beside a brace of six oxen that were hitched to a canvas-covered Conestoga wagon. Sitting on the wagon seat was a plain-looking woman who was obviously his wife. From behind her peered the faces of two towheaded young boys. Ever since Bozeman had approached Pendleton with the invitation to join the wagon train he was assembling, the man's wife had listened with intense interest. But not once had she presumed to offer any advice or opinions to her husband.

"We heard about your trail, Mr. Bozeman," Pendleton told him slowly, "but we also heard there might be trouble with the Indians up thataway." At the mere mention of the word "Indians," Pendleton's wife wore a frightened expression on her face. Her gaze shifted protectively toward her two sons.

"I wouldn't try to deceive you and tell you there's no chance of trouble with the Indians," Bozeman admitted, "but I won't say there's no chance of attack if you travel on along the Oregon Trail instead. I can tell you this. When the Indians won't listen to any other sort of reason, they do understand the logic of that thing right there." He pointed up to the rifle Pendleton kept in a boot alongside the wagon seat.

"We don't want no trouble," Pendleton declared, "but I do need to get the family settled into some sort of place before winter hits. It's gonna be rough for at least the first year."

"That's precisely the reason my partner and I blazed this new trail," Bozeman explained. "We know that when folks like you get his far west, you're in a race against time. Just think what you could do with an extra month on that new homestead of yours."

"I sure could do plenty," Pendleton agreed.

"Well you folks think about what I've said and talk it over between yourselves," Bozeman told Pendleton at last. "When you decide, you can join the rest of us about a quarter-mile north of here. But mind you don't think too long. Time's a'wasting and we're all eager to get on the trail north."

"I'll get word to you one way or the other," Pendleton promised as they shook hands a final time.

The broad smile remained on Bozeman's face as he turned away and started toward his horse. The Pendletons would likely be along within the next day or two to join his group, as would a good percentage of the other twelve or so families that he had talked to about his new trail that afternoon. It had been a good day, one of several he'd had in nearly two weeks of recruiting customers for the guide service that he and John Jacobs were now qualified to offer. It was only fair. They were due for a run of good luck after the miserable experiences they had lived through following their capture by Blue Eagle's band of Sioux.

After their stay in the Indian camp, the Sioux had sent them on their way with little but the clothes on their backs, plus three scrawny, reject horses that were scarcely up to traveling twenty-five miles per day. They were not permitted to take their firearms with them. So after the second day, when the horse No Tongue Girl was riding came up lame, they ended up killing and eating it. Butchering the animal with sharp stones instead of knives was an arduous task. Because they had no fire, they could do nothing but half-dry strips of the meat in the sun and then choke them down uncooked. The majority of the meat they carried spoiled before they could put it to use, and when six days later they finally straggled behind schedule into Deer Creek, they were a bedraggled, ravenous crew.

After gorging themselves with food at the stage station at Deer Creek, they sold their two remaining horses to the station operator, who had taken pity on them. While at Deer Creek, they learned that most of the westbound prospectors, settlers and freighters were using Fetterman's Fort as a stopping place before continuing their journey along the Oregon Trail. After spending two days recovering from their ordeal, they headed east on foot for the few miles' walk to the fort.

The scene there was as bustling and active as Bozeman had hoped it would be. One train of eighty-eight wagons was starting out along the Oregon Trail when they arrived. But at least fifty other wagons remained behind while their owners bought, sold and traded stock, mended broken axles and spokes and took care of other needed repairs before beginning the next arduous leg of the trip. The wagons were scattered out in various locations. Nearby were the small stockade, trading post and corral which comprised the "fort."

Here was the market for the services they had to sell, Bozeman realized. His initial move was to use the last of his cash from the sale of his horse to buy a new set of buckskin clothing. That way he *looked* like a frontier trail guide. Nobody was likely to agree to follow a man dressed in the ragged, cast-off clothing that the stage station operator at Deer Creek had given him to wear. Next he and Jacobs secured new horses for themselves at the fort, promising to pay for them out of the first fees collected for their guide services. Having made those simple preparations, they were ready for business.

The first few recruits for the wagon train they planned to put together were the hardest to convince. Everyone had heard how dangerously inhospitable the Sioux and the other tribes were to the north. And nobody relished the thought of traveling along the untried route with such a small and vulnerable group. It took four totally unproductive days of talking to pioneers and immigrants who were unwilling to gamble with their possessions and their lives before fate finally smiled on Bozeman in the form of the Anderson Exploratory Company.

The Anderson Exploratory Company was the pretentious title of a group of eighteen men who had banded together in Westport, Missouri, with the intentions of heading for the gold fields and hopefully striking it rich. The heavily armed, well-equipped and confident group was traveling with six wagons and sixty head of stock, including their wagon teams and riding horses. For the first time Bozeman found eager reception for his glowing descriptions of easy travel and abundant wood, water and grass along the new trail. The men in the Anderson Exploratory Company were in such a hurry to get rich that they were not about to let a bunch of sun-baked savages stand in the way of the early completion of that dream.

After a full day of negotiations and consideration, Bozeman led the group to the rallying point that Jacobs had established along a babbling creek a quarter-mile north of the fort. Once settled on that solid foundation he set out building the remainder of his wagon train.

By the first of June wagons were arriving at Fetterman's Fort almost daily. Some traveled in large trains that were already well organized and competently led, and he was unable to convince many people to leave those trains. But many others traveled in small groups of five to twenty wagons that usually had banded together somewhere along the trail for mutual support and protection—a few hardy souls had even undertaken to make the trip alone. It was from those ranks that Bozeman drew most of his new recruits.

As he rode north toward what was already being labeled the Bozeman Trail Camp, he was well satisfied with the progress he had made. The day of departure was enticingly close. Just the afternoon before he had upped his ante in the project by convincing crusty old Marlow Fetterman, owner of the fort and trading post, to stake him and Jacobs to two wagons loaded with staples desperately needed in the sprawling mining camps.

That was a gamble. He had rashly agreed to pay for the goods even if they were lost. But if theirs were some of the first wagons to reach any of the isolated camps, the potential profits were well worth the risk.

Near the end of his ride, Bozeman stopped his horse on a rise overlooking the camp. It took a moment just to survey the results of all of his and Jacobs' efforts. Bozeman smiled with satisfaction.

Thirty-eight wagons were scattered in the broad meadow below. The number fell far short of the two hundred wagons he had hoped to lead through on their maiden journey, but this at least was a start. And when this train got through in record time, as he felt utterly confident that it would, word would spread quickly about the many advantages of traveling the new trail. When he and Jacobs next returned to Fetterman's Fort in August, travelers would be coming to him, begging to join his next train.

By the time Bozeman reached their camp near the edge of the creek, No Tongue Girl had a rabbit stew cooking and Jacob was affectionately polishing his shiny new Henry .44 rifle. Both he and Jacobs would undoubtedly need weapons along the trail. For that reason he had armed himself and his partner, again on credit, with new Henry rifles and Starr double-action .44 revolvers.

"You're going to wear the bluing off that rifle before you even get all the misses shot out of it," Bozeman teased as he stepped to the ground and began unsaddling his horse.

"I never thought I'd ever own me a fine piece like this one," Jacobs exclaimed for perhaps the hundredth time since Bozeman had presented him with the new weapons a few days before. "I brung down that rabbit Girl's cookin' at nigh onto two hundred yards an' was still able to pick my spot on 'im. Damned if it isn't worth a whole summer's travel jus' to get my hands on this here rifle!"

"Well I hope your aim's as good if we meet up with Blue Eagle's bunch back out on the trail," Bozeman chuckled.

"Don't you worry none 'bout that," the old mountain man told him. "I'm hopin' the need don't arise, but if it does, I'll be ready to put this here fine piece of goods through its paces."

Bozeman hitched his horse on a long lead rope. Then he staked the rope near the creek where the animal could graze at its leisure along with Jacobs' mount. Jacobs had taken charge of choosing their horses. The two sturdy horses they had ended up with from Fetterman were well suited for the long trek they would be called on to make.

When Bozeman returned to the camp, Girl had a bowl of stew waiting for him. He settled on the ground near Jacobs to enjoy his dinner.

"Well I talked to about a dozen more people today," he announced after swallowing the first steaming mouthful, "and it seems likely that at least four or five more wagons will be joining us soon. That'll put us well over forty."

"It don't seem enough," Jacobs grumbled, "but I reckon it'll have to do. Cáp'n Morris come to me today an' said most of the folks are itchin' to get started."

The people of the train had elected a captain and four lieutenants among themselves to manage the majority of routine matters connected with wagon travel.

"That way," Morris had explained to Bozeman, "you and Jacobs will be freed up to be scouts and guides."

"I agree it's time we were heading out," Bozeman declared. "We've already held up the Anderson Company for more than a week. If they have to wait much longer they'll be wanting to strike out on their own. The whole train might just fall apart if that happened."

"Might be better if it did," Jacobs grumped. "I know you hate to hear talk like that at this point, but forty wagons jus' ain't goin' to give us no whoppin' big edge over them Sioux like you think it is. You was there an' heard what Blue Eagle had to say. When the time comes, they'll fight, an' they'll fight hard."

"I'm not trying to question your judgment or your experience with Indians," the younger man interjected tactfully, "but it seems to me that after scouting fifty-nine men in this party and sixty-seven weapons, the Sioux will think twice before they try to launch any major attack against us. Surely they'll realize the kind of losses they would suffer if they tried it."

Finished with his cleaning, Jacobs tenderly laid aside the Henry rifle and accepted his supper from No Tongue Girl. He ate a tentative first mouthful. Then he turned to Bozeman and told him reflectively, "I can see that for all your grand dreams an' drive, your education ínto the way things are in this big country ain't near complete yet, young feller. But on up the trail, mebbe a week or a hunnert miles from now, you'll see a'right. Mark what I say, John Bozeman! You still got yourself a thing or two to learn about wild red Indians a'fore you know it all!''

Lula Mae Pendleton's frenzied screams could be heard from one end of the camp to the other when she found her husband. When the first people reached her, they had to pry her fingers loose from her husband's clothing and drag her, bloodied and fighting frantically, from beneath the wagon. Within moments a crowd had gathered to survey the mess by the first light of dawn.

Jeremiah Pendleton lay on his back in a pool of blood. His eyes stared up vacantly at the floorboards of the wagon that had transported his family so far from their Ohio home. His throat had been slit, and so suddenly and skillfully that he hadn't had time to put up a struggle. The onlookers speculated that he had probably been scalped after he was already dead. A shallow set of moccasin tracks in the dirt led up to his body from the front of the wagon and back away again in the same direction.

Though absolutely horrified himself, John Bozeman took charge of the scene as quickly as possible. He assigned some of the nearby women to escort Pendleton's widow and sons away from the area. Then he instructed that the body be covered temporarily with a piece of canvas and ordered the rest of the people to return to their own wagons. When things finally calmed down, he told Captain Morris to call a meeting of all the men who had been on guard duty around the horse herd and the fringes of the camp the previous night.

All the guards related basically the same story in response to questioning. None had seen or heard anything. No one had any idea how the murderer had managed to slip in undetected, then slip back out again. It took nearly a half an hour of discussion before Bozeman and Morris were able to piece together what probably had happened.

When Pendleton's turn at guard duty was over sometime during the night, he had apparently piled down on the ground under the wagon to sleep, rather than disturb the rest of his family inside. The Indian killer either had been hiding nearby or had come across Pendleton as he lay underneath the wagon. The dead man's rifle was missing along with his scalp.

After conferring with Jacobs and Morris, Bozeman decided to keep the wagon train where it was for the day. Doing that would give everyone time to recover from the shock of the tragedy and opportunity to get Jeremiah Pendleton buried.

Practically every person in the wagon train had witnessed death in one form or another along the route. But the brazen attack on Pendleton confirmed in everyone's mind that all the rumors they had heard about Western Indians were true. Even the headstrong men in the Anderson Exploratory Company seemed shaken by this particular death. Already there were some rumblings among the less determined members of the train about turning back before it was too late.

For the four days they had been on the trail, Bozeman had been expecting something to happen. It was ridiculous, he thought, to believe that the journey would end without any contact with the Indians who claimed the land as their own.

Yet he had always pictured a daylight attack where he and his charges would have targets to shoot back at and a real chance to defend themselves. There were forty-two wagons in this train and ninety-two people, including sixty-three men, twenty-one women and eight children. In all they carried a total of seventy-four weapons and had about four hundred fifty head of livestock to ride and pull their wagons. But what use were all those numbers and all that firepower when one Indian could sneak into camp undetected and kill? Even Bozeman experienced fear, thinking of death striking unexpectedly.

But he wouldn't let the members of the wagon train break up their group. In that event, not only would they be greatly delayed in their travels west, but all of his and Jacobs' efforts during the previous two months would be for naught. They would be riding horses and carrying weapons they could not pay for. And they would have risked their lives scouting a trail no one ever again would consent to travel. No, the group would not disband, Bozeman promised himself. And to stop it he would take decisive action.

After the funeral services for Jeremiah Pendleton late that afternoon, Bozeman kept the entire train assembled for a speech. Standing on a slight rise near the plot where the widow had chosen to lay her husband to rest, Bozeman stared searchingly at the crowd. He read the apprehension on almost everyone's face. The people stood as still as prairie grass waiting to be swayed by an oncoming wind. Bozeman cleared his throat, wet his lips and began.

"A sad thing has happened among us today," he declared loudly. "One of our number, Jeremiah Pendleton, was killed without warning and his murderer goes unpunished. I'm aware that a lot of you are frightened and wondering if you or one of your loved ones might be next. The killing has got the whole train jittery and I've even heard talk going around about turning back toward Fetterman's Fort and the Oregon Trail.

"Well, folks, I'm standing up here to tell you right now that this wagon train isn't turning around just because one man has died. Now that we've given Jeremiah Pendleton a decent funeral, we're pushing on just like we intended to from the start. Now I won't promise you that along the way somebody else might not get hurt or even killed. The danger of our journey must be accepted. If you aren't prepared to face trouble then you never should have left your nice, safe homes back in Missouri and Iowa and Pennsylvania and such places. This is a risky piece of business we've taken on together. Chances are that time and again before we reach our destination you'll all be frightened and worried just like you are now. But we can't abide talk of quitting every time that happens.

"I won't try to stop anybody who decides to pull their wagon out and start back to Fetterman's Fort. But if any of you are considering it, I would like to offer these words of caution. It'll be a long, lonely ride you're undertaking. And if you think you're in danger now, just wait until two or three or even half a dozen wagonloads of you people are out of reach of our help. Then you'll *really* find out what it's like to be scared. Worse than that, I wouldn't take ten-to-one odds on a single one of you making it back alive.

"As long as we're together, we're strong. We might have to make adjustments in the way we guard ourselves and in the way we travel, and we might leave more graves along the trail behind us, but we all know what waits for us at the end of the line. I believe that rewards we find will be worth the risks we face now.

"All day most of you have been wondering what's going to happen. I'm going to tell you right now. Tomorrow we'll rise at dawn as usual, gather our stock, hitch up our wagons and push on. Our course is set and we're not going to stray from it."

With that pronouncement, Bozeman started down the hillside before anybody had the chance to voice his misgivings. Midway along his walk back to camp, Jacobs fell in beside him. The two men walked along in silence. After a moment Bozeman could not resist asking, "Well, John, what do you think?"

"Oh, it was a fine speech," Jacobs told him, hardly concealing the note of sarcasm in his voice. "You make a dandy stumper, boy."

"No, I mean what do you think about the situation now?" Bozeman corrected.

"Well, I think Blue Eagle an' his bunch have showed us what we can expect," the old mountain man told him, "an' I think we'd best start expectin' more of the same. Now the first thing we're going to have to do is start circlin' the wagons at night an' herdin' the horses in the middle for safety. That'll mean we'll lose at least three hours every morning while the stock grazes. But it'll be that or expectin' to lose horses almost every night. An' we'd best up the guard from twelve to twenty. . . ."

Despite the lost day, the caravan had advanced nearly a hundred miles by the end of the first week. The pace encouraged most members of the train to take heart and everyone crossed the Powder River without a mishap. By the evening of the seventh day, the travelers had pushed on to a campsite south of Lodgepole Creek that Jacobs had scouted out.

Two days of steady travel had already diminished the memory and pain of Jeremiah Pendleton's murder. The increased security measures had been reassuring to most, and each night when the men went out to pull their shifts on guard, their alertness was heightened. True danger lurked beyond the splashes of light thrown off by the evening campfires and everyone knew it.

A hearty laugh circulated around camp when Roland

Fitzsimmons, one of the best marksmen in the Anderson Company, downed a skulking timber wolf with a single shot, thinking it was an Indian. But privately many were glad that one of their guards had displayed such exceptional shooting ability.

On the morning of the eighth day, as the stock was being turned out to graze according to the new routine, Captain Morris sent out a detail of eight men in two wagons to cut wood for the camp. No one worried much about their safety because the men left in full daylight. Also, the cluster of pines they headed for was scarcely a quarter of a mile away. Yet no more than twenty minutes after the two wagons had disappeared into the grove of trees, a single shot rang out.

The sound was ominous. All through the camp, people abandoned whatever it was they had been doing and let their eyes rove in the direction of the pines. Probably one of the woodcutters had spotted a deer or an elk and decided to bring it down, they told one another. But despite the reassurances, anxious hands still reached for rifles left lying close by. In addition, the men tending to the livestock began considering whether to start herding the animals back toward the broad opening in the circle of wagons.

Half a minute later another shot rang out from the trees. A few seconds after that a barrage of fire erupted from at least half a dozen weapons. There was no mistaking what was going on. Despite instructions involving where to go and what to do in case of an attack, the entire wagon train seemed to explode into chaos as the gunfire in the trees continued.

In their haste to get the animals back within the ring of wagons, the five men tending the herd panicked their charges and a full third of the livestock went thundering out across the open plain. Panicky children screamed in terror as their mothers snatched them up and hurried them to cover. Rather than reporting to their assigned fighting positions, husbands raced to make certain that their families were safe. For a few minutes it was out of the question to consider sending any aid to the isolated woodcutters because nowhere in camp was a single horse saddled and ready to use. One man received a nasty wound to the thigh when he fell on his own rifle. Another ended up with a crushed foot and a broken arm when he was trampled by the incoming horses.

For a while, despite his leadership role, John Bozeman was unable to restore order. He could find no trace of Tom Morris anywhere and John Jacobs had not yet returned from an early-morning scouting excursion. What Jacobs said was true, Bozeman soon realized. If the Indians chose that moment to attack the train itself, his partner's most dire predictions of disaster would become reality.

When he did finally locate Captain Morris, Bozeman found the captain standing with a rifle in his hand just outside the western perimeter of the encampment. Bozeman stomped over toward him and demanded, "What in the ever-loving hell are you doing out here? We've got to get these people organized—"

"Look!" Morris interrupted, scarcely realizing that he was being shouted at. "Look up there!"

Bozeman glanced up in the direction Morris was pointing. At once a sudden elation flooded over him. A moment before he had been wondering whether it was too late to send any relief to the stranded woodcutters. On top of that he worried what depleting his forces might do to the organized defenses of the wagon train itself. Then suddenly he saw the two wood wagons emerging from the pine trees, racing at breakneck speed down the gradual incline. As the drivers urged their teams on to even more desperate efforts, the men in the back of the wagons were sending out a steady barrage toward the trees. There Bozeman could barely make out a number of dark forms creeping from one bit of cover to another as they returned the fire.

A cheer rose in camp as the two wagons raced through the opening in the circle and braked to a halt amidst the skittish livestock. As the crackle of the distant gunfire died slowly away, people raced from all sides to congratulate the woodcutters for their courageous escape. One of the eight men was dead and three others were suffering from various wounds, but the whole camp was in good spirits, having witnessed the careening dash to safety.

Bozeman leaped up to the back of one of the wagons and raised his hands for silence. When he had nearly everyone's attention, he called out, "Hold on! Now isn't the time for a long-winded speech. But it is the time for us to stop acting like a flock of panicked geese and start pulling together again. None of us knows what's really going on out there. What we do know is that we've got all our people together again and that if we defend ourselves according to plan we can hold our own just fine.

"The first thing that must happen is for you men to ready your weapons, get to your firing positions and *stay there*. You ladies get the young ones tucked away somewhere. Then get to work passing out food and ammunition like you were instructed to do. If we'd been attacked at any time over the past twenty minutes, it would have been pure slaughter, but from here on we're going to be ready. Every single one of us is going to perform the duties we've been assigned to do. Now get going!"

Bozeman was surprised and pleased to see how quickly and calmly everyone began to disperse following his speech. The initial wave of panic was over and the people of the train were acting responsibly again. Jumping down from the wagon bed, Bozeman called to Morris and together they began taking stock of their initial losses.

The long, tense morning progressed, but the expected massive attack never came. At one point a party of about fifteen mounted Indians appeared briefly to drive away the scattered stock that had escaped the herdsmen. Some of the men passed the time taking pot shots at the distant, hard-riding Indians, but none of the warriors went down and the entire group disappeared over a rise to the north.

In their haste to reach camp, the woodcutters had not brought back any wood, but Morris sent a heavily armed party about fifty yards outside the circle of wagons to bring back several barrels of water from Lodgepole Creek. They might run critically short of cooking fuel, but if this affair turned into any kind of siege, they would have enough water for at least several days.

About noon, Bozeman paused to eat a piece of bread and a hunk of meat with No Tongue Girl. In her own awkward way, Girl had expressed her concern over her father to Bozeman, but he had no news to tell her. The only thing certain was that Jacobs had left at dawn with the intention of scouting ahead. Because there were Indians in the area, the possibility existed that Jacobs had been captured. Bozeman shook his head doubtfully. The old mountain man was mounted on a fine, swift horse. There were plenty of tricks he could bring into play during a close, dangerous pursuit.

During the afternoon that followed, scattered groups of Indians began appearing on all sides of the beleaguered ring of wagons. At first Bozeman and Morris thought the warriors might be massing for an overwhelming attack. But women and children began appearing along with the Indian braves. And smoke from scattered fires started rising in the sky. Disbelievingly, the white travelers realized that the Indians were setting up their camps on all sides of the wagon train. Some of the most alarmed white men guessed that there were as many as a thousand Indians surrounding them now, but Bozeman more conservatively put their number at about four hundred.

No one got much sleep that night. Morris divided the men up into two guard shifts of thirty men each, but even the men not on guard stood gazing out at the distant flickers of light that marked the dying Indian fires. During the night, a rumor spread through camp that the Sioux preferred to mount their attacks at dawn. Believing that, nearly everyone was up by first light and prepared to fight for his life. But when it was bright enough to see the Indians, it was easy to observe that they were occupying themselves with the routine matters of eating a morning meal and tending to their livestock.

The entire second day, the situation remained the same. The Indians took no aggressive action against the wagon train. No one could figure what their plan might be and the tension increased. Perhaps, the white men thought, the Indians' intention was simply to keep the intruders under siege until they either starved or surrendered.

When evening arrived, Bozeman and Morris met to consider the possibility of sending someone through the Indian lines under cover of darkness. But the big question was, if a rider did slip past the Indians successfully, who could he go to with his appeal?

At that time of year, as many as two or three hundred men could be found in and around Fetterman's Fort at any given moment, but how many of them would be willing to take time and risk their lives in a mad dash north to rescue the people in Bozeman's party? The salvation of the wagon train was clearly a job for the military, but the nearest army garrison was at Fort Laramie, and that was over two hundred miles away. Considering travel time, it might take a contingent of cavalry as long as two weeks to reach them, and Bozeman hated to consider what shape his group would be in by then. He decided finally to call a meeting of the entire wagon train in the morning. A decision would be reached by vote.

The second night passed as tensely as the first, with the possibility of attack still hanging over everyone's head. Still, more of the men were able to grab a few hours of sleep, and Bozeman was no exception.

When one of Captain Morris's lieutenants shook him awake, he sat up with a start and reached for the rifle lying close beside him. The first thing he became aware of was that the eastern sky was just greying with the early light of dawn. The second thing was that there was no sound of gunfire signaling that an attack had begun.

"What's the matter?" Bozeman asked the man kneeling beside him.

"Rider coming," the man grunted.

"White or red?"

"He's too far to tell," the man reported. "But he's riding slow. Some of us think he might be some Indian coming to parley. Maybe we'll finally learn what those redskins are up to."

Bothering only to pull on his boots and snatch up his buckskin shirt, Bozeman hurried to the south side of the ring of wagons where a small group of men had gathered to watch the approaching rider. For a while the rider was barely visible in the scant light, but as he drew nearer, the hunched form of John Jacobs was easily identified.

"Praise the Lord!" Bozeman exclaimed as Jacobs drew within hailing distance. "We'd given you up for dead a full day ago."

"Well I ain't dead, but this horse of mine mighty near is after the workout I give 'im the past two days," Jacobs explained. "I figure I've covered right at a hunnert an' fifty miles since I left here day 'fore yesterday."

By the time he reached the wagons, it was easy to see the kinds of demands that Jacobs had made on his mount. The fine horse he had ridden out on was lathered with sweat and sagging from complete exhaustion.

"How in the hell did you get past all them Indians?" one of the guards asked Jacobs in amazement.

"I jus' rid right through betwixt their camps," Jacobs cackled with delight. "I guess if I'd been hightailin' it, they mighta come after me, but as slow as I was goin', they probably jus' figured I was one of their own. If daylight had of come ten minutes sooner, though, I couldn't of made it."

"Well where have you been?" Bozeman asked. "Do you have any idea what's going on or what those Sioux out there are up to?"

"It's easy enough to figure what they're up to," Jacobs snorted. "They're puttin' a stop to this here wagon train. That's what they're doin'. And as far as why they haven't attacked, I guess it might be 'cause they know they can get what they want without havin' to lose any of their men in the doin'. But I'd rather do my talking over a cup of coffee and a bowl of crimp cut. Why don't you get Cap'n Morris an' his helpers together. I'll run through my whole story while Girl's stirrin' up a fire."

Jacobs had been returning from his scouting trip when he heard the firing of the woodcutters' guns and saw the Sioux assembling to attack the wagon train. His first impulse was to break through before the ring of Indians had closed around the train. But then he decided that he might be of more use to everyone by staying on the outside of the trouble.

He didn't know if the Indians would waylay the train. But judging from their numbers he sensed that the only hope Bozeman's band had was if he traveled south fast enough to bring back help.

"But," Jacobs explained, "no more than ten miles back down the trail toward Fetterman's, I made a startlin' discovery. I'd just forded the Powder an' then swung west a few hunnert yards to a little cottonwood grove down by the water to be out of sight while I let my horse blow for a few minutes. You boys prob'ly remember the place, don't you?" Bozeman and the others confirmed that they did remember the grove.

"Well right there at the edge of the trees I found a spot where somebody had fit some sorta little battle. There was the ashes of three wagons an' a neat little row of eight fresh graves. From the looks of things about thirty Sioux had jumped a small wagon train there an' it looked like the Sioux had got the worst of the bargain. I saw places where a dozen or more of 'em had gone down, but the corpses naturally was all gone. An' there was tracks to show that five or six more wagons had lit out back south after the fight."

"A lot of that doesn't make much sense," Bozeman commented. "Did you ever get it all sorted out?"

Jacobs explained that he had caught up with the white survivors of the fight a few miles to the south. They explained the odd circumstances that Jacobs had discovered in the cottonwood grove. The leader of the group introduced his companions as a small band of Irish immigrants who had started west in January from New York.

Only two days after Bozeman's party left, they had reached Fetterman's Fort in their eight wagons. After hearing about the new shortcut, they had decided to strike out on their own and travel hard until they caught up with Bozeman on the trail. And they had almost accomplished that goal.

But on the banks of the Powder River, a medium-sized band of Sioux had struck them fiercely and unexpectedly just as they were preparing to break camp and cross the river. The Irishmen struck back as best they could, taking a decent toll on the Indian attackers during two lightning assaults. But then, just as unexpectedly, the Indians charged off across the river and continued their ride north, carrying their dead and wounded across the backs of their horses.

"Them Irishers couldn't figure why the Indians went on off an' left 'em alone," Jacobs reported, "but I think I know why. That bunch that lit into 'em was likely on its way here, prob'ly on the instructions of some Sioux chief—mebbe Blue Eagle or even Red Cloud hisself. An' prob'ly they were more concerned with stoppin' this main train than they were interferin' with a small group of stragglers like the Irishers."

"Did you make it on through to Fetterman's Fort?" Bozeman asked eagerly.

"Not quite," Jacobs replied.

"You mean you didn't get through to round up any help for us?"

"Help was on its way a'ready," the mountain man declared. " 'Bout forty miles north of Fetterman's I came across a troop of cavalry headed this way as fast as their gover'ment ponies would carry 'em. They'd been ridin' hard an' fast all the way from Fort Laramie. Their orders were to catch up with us an' bring us back."

"No!" Bozeman exclaimed, stunned by the announcement. "We can't go back now! Not after we've come all

70

this way! When the soldiers get here, they can help us break through this ring of Indians and then we'll press on. Perhaps we can even persuade them to travel along with us and escort us until we get clear of Sioux country.''

"Boy, do you know how many soldiers there were in that troop?'' Jacobs asked angrily. "There was sixty of 'em, an' that's all. When they get through to this train—if they get through—guarandamntee you they're goin' to be talkin' nice an' treadin' light around these four or five hunnert Sioux that got you penned up. They won't let you violate the treaty, at least not this time, 'cause *they* realize— if you don't—that if you press on another mile, these Indians will be onto this train like flies on dung. It's over, boy! We all tried, you most of all, but it's finally time to get it through your head that your train ain't goin' through an' your big dream is finished.''

Little more seemed left to be said. One by one Morris and his men began to wander off to spread the news. They were going to be saved, but their decision to follow Bozeman had cost them weeks of critical travel time.

None of the men had anything to say to Bozeman as they left. They were not angry with him, though that would probably come later. At that moment they merely were embarrassed to be in the presence of a man who had dreamed so grandly, only to have his hopes crushed in a few short minutes. Even Jacobs got up and wandered a short distance away, sensing somehow that his friend needed solitude.

Still squatting on the ground as he had been while they talked, Bozeman picked up a scoop of dirt in his hand. Slowly he let it trickle through his fingers. At last he looked up and gazed at the forty-two wagons that were the integral parts of his plan to become a wealthy and successful man. Within a few hours the soldiers would arrive to assure the Sioux they still held title to this barren land. And no later than the next morning, the wagon train would most likely be starting south.

But then a glimmer of something hopeful streaked through his thoughts. The trace of a smile danced across his lips.

"Finished, hell!" he exclaimed, rising to his feet and turning to where No Tongue Girl had just pulled the gurgling coffee pot off the fire. Watching Bozeman, John Jacobs merely glanced up from where he sat on the ground and shook his head.

Chapter 5

May, 1864

John Bozeman scratched reflectively at the full red beard
he had grown during the winter. With an almost paternal
appreciation he gazed at the distant Bighorn Mountains.
Traces of a late-winter snowfall still lingered along the
shaded northern slopes even as the early foliage of spring
was beginning to blanket the earth with green.

Bozeman glanced around. He had heard a teamster rip
out a chain of lively oaths at the team of ponderous oxen
that were pulling the wagon the man was driving. The
team had stopped in midstream during the crossing of the
Tongue River. For a moment, as Bozeman watched, the
wagon shifted and tipped at the mercy of the rushing
current. But the bullwhip that the teamster applied to the
rear ends of the lead animals prodded them into motion
again. Within a couple of minutes the wagon was safely
across the river.

Twenty wagons had already forded the Tongue to the

northern bank and about that same number remained on the south side waiting to make the crossing. It would take at least another two hours for all of them to complete the crossing. During that time, Bozeman planned to scout a couple of miles ahead to locate the best route for the wagons to follow.

The previous summer it would have been difficult to convince anybody that by springtime he would again be forging his new trail with a chain of wagons bound for the northern gold fields. Bozeman smiled to himself. He had never doubted it, even during the darkest hours.

The U.S. Cavalry troop had escorted Bozeman's first wagon train back to Fetterman's Fort. Arriving there, the disappointed, angry travelers were demanding everything from refunds of their fees to Bozeman's imprisonment or hanging. But Bozeman had envisioned the future accurately. He knew that somehow he would find a way to make another, more determined, try.

He had gone deeply into debt to Marlow Fetterman to make good on his obligations to the people of the wagon train. But Fetterman, a dreamer and schemer of sorts himself, had been willing to gamble a few hundred dollars on the expansive plans of a fellow visionary. Soon after, Bozeman had met with another disappointment as great as the forced return of his wagon train. John Jacobs announced that he planned to return to his wife's people, the Flat-heads, and would winter with them in their tribal territory far to the northwest.

In retrospect, Bozeman realized that from the start his partner's heart had never really been committed to the project. Discovering a new trail through Indian territory was simply not that important to him. Jacobs had come along for the adventure to be had. But the session in the council lodge of the Ogalla Sioux had soured him on the grand dreams he had attempted to share with Bozeman.

As was expected, Jacobs and his daughter left within a few hours. Bozeman was pleased that he and Jacobs parted on the best of terms. Both he and his companion were satisfied with what their three-month association had given them. Bozeman had firsthand knowledge of the trail he sought to explore. And Jacobs left with the finest two firearms he had ever owned.

During the busy fall and winter that followed, Bozeman remained on horseback almost constantly. His time was spent securing backers and making preparations to carry out his plans for the spring. Also during that time he spent many hours considering why he had failed initially and wondering what he could do differently the second time in order to insure success.

First, of course, old John Jacobs had been right in repeatedly advising him not to underestimate either the fighting ability of the Indians or their determination to defend their land against intruders. And secondly there had been the matter of setting out with such a mixed bag of people. Even though his group had been well armed, it had been impractical to expect dirt farmers and inexperienced Eastern adventurers to fight as skillfully as Indians who had lived their whole lives on a diet of violence and tribal warfare. In addition, the women and children along on the first trip had been a definite liability. Men tended to fight with less reckless courage when they had families to live for. And courage, in the final analysis, was the key to facing Indians on their own ground and holding them at bay.

So what he needed, Bozeman concluded at last, was a wagon company comprised of men who were knowledgeable of the West, skilled in the use of firearms and brave enough to put that skill to effective use. Such men were no rarity on the frontier. Bozeman realized that all he had to do was put out word of what he was looking for. He did this, and in no time teamsters volunteered who were willing to risk their lives in order to earn a considerably higher than average salary.

Financial backing was much more difficult, though not impossible, to obtain. In January of 1864, Bozeman had headed across the snow-swept Great Plains, carrying only two documents. One was a letter of credit. The other was a personal recommendation. Both had been signed by Marlow Fetterman.

Bozeman stopped first in Omaha, Nebraska. Then he traveled south to Independence, Missouri, where he finally persuaded a profit-minded wholesaler to back him on his venture.

If his plan succeeded, he told the wholesaler, then the rewards would be tremendous for all concerned. If it didn't, then the supplies would still be taken on the round-about route. And they would be sold for the usual profits, which were by no means paltry.

In late March, before the final blizzard of the season had roared its way across the Kansas plains, Bozeman started out from Independence with thirty wagons. The draft animals suffered from the scarcity of grass, and the teamsters suffered from the cold. But by the time Fetterman's Fort was reached, spring had also arrived and was making life much easier for all concerned. At the fort, Fetterman added ten wagons of his own to the train and Bozeman hired an extra twenty-five roughnecks whose primary duty it would be to defend against any Indian band that challenged them.

But now, two weeks after they had left the fort, they had traveled nearly a third of the distance to the gold fields without a single major confrontation. It was Bozeman's opinion that the Sioux knew it would be more difficult to turn back this wagon train than it had been to turn back the first one that had tried to cross their land.

Bozeman did his necessary scouting to the north. Then he rode in a wide circle around the train and headed south along their back trail, as he often did, to insure that no large band of hostiles was easing up behind them for a sneak attack. About a mile south of the Tongue River ford, he halted his horse on a gentle rise and surveyed the dozens of square miles of empty open country which lay spread out beneath him. It was almost too peaceful, he thought.

If he had turned back only a moment earlier, he would not have seen the lone horseman top a distant rise and come galloping toward him along the same route the wagon train had taken earlier in the day. But lost in his own thoughts, he had remained motionless on the hilltop.

When the horseman drew nearer, Bozeman recognized the man as Billy Buffalo, the Shawnee Indian he had hired in Kansas to work as an outrider for the wagon train. Billy was a "civilized," mission-educated Indian who had learned his tracking and scouting skills at an early age from his ancient grandfather, a former chief of the Shawnee tribe. Bozeman had sent Billy out to locate the Sioux.

The Indian had been away for two full days. That was not at all unusual. But now, seeing the hurried pace the Indian was setting, it seemed he was bearing important information.

Bozeman hailed the scout from a distance. When the Indian drew close enough, he asked him, "Well, what's the word, Billy? Any sign of the Sioux?"

"I saw them, all right," Billy announced excitedly. "A big band of about a hundred, braves only, riding about five miles south of here. But that's not all, Mr. Bozeman. There's another wagon train back there. It's just on the other side of the crest of that hill!''

"Well I'll be damned!'' Bozeman exclaimed. "We're being followed again!''

"It's only a small train,'' the scout put in, "eight wagons and fourteen teamsters. I talked to them and told them about the Indians, but they acted like the Indians didn't matter. They're crazy people back there, and the craziest thing is that their trail boss is a woman!''

"That *is* crazy . . . I won't argue that,'' Bozeman agreed. "Just what does the lady expect to do, sit there and be wiped out if those Sioux attack? Or does she have the wild notion that the fourteen of them can hold off one hundred Indians?''

"From the looks of the people with her, I'd say they'd make a lively fight of it,'' Billy speculated. "They're a rough-looking lot for sure, as tough or tougher than any we've got with us. And the woman fits right in with the rest. She's a looker, but she wears these two Navy revolvers in crossed holsters around her waist, and something about the look in her eye made me shiver.''

"She'll need to be some special kind of tough if those Sioux fool around and take her alive,'' Bozeman scoffed.

The two companions turned their horses north and headed toward their own train. Most of the way back, Bozeman wrestled with the problem of what to do about the tag-alongs and the Indian assault they would most likely be facing soon. It irked him that anybody would be so blatantly using him this way without bothering to pay a fee or even ask his permission to follow so close behind. His first inclination was to press on and abandon them to whatever fate their stupidity led them to. Yet here were white peole who would soon be in mortal danger from

Indians, and in this country any man with even a thread of a conscience just didn't turn away and ignore a situation like that.

By the time he and Billy caught up with the train, all of the wagons were across the river and just beginning to move northward according to the trail he had marked for them. He galloped to the front of the caravan and issued instructions for the wagons to circle on a grassy slope overlooking the banks of the Tongue. The maneuver took about ten minutes. When it was completed, he gathered his teamsters and guards within the circle for a discussion.

"Billy Buffalo has just informed me that we're not alone on the trail," Bozeman announced to the others. "There's a small wagon train coming up behind us, and Billy says a big band of Sioux are just about on top of them ready to attack."

"So what're we s'posed to do 'bout that?" asked a heavily armed rider named Burlanger, whom early on in the trip Bozeman had made second-in-command of the extra guards. Mainly it was Burlanger's burly size and toughness that made him a figure worthy of respect. "If those dumb jackasses are stupid enough to come out into country like this with only a small band, I say they deserve what they get."

"Part of me wants to agree with you," Bozeman conceded. "We're in this for the money and we all want to make it through to the gold field alive. But another side of me says we can't push north knowing that a train of white people is being slaughtered only a few miles behind us. If it was us, we'd expect help."

"But it ain't us," Burlanger scowled. "Listen, Bozeman, we hired on to fight for you an' your train, but I don't see no damn good reason to ride out an' fight for no strangers that won't be payin' none of us a plug nickel for savin' their hides.''

Bozeman had realized from the start that the only way to deal with Burlanger was to be as tough as he was and a little bit tougher, too. But until that moment it had not come to the point of the two of them standing face to face in a contest of wills.

"Listen, Burlanger," Bozeman retorted, letting his hand stray to the hilt of his Starr revolver, "your one responsibility is to do whatever I tell you to until we get these wagons to the gold fields and you draw your pay. It's the same for you and every other man in this outfit, and if you don't like that bargain, then you can just saddle up your mount and ride on your way."

Burlanger's expression deepened to a deadly-looking frown and he said, "I don't like it! I don't see no reason for a lot of us to get shot up for a damn bunch of strangers."

"The reason is because I say that's what we're going to do," Bozeman came back steadily. "Now you've got two choices. Stay and help me plan this thing out or pack your kit and go!"

For a moment the possibility of gunplay was very real. But finally Burlanger replied, "I reckon if we did it right, we could catch the Indians off guard an' keep our losses down."

"Hopefully," Bozeman agreed, holding no grudge. "They've got the edge in numbers but I'd guess they aren't nearly as well armed as us. And I don't think they'll be willing to fight to the last man simply for the thrill of taking a small wagon train."

Within a few minutes Bozeman and the others had worked out a plan. A full half of his company was organized to ride out to the rescue of the wagons a few miles back along the trail. Thirty men would stay behind with good repeating rifles and plenty of ammunition. Within minutes the designated men were saddled up, armed and on their way to the defenseless train.

About two miles south of the Tongue River, the riders began to hear the sound of distant gunfire. Though they could not yet see where a battle was taking place, it was obvious by the sound of things that the members of the small wagon train were making a lively fight of it.

When Bozeman's men finally topped the hill and gazed down at the scene below, they realized how difficult and costly it would be for them to try to break through to the wagons themselves. The Indians had caught the train in a broad, open meadow midway up the hillside. They were rushing in on desperate forays, trying to get close enough to fight hand-to-hand with the teamsters. The bodies of half a dozen downed Indians littered the open area around the wagons and testified to their lack of success thus far.

Instead of having his men charge in, Bozeman ordered them to dismount and take up firing positions in the small cluster of boulders near the crest of the hill. The actual fight was taking place nearly three hundred yards away, but the attackers were still within range of the new repeating rifles the white men carried. Within moments their heavy fire was beginning to empty Sioux saddles.

As Bozeman had predicted, the Indians soon began to withdraw. Their last desperate charges were to claim the bodies of their downed comrades, and a short time later they disappeared across a long, low ridge to the west. It seemed likely that they would plunge on directly into the mountains to lick their wounds and would cause no more trouble to the travelers for at least a few days. But just in case that wasn't their plan, Bozeman instructed Burlanger to lead all but five of the men directly back to their wagons. Then he and the rest of the group rode down the hillside to see how badly the small group had been bloodied.

The members of the wagon train had barely found the time to circle their wagons and herd their stock in before the attack began. But even after undertaking that defensive measure, they had suffered several losses at the hands of the hostiles. Four of the fourteen men were dead, and two others were seriously wounded. Those casualties left only one man to drive each of the eight wagons that the group had brought along. Several head of oxen and horses lay bloodied on the ground. A few other animals suffered from bullet wounds inflicted by random gunshots fired by the Indians.

When Bozeman and his men reached the circle of wagons, they stopped for a moment, surveying the chaos before them. Some of the uninjured men were on their knees helping the wounded. Others were working their way around, taking account of the stock and mercifully killing the animals that were critically hurt.

Finally Bozeman jumped to the ground. He went over to the man nearest him, who was fashioning a clumsy bandage over the gushing arm wound of a comrade. "I heard tell there's a woman in charge of this outfit," he remarked, introducing himself. "Where is she?"

Hardly glancing up, the man motioned with his head toward the far side of the ring of wagons. Bozeman gazed over in that direction but could see no sign of a woman anywhere. "Kate?" the man called out. "Feller here wants to see you."

A form that had been kneeling over one of the casualties rose. She turned toward them and Bozeman realized immediately why it had been so difficult to recognize her as a woman amidst this band of hard-bitten teamsters.

Standing nearly as tall as some of the men who

worked for her, she was dressed similarly to the drivers. Whatever figure she had was hidden beneath a heavy flannel shirt, loose trousers and high-topped leather boots. Yet beneath all that clothing it was possible to tell something about her slender, healthy proportions.

The woman wore her hair piled up beneath a worn, shapeless felt hat. But as she started toward Bozeman, she removed the hat and mopped a sleeve across her sweating brow. At once her sun-streaked brown hair cascaded down her back.

Her face was pretty, but not in a passive, overly feminine sort of way. She was no example of any customary male ideal of beauty, and Bozeman thought that perhaps the adjective which more properly described her was "handsome." Beneath an aquiline nose, her mouth was full and expressive. Her high cheekbones were almost Indian in their shape and proportions. Her skin was tanned a rich honey-brown and the gaze of her large dark eyes was probing and cautious.

When she reached Bozeman, she greeted him with a firm handshake and announced, "The name's Kate Lancaster. You must be part of the bunch from up there in the rocks."

– "That's right," Bozeman informed her, and he told her his name. Then he paused, permitting her time to express her thanks if she wished to do so. She did not. "It looks like they bloodied your outfit pretty good," he noted.

"We did all right, considering the odds," Kate judged. "I lost four men and a few head of stock, but we can still go on. It could have been worse."

"That's right, it could have," Bozeman observed. He was both amazed and angered by the woman's apparent unwillingness to offer any sort of gratitude for the help she had received. It was as if she hadn't noticed that he and his men had assisted in any way, let alone that they had most likely saved the lives of her and her men. Beside him Billy Buffalo had drawn back a couple of paces, not wanting to deal with a strange woman of Kate Lancaster's sort. The other three men were also holding back in a similar manner.

"Listen, Miss Lancaster," Bozeman went on at last, deciding to be as blunt as the wagon leader herself had been. "I don't know what kind of madness inspired you to start out in this country with such a small party—even as tough a bunch as you appear to have with you. But I do know that we almost didn't come back to lend you a hand. To be honest, I don't like anybody thinking they can get a free ride along this trail on my shirt tails, not after all the trouble and expense I've been through to get my train organized."

"Excuse me if I'm mistaken, Mr. Bozeman," Kate shot back, casting him a cool, defiant look, "but I failed to see your 'No Trespassing' signs when we started this trip. Do you *own* this land?"

"Of course not!" Bozeman snapped. "It's public land, or Indian land, depending on how you want to look at it. But I am one of the few men who knows the trail across this territory and I expect to get paid when I guide someone through. Lady, I don't know who you are or what kind of shenanigans you think you're up to, but I do know I'm not about to let somebody slide through on my back trail absolutely free, especially when I have to swing back around and lose time to save their bacon from the Sioux. The best thing for you to do, Miss Lancaster, is turn your wagons around while you've still got some men to drive them. Then head for Fetterman's Fort like the devil was riding your tailgate."

"Nobody asked for your help," Kate reminded Bozeman curtly. "We just about had those Sioux whipped before you and yours even showed up. So now that it's all over, don't come wagging around here expecting a lot of gratitude."

"Woman, you're incredible!" Bozeman exclaimed. "I can't believe I'm hearing you right!"

A few feet away, one of Kate Lancaster's teamsters glanced up with a dark look on his face and asked, "Trouble, Miss Kate?" Bozeman noticed that the man already had his hand on the hilt of his revolver, and around the circle of wagons the rest of the crew began to pay close attention to the heated conversation.

"It's not a thing I can't handle, Jake," Kate assured him. Then, returning her attention to Bozeman, she continued, "Mr. Bozeman, you don't own this trail and you don't own me. I have no use for your sage advice or your words of wisdom. I may be a woman, and only twenty-two years old at that, but don't fool yourself into thinking that because of my lack of years I don't know what I'm doing here. I've been traveling and trading and handling freight on the frontier since I've been fourteen years old, and I can take on anything that these Indians or any highhanded roughnecks like you throw in my direction and still get done what I set my mind to do."

Bozeman stared, infuriated but unwilling to keep up the exchange any longer. He could sense that behind him his men were tense and bristling for a fight. The situation easily could erupt into a renewed round of gunfire.

"All right, lady," he conceded at last, "have it your way. Me and my men butted our noses in where we had no business, but you can be assured we won't make the same mistake again. The next time you and what's left of this ragtag outfit of yours meet up with the Sioux, you won't have to worry a bit about sharing the glory with anybody. I've got a lot of brave men in my bunch, but none so crazy they'd be willing to risk their lives a second time for a bullheaded, ingrate hussy like you!''

Kate Lancaster took a quick swing, not with her palm open for a slap but with her fingers clenched into a fist like a man. Half expecting such a display, Bozemen sidestepped and the blow glanced off his shoulder. Before Kate could regain her balance for another try, he spun and marched outside the ring of wagons to where the horses waited. His men followed close behind him, the sight of their backs defying Kate's crew to do anything about the parting insult.

As the days passed following the confrontation between him and Kate Lancaster, Bozeman became convinced that the young woman must lead a charmed life. Depending on the weather, wagon breakdowns and the condition of the wagon stock, Kate's group remained anywhere from one to ten miles behind his at all times. And no matter how much distance separated the smaller group from the larger, the Indians in the area made no further attempts to capture Kate's wagons.

Twice Billy Buffalo returned from distant scouting trips with reports of Indian sightings in the Bighorn Mountains to the west. But neither time did the Indians advance down to the rolling hills and plains to threaten either of the wagon trains. Probably, Bozeman decided, the Sioux still thought that the two wagon trains, though not traveling together, would still come to one another's aid in case of attack.

All during the journey Bozeman's men kept coming to him with schemes to delay or halt the smaller train. Burlanger suggested that if they picked an appropriate water hole and dumped a couple of dozen bags of salt in it, it would probably kill some of Kate Lancaster's stock and make the rest so sick that it would take them days to recover. Another of the men proposed that they pick a hot, dry day when the wind was right and set the prairie grass on fire behind them. A few of the men even expressed their willingness to sneak back at night and see what sort of damage they could do with their rifles to Kate Lancaster's livestock and drivers.

In the end, Bozeman decided to do nothing vindictive. He claimed that Kate's presence simply wasn't enough of a bother to warrant any action against her. If she arrived at all, she would reach the isolated mining towns after his train. By then the amount of freight she had to sell would amount to only about a quarter of what he had brought along.

In his own mind, however, Bozeman was not completely sure why he did not want his men to harass Kate and her drivers. She frustrated him with her bullheadedness and her lack of appreciation for the risk he had taken for her at the Powder River. Nevertheless, he felt something akin to admiration for her independence and her utter courage in the face of great danger. A part of him, he decided, believed that Kate Lancaster *deserved* to get through with her freight and make a decent profit on it—just so long as nothing she did interfered with his business.

Chapter 6

The rough hemp of the rope ground at Hank Mandell's throat like sandpaper, but it was impossible for him to reach up and relieve the irritation. His hands were tied firmly behind his back. Beneath his feet, the tiny, three-legged stool wobbled precariously, threatening to collapse from his weight even before anyone could step forward and kick it from under him.

Mandell stared out defiantly over the faces of the crowd surrounding him and thought, You bastards have yourselves a real, live badman to string up and you're loving it, aren't you? He could see the lust for violence in their eyes. Not even the twelve members of the "council" who so soberly had condemned him to death could conceal the rush of excitement they were feeling at witnessing his sanctioned execution.

There was no trace of submission on the rigid features of Mandell. His gaze was fiercely cold despite his helpless situation and he could sense fear in the emotions of those men whose gaze met his. The reaction was something he was used to.

The hard life he'd led had honed his tall, husky frame down to a compact assemblage of muscle and bone. Even standing still, as he was now, he conveyed the impression of a man whose reflexes were as quick and accurate as those of a striking cobra.

In their haste to get Mandell hanged, the onlookers had not even bothered to build a gallows. Nor had they permitted their prisoner the customary last meal. Once his sentence had been determined, they simply had shoved him into the vacant shell of a half-finished building, pitched a rope over a heavy beam and tied the loop around his neck.

During what seemed to be the final moments of his life, Mandell was surprised to discover that the thing that bothered him most about this situation was seeing the yahoos who stood in front of him getting so much enjoyment from the whole affair. Over the past three years he had seen plenty of men die, allies and enemies alike, but he could never recall a single instance when he felt any real pleasure in the experience.

In Lizard Gap, where he faced his own death, it seemed like his execution was the biggest event to have happened all spring. Men had left their sluices unworked and their businesses untended to witness it. Mandell guessed that when he finally did make that short fall into eternity, he'd have just about the whole population of the town as his audience.

He wished for one free hand. What a fine thing it would be to go out making a last expressive gesture and show the crowd what he was thinking.

A lot of things had happened in a hurry since he had ridden into Lizard Gap just two short hours before, and not a single one of them had anything to do with the plans he'd made for himself during the difficult, four-day ride over into the mountains from Bannack City.

*   *   *

He had figured correctly that by heading west into the mountains early in the spring he would beat the rush of greenhorns from back east who would begin arriving in early June. The extra time would give him a chance to check out the job opportunities at the gold-producing sluices around Lizard Gap, and also, if he was lucky, to stake out a claim for himself somewhere along one of the prime stretches of nearby Bohannon Creek. Some of the most fortunate of the miners along the creek were already said to be sluicing out up to a hundred dollars a day from their hundred-foot-long claims, and that was even before the ground had thawed sufficiently for them to dig down to bedrock where the real deposits were.

Lizard Gap had sprung to life the previous summer in a small meadow conveniently close to where several prospectors had discovered placer deposits of gold in a twisting mountain stream. No thought or planning had gone into the layout of the town. As a result, men had built their cabins on any spot of ground available. A main street of sorts had evolved and eventually had become the center of what commerce there was to be found in Lizard Gap. Along that thoroughfare were three general merchandise stores, a blacksmith's shop, half a dozen boarding houses, two restaurants and two saloons.

The two-hundred-plus residents of the town had suffered mightily during the winter, both because of the severe mountain cold and the shortages of everything from flour to chewing tobacco. But with the arrival of spring, food and supplies were more plentiful and a new influx of fortune-hungry hopefuls had begun to pour in in search of any opportunities that were available in the ramshackle metropolis.

Hank Mandell had been one of the stream of travelers. They had arrived in the mountains from Bannack City in the west and Fort Benton in the north. But his luck had turned sour on him almost the minute he'd reached Lizard Gap. After no more than half an hour in town, he had gotten himself mixed up in an argument with a drunken miner. The miner had decided it was his right and obligation to flog a local doxy named Lydia with the ramrod of his rifle because she had not performed up to his expectations. Lydia had fled half-naked out the front door of the man's cabin and collided with Mandell. Once Mandell had evaluated the situation, he had tried to save Lydia from a painful beating. The argument had exploded into gunplay and Mandell had laid the miner out with one quick shot to the center of his chest.

That should have been the end of that, but the woman Mandell had fought to defend immediately turned on him. Angrily she insisted that without just cause he had interfered in a bit of personal business between her and the dead miner. The woman's testimony before Lizard Gap's hastily convened council had been utterly damning. Some of the dead miner's friends already had the hangman's knot tied with a fresh coil of hemp rope before the proceedings were even finished.

It was crude justice. But it was the only kind available in an area like Lizard Gap. There the westward thrust of exploration and commerce had far outdistanced the system of laws that prevailed in other more settled areas. Nobody had really given much thought to the finer points of Mandell's case, such as whether or not he had actually fired in self-defense. They were more concerned with the fact that he seemed to be too dangerous a man to have around and decided to remedy their concern by disposing of him quickly and permanently.

"Well, young fellow, it looks like you've bought the

farm," a man teased from beside Mandell's perch atop the stool. "But in case you're wondering, after it's all over we'll sell off your guns and horse to pay for your burial."

The man's name was Sims Lawton. He was the fifty-year-old owner of the largest merchandise store in town. As chief of the Lizard Gap Council, he had presided during the trial and sentencing. Now it seemed that he would also serve as executioner.

"You got any last words you'd like to say?" Lawton asked.

"I can't think of a damn thing," Mandell growled.

"Well one fellow we strung up last November used his last breath to give us a good cussing," Lawton chuckled. "It seemed proper for us to let him do that then, just as it would be for you to do it now. So go ahead and rip a few out if you feel like it."

"I don't see no use in it."

"How about a smoke, then?"

"Not a chance. Just do what you have to and be damned," Mandell snapped, tired of reading the growing excitement and anticipation on the spectators' faces. At least after he took the fall he wouldn't have to feel like a side of beef hanging in the meat shop window.

"Well if he won't speak up for himself, I will!" a voice called out unexpectedly from the back of the crowd. Mandell looked over and saw a man pushing his way hurriedly to the front.

"What's any of this got to do with you, Henry Morton?" Lawton inquired. Mandell was wondering the same thing, but he didn't mind the interruption.

"Well I been standing back watching," Morton replied, "and all the time I've been wondering why this Mandell fellow looked so familiar. Then it hit me. Crop his hair off shorter, add a beard and a mustache, and he's the very same man that saved the lives of me and my two partners two years ago down along the Gros Ventre Range.''

A puzzled expression shadowed Mandell's face. Two years before, as he recalled, a company of Confederate Cavalry he was leading had been lined up along the bluffs above the Tennessee River at a place called Shiloh. They were hoping to push General Ulysses S. Grant back into the river with their next charge.

Mandell's expression deepened. Until that moment he had never even heard of the Gros Ventre Range. Nor had he ever seen the man who was now speaking out in his behalf. But whatever Morton's game was, he saw no harm in playing along.

''Yessir,'' Morton continued, ''that was one hairy scrape we got ourselves into down there.'' He turned to address the whole crowd behind him. ''Them three road agents had us cold along a narrow mountain trail. They were ready to haul away everything we had. But then this man here come along unexpected and when the lead stopped flying them three owlhoots lay dead on the ground. So you see, men, I owe this Hank Mandell my life and I ain't all that particular fond of seeing him hanged.''

Morton's tale aroused mixed emotions in the crowd and also in the council members who had condemned Mandell. Thieves and road agents were a constant threat in those parts. Some of the men believed it was a fine thing that Mandell had done. But others were unwilling to forget that he also had killed a resident of Lizard Gap less than two hours before.

Morton stroked his salt-and-pepper beard while contemplating the problem. Then he turned to the members of the council with a suggestion. ''I can see why you men would get antsy with a fast draw and a straight shot like Hank Mandell right here amongst you,'' he said, 'but how

94

would you feel if I ridded you of Mandell without you having to swing him down from a crossbeam?''

"Well, I . . ." Lawton began hesitantly. He turned to glean support from the other members of the council who stood nearby. But none of them wanted to be the first to speak up.

"It ain't no crime to be a good shot," Morton insisted. "Hell, you found that dead man's gun laying right by his hand. Don't it make sense that Mandell was defending himself?''

Without receiving permission from anyone, Morton drew his sheath knife and sliced through the rope that circled Mandell's neck. At the same time he announced, "Me and my partners can use this man on the prospecting trip we're heading out on. That will get him out of everybody's hair quick enough. And when the trip's finished, I think Mandell will have better sense than to ever come back here again." Morton cut Mandell's hands loose with the knife and retrieved his rifle and two pistol belts from the council member who had confiscated them. "Does that idea suit everybody?" he asked at last.

With their prisoner already practically free, Lawton and some of the other council members scowled as they tried to figure out what they were really feeling, but none moved to stop Morton.

"He just better not ever come back and try to shoot none of our folks," Lawton threatened at last. "We won't abide it."

"Come on," Morton told Mandell, ignoring the comment and leading the former captive into the crowd. "My horse is near yours over by the saloon. I'll let you have your guns back once we get clear of town."

All the time that they were mounting up and riding out of town, Mandell kept expecting the people of Lizard

95

Gap to have a sudden change of heart and come surging after him to complete their deadly work. But it didn't happen. He stayed silent until they had cleared the last cabin at the edge of town. Then he turned to the man riding beside him and said, "Fella, I don't know how or why you did what you just did, but I can tell you this—you just made yourself a friend for life!"

"Friends are something a man can't have too many of," Morton tossed back with a grin.

"But just exactly why did you do it?" Mandell asked after they had ridden along for another minute. "We've never met before. For all you know I could be the stone-hearted killer that all those morons back there had themselves convinced that I was."

"That's right," Morton agreed. "But have you thought that maybe I didn't do what I did so much for you as for my own self?"

"I'd have some trouble understanding that," Mandell admitted.

"Well you see, last fall I had this young feller working for me," Morton began. "His name was John Tabor and his head was as thick as an ironwood tree, but at the sluices he could put in a day's work that any two other men would be proud to take credit for. One night John got drunk and rowdy and the next morning one of the town whores turned up strangled to death. John was the last one anybody could remember seeing her with, so after a trial like yours he was strung up for the crime.

"Two days later a drifter tried to sell some of the dead girl's jewelry to a drummer, and after he got himself caught, he admitted strangling her. Well that set me to feeling mighty guilty about how I hadn't stood by John or believed him when he swore he hadn't committed any crime. After that time, I told myself I wouldn't be quite so quick to go along with a crowd when they decided they'd like to stretch somebody's neck.''

"Well, I guess I owe my thanks to you *and* to John Tabor," Mandell returned.

"You might say that," Morton answered. Then, after a moment of consideration, he added, "Yeah, John might have liked thinking that. That big dumb brute had a good heart. It would have pleased him to know that after a year his death did finally count for something after all."

The two men were riding up a steep grade to the east, right into the heart of the Gallatin Mountains. When they neared the crest of the small rise that would put them out of sight of the town of Lizard Gap, Mandell didn't even turn around for one last look.

They rode on and Morton explained that the other six men in his group were camped about a mile ahead, eager to strike out on their prospecting trip. Only the rarest stroke of fortune, Morton said, had delayed them and brought him into town one final time before they left.

Earlier that morning, as they were preparing to leave, one of the horses had reared as it was being packed. Their only bag of salt had fallen to the ground and spilled. Because their group planned on an extended stay in the wilderness and didn't want to go so long without salt on their food, Morton had been selected to make one final trip into town.

Morton chuckled. "Except for that coincidence, me and my men would now be at least ten miles into the mountains and you would be swinging in the breeze with a rope around your neck."

Mandell shrugged good-naturedly. He had learned long ago that often fate had its own way of arranging and rearranging a man's life, with or without his consent. It was a fact of life that he had grown accustomed to. Believing that, a man could simply take things as they came.

He had known all along what the stuff would look like, but now that he was actually gazing down at the tiny flecks of yellow metal in the bottom of his pan, Mandell was flooded with an unexpected rush of excitement. Despite himself, he let out a shout to his companion. In a moment Luby Anderson, his sometimes partner on the trail, came rushing down the creek bed to him.

"It's gold, Luby!" Mandell proclaimed excitedly. "I actually found some gold!"

Anderson looked down at the half a dozen minute flecks in the bottom of Mandell's pan. Then he glanced up at his companion, wearing a patronizing grin. "It's gold all right, Hank," he chuckled. "Hell, another two hours of panning up treasure like that and you'll have enough to buy yourself a drink of whiskey!"

"What are you talking about?" Mandell asked, more than slightly angered by his companion's lack of enthusiasm over the find. "If this was here," he snapped defensively, "then there's bound to be more."

"Sure there is," Anderson agreed. "Hell, it could be our first step in finding the mother lode that'll make us all rich. But more likely not, Hank. Just don't get your hopes built up too soon, not until we work this area out and find out if we're onto something worthwhile or not. Right now I'm going to go get my shovel and pan and we'll start working our way upstream to see if the colors get any richer the higher up we go."

During the four days that had passed since they left the camp near Lizard Gap, it was Luby Anderson Mandell had found himself pairing up with most frequently when the party split up to check out the various streams and creeks. The thirty-year-old Irish immigrant had a quick, dry wit and he had been at this prospecting business for nearly two years. That made him a man who could teach a great deal about prospecting. Sometimes when they worked, the two men spent hours at a time without exchanging more than a dozen words. But in camp or during the long rides, Anderson often kept the entire party entertained with his wealth of yarns about the men he had fought, the places he had seen and the women he had loved. That fact alone made him ideal company for a man who preferred to talk as little as possible about himself or his past.

During the four hours that they worked the bed of the mountain creek, Mandell found himself growing more and more discouraged by the results of their labors. No matter how deep they dug or how promising the silt they panned seemed, the creek bed refused to yield any more than an occasional trace of gold dust.

When noon finally arrived, the two men decided to stop and return to camp a mile or so away. There they would discuss their minor find with Morton and the others, and then they could better decide whether to investigate the vicinity of the creek more thoroughly or give up and press on in search of richer deposits elsewhere.

Mounting their horses, they followed the steep, tumbling creek down to a broad valley below, where Morton had chosen to camp in an aspen grove on the banks of a clear, shallow stream.

As Mandell and Anderson neared to within a few hundred yards of the camp, they saw four of their six companions kneeling on the ground in the edge of the grove. The men appeared to be engaged in a discussion as they tended to a pot of stew cooking over a low fire. But as he and Anderson rode closer, Mandell began to feel uneasy. At last he stopped his horse and quietly told his partner, "Wait a minute, Luby. There's something about this situation I don't like."

Anderson reined up and leaned forward in his saddle, staring intently, trying to detect a sign that anything was wrong in or around the camp. "I don't see anything," he said at last.

"What's the first thing a man would usually do when he got to camp?" Mandell asked worriedly.

"I don't know. Step down, I guess."

"All right, and then what?"

"Check the pot, I guess, or maybe get a drink of water or take a leak. . . . Hell, I don't know. What are you getting at?"

"What would you do with your horse, Luby? Would you turn him out to graze while you ate?"

"Well sure, but . . ." And then he realized what Mandell was getting at. The horses of the four men had not been turned loose to graze in the thick grass near the camp. They were all tied to trees within a few feet of where the men now knelt.

While he was prospecting, Mandell always wore one gunbelt strapped to his right leg. Now he reached back to get his second pistol and gunbelt out of his saddlebags and strap it around his waist. He loosened the flap that secured his rifle inside the boot on the right front side of his saddle.

By that time all four men in camp were staring toward them blankly. None had stood up or made any sign of greeting.

Beside Mandell, Anderson drew his Henry .44 from the boot. Then he stated, "As I see it, we've got two choices. We either ride on in and try to shoot it out with whoever has the drop on our friends there, or we turn around and haul on out of here before somebody tries to knock us out of the saddles.''

"A general I served under once years ago told me he had one basic tactic in warfare,'' Mandell put in. ''When in doubt, charge!''

"Do you figure he knew what he was talking about?''

"I think he probably did. His name was Robert E. Lee.''

"All right, then . . .''

But before either man could spur his horse toward the camp, one of the prospectors at the campfire rose suddenly and raised his arm. It was not quite a wave, more like a signal of some sort that neither Mandell nor Anderson could understand. The man began walking forward and they recognized him as the leader of their group, Henry Morton.

Mandell and Anderson dismounted. Then they stood with their horses partially concealing their bodies as they waited for Morton to reach them.

"What in the hell's going on?'' Anderson asked when Morton was close enough to hear.

"It's Sioux,'' Morton told them darkly. ''When me and Ben Hardesty got back to camp about half an hour ago they was hiding close by and got the drop on us right off. Then they made us stay out in the open like everything was fine so they could lure everybody else in. Blankenship and Peabody rode right into the trap, but I guess you two weren't so easily fooled.''

"We knew something was wrong,'' Mandell told him, ''and we were just trying to decide whether to come in shooting or turn tail and head the other way.''

"That's why they sent me out here,'' Morton told them. ''There's a rifle trained on my back right now, and

101

the same goes for them other three. They said if you don't come on in and turn your arms over to them, they'd shoot all four of us down." Morton paused a moment, then looked steadily at both men before adding, "But I'd advise you to make tracks anyway. From what I know about the Sioux, I'd say the four of us are goners any way you look at it."

"Well what in the hell are the Sioux doing in this neighborhood?" Anderson asked. "I thought their country was farther to the south and west of here."

"I guess they pretty much go where they damn well please," Morton replied. "I've known of them ranging as far north as Fort Benton and as far west as Bannack City. But I don't suppose all that makes much difference anyway, because they're here now. At least twenty of them are hidden in the trees back there, and I'd guess there's others out in these hills nearby."

A shot rang out suddenly from the trees behind Morton and a bullet plowed a furrow in the dirt no more than a foot from where he stood. "I guess they're trying to tell me that we've talked enough," Morton remarked dryly. "It's up to you now."

"I'm going in with you, Henry," Mandell announced without hesitation. "A full week hasn't passed since you cut that rope and got me out of Lizard Gap. After a thing like that I'd have to be some kind of belly-crawling no-count to turn around and leave you to die."

"I guess I'd just as soon hang in with the bunch I came out here with, too," Anderson announced.

When the three men reached the camp, it took the Indians only a minute to disarm Mandell and Anderson and put their horses with the other mounts. Then the captors ordered the two new arrivals to join the four others so that once again the trap would be baited. It was clear that the Sioux already knew how many prospectors were in the group and intended to take them all captive.

But as Mandell was preparing to kneel, one of the Indians restrained him with a grunt and a firm grip on his upper arm. The Indian had his eyes fixed on the tooled leather belt and silver buckle Mandell wore, and his intentions were obvious. He pointed to the belt and growled an order in Sioux, apparently expecting the belt to be surrendered without protest.

"Damn you!" Mandell snarled at the man. "You already took my guns. I'm not about to hand over every single thing you decide you like."

The Indian repeated the order in even more harsh, unmistakable terms, drawing his heavy sheath knife at the same time.

"Better give him the belt," one of the other men advised hoarsely.

"The hell I will!" Mandell protested. Without warning he drew back one fist and smashed it hard into the face of the startled Indian. The man went down like a log, but only an instant later a pistol barked from somewhere to the side. Mandell felt a searing pain across the back of his skull and everything went black.

Chapter 7

No one had to tell Hank Mandell how much his act of defiance had angered the Sioux. He realized it the moment he began to regain consciousness in the Indian camp.

They had him tied upside down between two posts set firmly in the ground, and it seemed as if every fly in the northern Rockies had already found its way to his honey-smeared body. His belt and buckle were gone, of course, as were his shirt, pants and all the rest of his clothes. Practically every inch of his skin was alive with a multitude of buzzing black insects, and it was impossible for him to do a thing to dislodge them with his arms and legs splayed so rigidly out from his body.

As his attention focused on the throbbing pain in his head, he recalled the roar of the pistol that had sent him spinning away into unconsciousness and began to wonder why he was still alive. He decided that the bullet that had been meant to kill must merely have grazed him.

"Hank? Have you come to?" a voice asked from nearby. Mandell tried to open his eyes, but the flies made that difficult. And when he parted his lips to speak, a dozen or more insects immediately decided to investigate the cavern of his mouth, so, frantically, he shut it again.

"Sorry, but we can't do a thing for you," the man rasped. Mandell recognized the voice of Henry Morton, but still did not try to respond. "They got us trussed up over here like steers ready for branding, but they was kind enough to put us where we could see the show. Two braves tied you up like that, but it was the kids that had the bright idea of smearing the honey on you."

"Where are we?" Mandell managed to grate between pursed lips.

"We're in the main camp of none other than Red Cloud himself," Morton explained. A note of awe was evident in his voice. "It's a big camp, too, deep in the mountains about twenty miles from where they took us prisoner. Everybody else is all right so far—the Indians managed to get their hands on Wilkins and Smith, too. But we can't figure what they're up to. All we've seen since we got here are the squaws that came to pick through our pockets for what they wanted, and the kids that come to pester us. They stuck some red ants down the front of Peabody's britches and then had them a high old time just sitting back watching him squirm."

"The little jackals learn early how to devil a man," Peabody added bitterly. "I feel all puffed up down there."

"And they beat the bottoms of my feet with some damn little wooden paddles," another man chimed in.

"I guess they would have eventually gotten around to all of us," Morton remarked, "but finally an old squaw woman came. She ran them off and gave us all a drink of water. It's the only decent thing that's happened to any of us since we got brought here."

Time dragged on for what seemed like an eternity,

but Mandell took no part in the occasional nervous conversations. The consensus among the men was that they would eventually be tortured to death. But if that was to be the case, they wondered, then why hadn't the festivities already begun?

Listening to the exchanges, Mandell could tell that Smith and Blankenship were falling apart pretty quickly from the strain and that none of the others was faring much better. Only Morton, the oldest member of their group, seemed to hold out much hope that any of them would survive their captivity.

Because of the position he was in and the length of time he had gone without water, Mandell began to fade in and out of consciousness once more. His mind quit trying to hold onto and understand the words that were being spoken nearby as wild, dreamlike illusions began to drift through his mind like passing storms.

A dozen men were crammed into a cell so small that some were forced to sit up so that the others could lie down and sleep. Food was shoved in through a small hole in the door once a day and the strongest took the lion's share before permitting the weaker to have the cast-off scraps. The air in the cell was thick and putrid with the odor of stagnant waste. Filth coated the prisoners' bodies. One of their number had passed beyond the point of screaming into uttering senseless mumblings that all knew preceded death. It was a hell more vivid and miserable than any mind could conceive without experiencing it personally, and for a time Mandell was back in that cell waiting to die.

The buckets of water splashing across his body jolted Mandell back to reality. But before he could quite grasp

107

what was going on around him, his limbs had been cut loose from the posts and he fell suddenly and painfully to the ground. His arms and legs ached from their stretching and his head felt as if it was in danger of exploding internally. He couldn't move. Strong hands grasped him by his arms and hauled him to his feet.

"Hank, are you with us?"

Mandell's throat was dry and constricted. He couldn't speak, but he responded to the question with a harsh, rasping sound.

"Luby, get that bucket of water and see if they'll let us get away with giving him a drink."

Water was splashed across Mandell's face and chest. When some reached his mouth, too, he swallowed it greedily.

"You going to make it, Hank?"

"Yeah. Yeah, I'll make it," Mandell managed to say at last. His legs and feet felt leaden beneath him, but eventually they began to accept the responsibility of supporting him and he opened his eyes and looked around.

Morton had not exaggerated when he said that the Indian camp was a large one. From where they stood, Mandell could see that the pointed hide tepees of the Sioux band covered nearly two acres of open ground in a broad, grassy mountain valley. They had been held near the lower, eastern end of the camps, and farther on down the valley hundreds of horses were grazing peacefully.

In addition to the seven other white men, at least a dozen armed Indians now stood nearby, watching impatiently as Mandell slowly regained his strength and sensibilities. When at last he was able to stand alone, one of the Indians pitched him a pair of greasy leather pants and gestured for him to put them on. Then in Sioux he gave a command to all the men and pointed toward the center of camp with the rifle he held.

"My God, Henry! What are they going to do with us?" Tim Smith asked unsteadily.

"How in the hell should I know?" Morton responded. "Maybe they got a buffalo roasting and this is their way of giving us an invite to supper."

"More likely they're ready to roast *us*," Anderson muttered.

"Well, whatever," Morton added matter-of-factly. "I never claimed to know much about these savages, but I do know that the first man who cracks and shows he's yellow is likely to catch the worst of things when it comes time to deal with us. I've heard it said many a time that there's nothing an Indian despises as much as cowardice. Some of you had best keep that in mind from this point on."

Mandell recognized Morton's words as good advice, but he also knew that what his friend suggested was something more easily said than done. He had seen men crack under all sorts of circumstances and situations. Every man had his own limits of courage and endurance. Beyond that point, each was susceptible to the primeval fears of unbearable pain or death.

They were taken to a council lodge that was much different in construction from the pointed tepees the Indians lived in. This headquarters of sorts had been constructed of vividly painted animal skins stretched over a rectangular frame about fifteen feet long and ten feet wide. When they reached the lodge, one of the Indian escorts went ahead for a moment. Then he came back out and prodded the prisoners inside with the barrel of his rifle.

In the center of the lodge, a small, ceremonial fire was sending up a thin cloud of pungent white smoke. About twenty Indians sat cross-legged in a semicircle along the back and two side walls facing the prisoners. They were a stone-faced lot, mostly older men who appeared to be the elders and leaders of the tribe. It took Mandell only a moment to pick out the one who must be the famous Chief Red Cloud.

Red Cloud sat in the center of the group. He wore a fringed buckskin shirt and trousers, as well as a massive feathered headpiece that stretched nearly to the ground behind him. He appeared to be a man of about forty, and the lined, blocky features of his face could have been carved from a solid chunk of granite for all the expression they held. Only Red Cloud's eyes moved, wandering with calm disdain from the face of one prisoner to the next.

No white man lived long in the northern Rockies without hearing about Red Cloud. He was said to be the unofficial chieftain of the Ogalla Sioux nation and at once was the most feared and warlike of all the great Indian leaders in the Northwest. Fear and respect mingled in men's voices when they spoke his name. And most believed that capture by any party of Sioux he led was tantamount to a death sentence.

Flanking Red Cloud on his right side was a bizarre-looking character whom Mandell took for the medicine man of the tribe. The Indian wore his hair in an elaborate, oddly braided topknot, and the skin of his face and arms had been ceremonially scarred with a variety of shapes and symbols. Half a dozen small bowls in front of him contained various whitish and grey powders. A larger vessel was filled with a thick, reddish liquid that had the unmistakable look of blood.

Henry Morton, who had decided that it was his place to act as spokesman for his party, held up one hand and began a greeting. But before he had spoken three words, a brave standing behind him brought him to his knees with a vicious blow from a rifle butt.

At last the medicine man took a small handful of powder from one of his bowls and pitched it on the smoldering fire. The powder flared briefly, sending upward a round cloud of smoke. Then the medicine man dipped his hand in the bowl of blood and began letting it drip from his fingertips onto a small, bleached skin spread before him.

His words, when considered with his expression, appeared to be a tirade against the eight white prisoners, in combination with an interpretation of the bloody divinations on the skin. The other Indians, including Red Cloud, listened to him solemnly, nodding occasionally as they continued to stare at the captives.

The medicine man's speech lasted for at least a quarter of an hour. When he was finished, the prisoners were herded outside again by their guards without ever having had the opportunity to say a word in their own defense. The guards permitted them to get drinks of water from a large pottery crock. Then they were allowed to settle in the shade of a spreading cottonwood tree.

"Wonder what that was all about?" Ben Hardesty asked.

"I'd say they must have brought us in to decide what to do with us," Morton speculated.

"Well, there ain't no doubt how that one fellow with the bloody hand is going to vote," Luby Anderson scoffed. "A man don't have to understand a word of Sioux to get the gist of what he was saying."

Off to one side, Roland Smith was struggling to control a fit of trembling as he listened silently to what the others were saying. Mandell watched him sympathetically for a moment. Then he turned his head away and gazed off toward a string of mountain ridges to the south. If it did come to torture, he knew that only a couple of his companions would take it even halfway well, and he was not even sure how he himself would act.

He rose at last and wandered off a short distance, as far away from the others as the guards would permit him to go. Stark memories were beginning to rush back at him once more.

The whipping post in the main yard of Locksly Prison was about two feet in diameter and eight feet high. When the guards tied a man to it, they stretched his arms around it with a rope until they felt like they were going to be pulled from their sockets. Then when all the prisoners were assembled in ranks in the yard, Mule Grimes, the head guard, would go to work with his whip. When four or five men were lashed in a single day, the ground for five feet around the post would be splotched with the rusty brown splatterings of their blood.

The screams were the worst part, even worse it seemed than seeing a man's back laid open with the heavy bull whip that Grimes used. After a while the sounds began to lance a man's mind like spears of fire.

"I guess maybe you're thinking right now that I didn't do you such a favor after all, cutting you loose from that hangman's rope," Morton jested to Mandell. "It sure would be an easier way to die than what we might face here."

"No, Henry," Mandell assured him. "What you did still stands out in my mind for exactly what it was—a good deed by a brave man. I was thinking about other things, things that happened a long time ago."

"You know," Morton went on, "I've never been a

particularly nosy man, but I do catch myself wondering about people sometimes, particularly when I meet a quiet, curious sort of fellow like you. Your past weighs pretty heavy on you now and again, don't it, Hank?''

"There's a thing or two that I did way back that I'm not so proud of,'' Mandell admitted with a burst of candor that surprised even himself. "When I came west some months back, I was figuring on living it all down and making a new start, but it seems like a man just goes on carrying that sort of baggage with him wherever he goes.''

A lot of men in these parts are on the run from something,'' Morton acknowledged, "whether it be the law, the army, a woman or whatever. What are you on the run from, friend?''

It had been a long time since Hank Mandell had placed his trust in any man. The secrets of his past had been his alone. But now, suddenly, he found himself opening up to Henry Morton, telling him things that a short time ago he believed would be his solitary burdens until he carried them to the grave. He did not really understand why, but he thought it probably had something to do with the camaraderie that sometimes existed between men who were about to die together.

"I've come across too many Southerners in these parts to ever talk much about my past,'' Mandell explained. "I'm a deserter of sorts from the Confederate Army and I knew if word got out, I'd be a marked man. There would be no end to the fistfights and gunfights I'd be facing everywhere and eventually somebody would get the job done. But I'm not a coward, Henry. I didn't just run away.''

He glanced over at Morton to see how his first few remarks were being received, and in the other man's steady

113

gaze he could see that his friend was not trying to judge him.

"I enlisted in the Confederate Cavalry nearly three years ago," Mandell continued. "I was only twenty-seven at the time, but it seemed like I had a knack for leading other men and I worked my way up through the ranks pretty fast. Within a year I was the captain over a company of a hundred and fifty men. They were a rough lot, but they were topnotch fighters and we made a name for ourselves by being able to hit the Yankees as quick and as hard as any outfit in the CSA."

During Mandell's term of service, General Ulysses S. Grant had been in charge of the Union Army's western front. Month after month Mandell had seen his fledgling country's fighting forces pushed farther and farther back into their own heartland.

In early May, 1863, he and his company had been ordered to the west-central part of Mississippi to help defend the river city of Vicksburg, around which Grant was throwing an ever-larger cordon of Union troops and artillery. From within the city's defenses he and his men had watched for six weeks as the Yankee cannons battered the besieged and starving bluff city into submission.

On July 2, only two days before Vicksburg was finally turned over to the northern forces under Grant, Mandell made a decision he knew even then would have a devastating effect on the rest of his life. In a fit of drunken depression and rage the night before, his commander, Colonel Block, had decided to commit one final act against the enemy before the inevitable happened and Vicksburg surrendered. He ordered Mandell to assemble his company for a dawn charge and announced that their target would be the headquarters of none other than General Grant himself, a site that lay beyond a battery of eighteen Union cannons to the northwest of the city. If a single man was able to survive and get through to take Grant's life, Block assured Mandell, then the charge would be well worth the devastating toll in lives it would cost.

At dawn the next day Mandell had his men assembled as ordered. But at the final moment before they mounted up, he gave his company new instructions. Moments later they rode out. Yet instead of charging suicidally at the muzzles of the Union cannons, they began to scatter in all directions, riding frantically toward the various undefended gaps in the Union offensive lines.

Mandell never learned what happened to the majority of his men, but believed that most were able to scatter out into the countryside and escape capture or death. He himself was arrested only a couple of weeks later just after he'd succeeded in making it back to the distant Confederate lines in the eastern portion of the state. During a brief court-martial he made no attempt to deny the treasonous orders he had given his men. Following the proceedings, he was sentenced to prison.

Locksly Prison was a hellhole Confederate stockade in the southern part of Alabama. After only a brief time there, Mandell realized that death would have been a far more preferable punishment. Two thousand criminals of various sorts were confined in quarters at Locksly, a structure that originally had been built to house four hundred men. And few if any ever spoke of the possibility of release once the war was over or their sentences were finished. Those who somehow escaped the diseases that ravaged those in the camp were inevitably reduced to human skeletons by the poor food and the lack of fresh air and exercise.

After his first month at Locksly, Mandell realized that

he would prefer to die trying to escape than go on living in such a place. He had already lost nearly sixty pounds from his two-hundred-pound frame and he saw in the gaunt, skeletal faces of the long-time survivors around him an image of what he would become if he remained imprisoned much longer.

He made his bid for freedom spontaneously one evening when two guards took him out of the packed cell he was in to help carry off the body of a man who had died. In the prison's sprawling cemetery, which lay outside the barbed wire perimeter, he was given a shovel to dig a shallow grave. One guard remained to watch him while the other returned to the compound.

It was surprisingly easy to kill the armed guard with the shovel. All it took was patience enough to wait for the moment when the man's attention had been diverted. But one of the guards in a tower along the prison perimeter spotted him as he sprinted for the edge of the forest a hundred yards away. It was fortunate that in the dusky evening light the man was unable to bring him down with any of the four rounds he got off.

Once he reached the forest, Mandell decided to try a risky ploy. He made straight for a murky swamp about a quarter-mile away, but once he reached the water's edge, he turned and backtracked several hundred yards along his original path. When he found a tree to suit his purposes, he made a leap for its lower branches and climbed as high as he could.

The bloodhounds that the guards released raced by below only moments later, and when they tracked Mandell to the edge of the swamp, the guards assumed he had plunged into it. The search lasted through the night and well into the next day. As more time passed, the guards spread out over a broader and broader area.

During all that time, Mandell never budged from his treetop perch which, during daylight hours, was practically in sight of the Locksly Prison fence. When the guards finally began to filter back through the swamp and woods late that afternoon, he knew he was close to being a free man.

The next month was a difficult one. As Mandell made his way west on foot across the lines of two embattled armies, he was forced to live off the land and travel mostly under the protective cloak of darkness. He began to feel safe only when he crossed the broad Mississippi River and made his way north into the boot heel of Missouri.

Outside the town of Hayti, he'd waylaid a Union dispatch rider on a deserted road. After tying the man to a tree beside the road, he'd taken his horse, weapons and money. Over the next month he'd continued to head west, keeping to the wilderness regions of the Ozark Mountains as much as possible and trading horses frequently to confuse those who might be following him. It took him well into the winter months of 1863 to finally reach the mountain regions above Denver. But he pressed on through the snows and miserable cold. It was only in the new gold fields of the northern Rockies, he realized, that he would feel safely anonymous again.

It was a long tale, but Henry Morton listened with interest. When Mandell was finished, he commented, "I don't guess it'll probably matter much to any of us now, but hearing all that does make a whole lot of things begin to fit in place. During all this time I wondered why you never talked about where you'd come from or anything that had happened to you in the past. I was right curious, too, about where you'd learned to handle guns so well."

"It was shoot straight or die in some of the places

I've been," Mandell explained. Now that his story was out, he felt vulnerable and yet relieved that in the simple telling he had developed a feeling of closeness with Morton. Not since he and the men in his company had scattered to the four winds on that battlefield outside Vicksburg had he felt anything even resembling a sense of friendship with another man. The feeling might even help him die better, he thought grimly.

A short time later a message came from the council lodge and again the guards herded their eight prisoners inside. The leaders from the earlier meeting were seated and waiting. It was apparent they had been engaged in serious deliberation.

"I think the goose is over the spit now," Henry Morton muttered quietly to Mandell as they filed inside and took their place before their council. "Look at old 'bloody hands' there. He's grinning from ear to ear."

The medicine man seated beside Red Cloud was indeed sporting a savage grin of satisfaction. His expression indicated to Mandell that his arguments, whatever they might have been, had met with the approval of the council. The Indian was silent for a moment, but when he did speak, it was in broken English.

"Bad you come Indian land!" he exclaimed. "All die! Die slow, Indian way." He paused as his eyes roamed up and down the line of eight men. Then he announced, "Him first!" and the bloody finger he raised in condemnation was pointed unmistakably at Henry Morton.

The other men turned toward Morton apprehensively. Hank Mandell was the only one to react actively to the fatal proclamation.

"You'll be in hell before him, you son of a bitch!" Mandell snarled, leaping forward across the chamber. Before any of the Indians had a chance to stop him, he had

118

snatched up the crock of thick blood and dashed it across the medicine man's face and chest. Then he smashed the vessel itself across the Indian's head. In the wake of that attack, chaos erupted immediately.

Two of the guards pushed past their prisoners and lunged for Mandell. But before they could reach him, Anderson and Peabody grabbed them from behind and wrestled them to the ground. In the meantime Mandell had spun back around and was racing toward the door. He shouted to the others, "If we have to die, let's go out fighting!"

Even as the members of the council were leaping to their feet, stunned that their sacred chamber and their holy man could have been so savagely violated right before their eyes, the eight captives were rushing out. But from everywhere, it seemed, Indian men were beginning to hurry toward the council lodge. They had been alarmed by the commotion. The white men saw that any chance of escape was impossible and gathered in a tight double line outside the lodge, where they stood back to back and held their ground. Within a minute they were surrounded by dozens of Indians. Some were armed with rifles and pistols. Others held knives. And all were poised and ready to strike.

A one-word command from the doorway of the council lodge held the Indian braves at bay. Mandell glanced in that direction and saw Red Cloud studying the scene with the same stoic gaze on his face that he had worn inside. In a moment the medicine man appeared at his side, holding one hand across his damaged and dripping head. Together the two Indian leaders strode over to stand directly in front of Mandell. Mandell matched the Indians stare for stare.

Red Cloud spoke a brief phrase and the medicine man told Mandell, "Chief Red Cloud say you crazy brave man."

"I've got nothing to lose," Mandell replied. "None of us do, so come ahead and try to take us. I'm sure you can, but there'll be a few less Sioux in the world before the job's finished."

When the medicine man translated, Red Cloud's gaze narrowed slightly. His stare was penetrating. Then suddenly a broad grin spread across the chief's face. He raised a hand to take a firm grip on Mandell's shoulder. When he spoke, he raised his voice so that he could be heard by all the members of the tribe who had gathered nearby.

"Here is a white Sioux man!" the medicine man proclaimed.

The string of horses belonging to the prospectors had been assembled at the western end of the Sioux camp. Each bore the same saddles and loaded packs they had previously carried. In preparation for their departure, Henry Morton and his men were making a final check of their gear. They were still amazed that every item which had been taken from them after their capture had now been returned. Twenty-four hours before, none of them had held out hope that they would live to see the next day, let alone that they would be departing from the Indian camp under the safe conduct of the most ferocious of all the local Sioux chiefs.

Hank Mandell stood off to one side and watched his companions make the few final adjustments to cinch straps and pack ropes. He wore the same leather pants the Indian guard had given him, but now out of preference. Nearby his clothing and other belongings lay in a neat pile on the ground.

The previous day Mandell had been as surprised as anyone over the results of his violent act. At best he had hoped that, because of what he did, he and his companions would meet with sudden deaths rather than having their dying prolonged by the Sioux methods or torture. But instead his act had brought him the respect, and even the awe, of the majority of the Indians in the camp.

Out of deference to Mandell, Red Cloud had ordered his people to bring food and water to the white men. Then he had instructed that none of them was to be harmed in any way. Mandell had been taken into the council lodge. In a very solemn ceremony he had been offered the brotherhood of the tribe and was invited to live among them. The presence of a man whose courage and magic was so great, Red Cloud explained through his interpreter, Angry Dog, would be a good omen for the tribe.

A bargain was struck at last, though Mandell had chosen not to explain all the details of the arrangement to his friends. He would stay among the Sioux if they returned everything to the other white men and permitted them to continue their journey through the mountains. The contract was sealed by the smoking of an exotic herbal concoction in a long-stemmed ceremonial pipe.

Mandell had no regrets about agreeing to stay with the Sioux. Beyond his efforts to save his fellow prospectors from death at the hands of the Indians, there was something about the savage, nomadic life of these people he found alluring. Deep within him he could already sense a feeling of kinship with these red people.

Now as he watched the men he had traveled with preparing to depart, he felt no urge to be going with them. Within a short time they would again be occupied with their pursuit of gold. Mandell shook his head wistfully. He had never really shared their plans. Going with them represented to him a senseless journey from one lonely place to another.

When Henry Morton's horse and gear were ready, he

came over to Mandell. "I know this is about the tenth time I've said this," Morton told him, "but let me ask you one more time. Are you sure you know what you're doing in staying here? I've thought about it every whichaway, but it still don't make no sense to me."

"I'm not asking you to understand," Mandell answered warmly. "Just try to accept what I've decided."

"All right, my friend, but take warning. These redskins can be a two-faced lot sometimes. They might treat you like a prince today, then tire of your company tomorrow and decide to scalp you."

"I'll face that if it happens," Mandell replied. "But even if it does, I don't suppose it's all that much worse than a lot of things that our own people do to one another. Whatever these Sioux might decide to do to me couldn't be much more two-faced than what the upstanding, civilized folks in Lizard Gap wanted to do to me for trying to save their town whore from a beating."

"Maybe you're right, Hank," Morton conceded. "Maybe you do know what you're doing after all."

The two friends parted with a final round of handshakes. Then Mandell stood watching until the line of mounted men had passed from sight through a pass above the Indian camp.

Chapter 8

Kate Lancaster raised her head cautiously over the rocky edge and gazed down into the valley at the two Indians several hundred yards away. Each of the Crow braves was riding on an opposite side of the Yellowstone River. They studied the ground carefully in front of them as they moved along in search of any sign of her trail.

Kate chuckled softly to herself. "Too bad, fellows," she murmured. "You thought you'd have yourselves an honest-to-goodness white woman to carry back to camp as a prize, didn't you?"

The two Indians had been dogging her trail for nearly half a day. They had ridden their mounts nearly to death trying to best the pace of her sleek, husky appaloosa, and along the way she had pulled a variety of tricks to further confuse them. In one place she had stampeded a small herd of buffalo, then ridden among them for a time before cutting away in a separate direction along a shallow, rock-bottomed creek. She had also crossed the Yellowstone on two separate occasions, swimming her horse far downstream each time so that the Indians would have to scout around to pick up her trail.

Now, watching the two Indians from a vantage point overlooking the river, she could tell that their horses were about spent and that she would have no trouble outdistancing them with straight, steady riding. Within another four to six hours she would be back among the teamsters who were driving her wagons and these Crow would not be causing her any more delay.

Four days before, she had left her outfit behind and set out alone on horseback to determine how close the wagons were to the mining towns at the end of the trail. It was there she planned to sell the supplies and equipment that they carried. A couple of the newer men in her group had been amazed and alarmed that she would undertake such a journey alone, even here near the end of the trail where Indians were not nearly such a threat as they had been farther to the southeast. But the men who had worked for her in the past simply laughed at the concerns of the new drivers. And afterward they enlightened them about the abilities of their lady boss.

"She's the best 'man' among us," they'd chuckled.

After spending nearly two thirds of her twenty-two years in the wild northwest country, Kate Lancaster was more at home in the mountains and forests than she had been in any town or city. She was a crack shot with both the short carbine and the long Sharps .50 rifle she carried. And more than one overeager frontiersman had discovered when they tried to force their attentions on her that the six-inch sheath knife she wore on her side was not just for show.

Kate was eight when she and her family came west in 1850. Her father, a burly, temperamental Irishman named

Sean Lancaster, had been a shipyard foreman in New England. His dream had been to carve the towering, hardwood timber of the Northwest into sleek sailing vessels for the growing West Coast shipping trade. He settled his family along the Columbia River near the Dalles and began the realization of his goals in a small way by building longboats suitable for plying the broad, swift Columbia.

Kate was orphaned four years later when Cayuse Indians who roamed the area slaughtered her father, mother and two older brothers during a drunken rampage, then burned the family's cabin, outbuildings and boat sheds. Only Kate managed to survive. She had hidden in the storm cellar that was located in the woods a few hundred feet behind their home.

After burying the members of her family, Kate Lancaster, then only twelve years old, set out to begin her new life with the entire legacy remaining to her—three fourteen-foot boats her father and brothers had completed before the attack. Tying the boats together, she navigated them downriver to Fort Vancouver, where she traded them for a saddle horse, two pack mules and a full load of metal implements, including plowshares, axe heads and cast-iron cooking pots.

Despite the warnings and the dire predictions of disaster from the men at the fort, Kate set out a few days later on her first trading trip, working her way down the Pacific coast from one small settlement to another. Even then she was tall and looked older than she really was, and she had learned quickly that with a weapon in her hand and the willingness in her heart to use it, she could be as formidable an adversary as any man.

Somehow she had survived those years of transition into womanhood. The unique wandering life she had chosen for herself helped develop her into a fiercely independent, cunning trader, as capable as any man around her in dealing with the countless threats and challenges of frontier life. Her trading endeavors had led her as far south as San Francisco and as far west as Salt Lake City. But in the fall of 1863 she decided to wander even farther afield into the burgeoning mining districts of the northern Rockies. Experience had taught her that in such places quick profits could be accumulated by anyone who could get through with the types of goods that were always so desperately needed in the remote mining communities.

She traveled that fall to Omaha, Nebraska, carrying her entire fortune, forty-six hundred dollars, in two saddlebags strapped across the back of her saddle horse. By early spring she was heading back west with eight wagons loaded with tools, mining implements and various supplies she knew were in short supply along the frontier.

Traveling along the Oregon Trail that spring, she began to hear talk about the new trail that a man named John Bozeman had blazed north through Indian territory. Rumor had it that despite his failure of the previous summer, Bozeman was trying to use the trail again, and Kate knew that if he made it through, his profits as the first trader to reach the mining district would be tremendous. By the time she reached Fetterman's Fort, she had resolved to take the same gamble Bozeman was taking. From the fort she veered her wagons north, following along in the ruts his wagons had laid down in the soft prairie soil only a few days before.

The sortie just south of the Tongue River had almost ended her venture for her, but after it was over she had pushed on for nearly two weeks and experienced no further confrontations with the Indians. Things had gone quite well in fact, and now she believed that within a few days she would have three or four times the forty-six hundred dollars she had started east with the previous fall.

With the pesky Crow Indians far behind her, Kate headed due east again along the south side of the Yellowstone River. The strong legs of her appaloosa gobbled up the miles and by dusk she was in the vicinity of the area she knew hers and Bozeman's wagon trains would be.

Topping a rise above a grassy meadow east of Stillwater Creek, she stopped her horse a moment and gazed down the hillside to where John Bozeman's teamsters were just beginning to circle their wagons for the night and release their stock to graze. She and her people had not had any contact with Bozeman's group since that brief exchange near the Tongue River, but she realized how angry Bozeman must have been by then over her unsanctioned use of his pathfinder services along the trail. No matter. What she was doing would be good for business. And she had learned over the years that when matters of finance and trade were concerned, the only way to beat out the competition was to take advantage of resources that were available.

The time had come to again make contact with Bozeman, but Kate wanted to make a few preparations before they met face to face once more. Instead of riding down toward the wagons, she wheeled her horse around and rode in the opposite direction, heading toward a sheltered grove along a creek she had spotted earlier.

Once she reached the grove, she tied her horse to a tree. Then she drew her carbine from the boot on her saddle and laid it on the ground near the water's edge. Finally she began to undress, laying her clothes on the bank near the rifle where they would be within easy reach in case unexpected company arrived while she was bathing.

Her body was slim and firm, indicative of the active life she led. Her face, neck and arms were deeply tanned from almost constant exposure to the sun, but the parts of her body that were protected by her clothing were pale and soft. Her back was straight and strong. And though her shoulders were too broad to give an impression of delicate femininity, they did serve to present her full, firm breasts to best advantage.

Though she was most accustomed to wearing functional male clothing and seldom found it necessary to don a dress for any occasion, Kate did take pride in her body. The life she led often demanded that she adopt the rough ways of rugged men. But at times when she was alone and at her leisure, she enjoyed the knowledge that she was an attractive woman.

She sat down in a small pool about two feet deep and splashed the cool creek water up onto her face and shoulders. Taking up handfuls of sand from the creek bed, she rubbed them on her body, scrubbing off weeks of trail dust and grime. This was the first bath she had enjoyed since Marlow Fetterman had permitted her to use the ornate porcelain tub in his private quarters at the fort.

When her body was clean, Kate dug some soft mud from the creek bank and worked it gently into her long, brown hair. The mud absorbed the oils from her scalp and hair. When it was rinsed out completely, it worked nearly as well as soap.

Kate emerged dripping and clean from the pool and let her body dry a moment in the cool evening breeze before taking a clean set of clothes from her saddlebags and putting them on. This outfit of clothing was her finest. She had brought it along with the specific intention of wearing it to her meeting with Bozeman.

The shirt, one of the two she'd had tailored for her in

Omaha over the winter, was of a bright plaid material and fit her upper body with flattering snugness. The light denim trousers, though entirely too tight for any extended rides, conformed themselves to the shape of her hips and legs.

By the time Kate had ridden up and dismounted at the Bozeman ring of wagons, the evening camp already had been set up. In the darkness, she tied her horse to the wheel of a wagon, then had one of the men lead her to where John Bozeman was squatting on the ground by a blazing campfire, sipping his first cup of fresh coffee.

When Bozeman glanced up, anger mingled with an expression of surprise. He took another sip from his steaming metal cup, nodded curtly and mumbled a terse, "Evening, miss."

"Good evening, Mr. Bozeman," Kate returned. The smile she issued was a casual one and she did not allow it to remain on her face too long. "May I join you?"

"I can't stop you," Bozeman told her coolly, "seeing as how neither this trail nor any of the land along it belongs to me." Bozeman's reference to the accusation she had made the day of the Indian attack was unmistakable, but Kate calmly let the bit of sarcasm go by.

"I've felt bad about that day, Mr. Bozeman," she came back evenly. "I know I acted terribly. But I decided then that probably you wouldn't have been very receptive to any apology." She knelt to the ground across the fire from Bozeman and folded one leg under her to sit on.

"Well, I learned my lesson that day about offering help when it wasn't asked for," Bozeman responded. "From then on I haven't worried much about you either way, but I'd say you're damned lucky you didn't get hit again and need to make some friends quick. You probably would have found them in short supply."

"Perhaps you're right," Kate answered, "but that's all behind us now. I'd like to think the entire incident could be forgotten. Actually I stopped by here tonight to discuss another matter." She paused and glanced down at the steaming coffee pot near the edge of the fire. "May I?" she asked.

"Bozeman shrugged.

Once Kate had her cup of coffee poured and was enjoying the first refreshing sip, she launched into the real reason for her visit.

"I've never been through this country before like you have," she told Bozeman, "so I've spent the last few days riding on ahead to see what's in front of us. I got as far as a place called Buffalo Leap before I finally turned around and started back to meet my wagons."

"John Jacobs and I passed through Buffalo Leap when we set out to scout this trail last spring," Bozeman put in. "Only about a dozen prospectors were dipping their pans in Tobiah Creek there then, but they were finding good colors and I was hoping the place had grown. I planned to make that my first stop."

"It *has* grown," Kate confirmed. "I counted forty-two cabins in Buffalo Leap and about twenty-five sluices along a mile-long stretch of the creek." She took another drink of the coffee, then set the cup on the ground in front of her. "But I want to tell you, Mr. Bozeman, now that we're so close to the end of the line, you don't have to worry about a race to the first town ahead of us."

"I did wonder about that," Bozeman admitted, "but the prospect didn't worry me much. I know you're short of harness stock, and my scout has told me that your wagons are in pretty bad shape. If it came to a race I knew we'd win."

"That's right, but I want you to know that's only part

of the reason why I'm going to tell my drivers to ease up and let you pull on farther ahead. The rest of it is that I want to make some sort of gesture to let you know how I feel about things.

"I knew as soon as I set off behind you down at Fetterman's Fort that my following was bound to rankle you, but I honestly couldn't see paying you any money when the trail was already there for anyone to use for free. Now that we're near the markets, though, it seems like you should have a right to pull on ahead and get to Buffalo Leap first. It only seems fair."

Kate Lancaster's attitude confused Bozeman. For a moment she could tell by his expression that he remained suspicious. But, sipping her coffee, she gazed across the fire at him and waited for the wave of doubt to pass. In a sense, she knew her offer was an empty one. Both she and Bozeman knew that with the wagons and animals she had, she could not possibly outdistance him and reach the town first. But that simple fact, she was confident, would also serve to erase the suspicions from his mind.

Bozeman reached out to pour himself another cup of coffee. Afterward he drew the stub of a half-smoked cigar from his shirt pocket and lit it with a flaming twig from the fire.

"Fifteen or twenty miles back should suffice," he told Kate. "That will give us nearly a day to sell what goods we can in Buffalo Leap and then move on a few miles toward the next place down the line. With any luck there still might be a market for some of the freight you're hauling."

"Perhaps," Kate replied. "This is a big area. In one place or another I'll get my goods sold."

When the discussion was over, Bozeman did not offer Kate Lancaster an evening meal or a place to sleep for the night. And she requested nothing. Even by starlight, Bozeman's back trail would be easy to follow, and she was in a hurry to get back to her own wagons. There were plans to make and things to do.

The cabin door hung slightly askew on its leather hinges. That and a mound of leaves that the wind had piled in the doorway told Bozeman that the dwelling had been abandoned since the previous fall. In his anger, he grabbed the door with his hands and ripped it loose. Then he flung it against a nearby tree which bore a hand-lettered sign identifying the town as Buffalo Leap.

Bozeman knew there was no need to check any of the forty-odd other cabins that were scattered randomly through the thick pine woods. Nor would it do any good, he realized, to ride on to the far side of the woods and check to see if anyone was working the sluices along Tobiah Creek. The signs were everywhere that Buffalo Leap was an abandoned town, plain and simple. The gold had played out and the people had moved on.

Earlier that afternoon he had left his wagons a few miles behind and ridden on ahead to Buffalo Leap. He'd been eager to see how the place had grown and to announce the upcoming arrival of his train of goods. What he had expected was a rousing reception from the people of the town who, he believed, would most likely be starving for the staples that his wagons carried. He was fortunate. Because his would be the first wagons to arrive that spring, within a short time the profits he had promised Marlow Fetterman and his backers at Fenwig, Price and MacDonald would begin rolling in.

But a feeling of dread had swept over him when he first rode in sight of Buffalo Leap. No smoke curled up from the stone chimneys of any of the cabins. No stock of any kind grazed in the grassy meadows near the pine forest. From a distance the place looked disappointingly vacant, but even so, Bozeman had refused to admit that certainty until he had actually ridden closer to see for himself.

He knew well that it was the fate of most small mining towns to be abandoned once the brief runs of bustling glory were over. In Colorado he had seen entire towns vacated overnight by rumors of new finds just over the next peak or beyond the next ridge.

But things should have been different here. Hadn't Kate Lancaster told him just three days before that she had seen Buffalo Leap? And hadn't she backed her wagons off, as promised, so that he could reach the town a full day ahead of her? None of the story she'd told him that night in his camp made any sense to him now. Was her telling of it a prank she had dreamed up to spark his hopes of great profits prematurely? If so, it was a silly, empty joke. Wasn't he so far ahead of Kate Lancaster now that he could still reach the next mining town ahead of her?

Bozeman wandered idly around Buffalo Leap for a while. At last he came to a long, log building that had once served as a general store. Rats now infested the debris-strewn floor and shelves inside, but he did find one interesting area along one front wall by the door. There various miners and travelers had left messages for relatives and friends whom they believed might pass this way in search of them. Bozeman started glancing over the messages, only casually interested. Then he noticed one name mentioned repeatedly in note after note.

To the friends and kin of Arthur Brisbain:

I am leaving today, Sept. 4, 1864, for Tumble Mountain Gorge and expect to stake a claim and winter there.

* * *

To Michael J. Johnson:

My partners and I have had no luck here and will leave tomorrow for Tumble Mountain Gorge where we hope our prospects will improve. Please join us there. Sept. 11, 1864.
Your brother, Robt. P. Johnson

To Cyrus Latigan:

Have arrived of late from our home state of Alabama and am bearing letters for you from your family at home. If you read this, look for me at Tumble Mountain Gorge.
Sept. 1, 1864

Message after message mentioned Tumble Mountain Gorge. At last it became apparent to Bozeman what had happened. During the previous summer, people probably had poured into Buffalo Leap, lured by the rumors of the gold. Though the placer deposits of gold in nearby Tobiah Creek had undoubtedly been small ones, by the fall, when word began to arrive about new discoveries in Tumble Mountain Gorge, an immediate migration had started.

Most likely a new town had sprung up at Tumble Mountain Gorge, but where in the world was it? Bozeman wondered. At last he came across a message in which a man had left instructions for a friend on how to get there.

"Follow Tobiah Creek s.e. about six mi. until it plays out in a broad meadow called Goose Valley," the instructions read. "Turn due east and cross two hills, then turn southeast eleven miles to Tumble Mountain Gorge. There is a rough road which will handle wagons with strong teams and experienced drivers. Distance, abt. twenty-five mi."

A broad grin spread across Bozeman's face as he began to consider this new settlement. Because the people who headed in that direction had started out in the late fall, most of them had probably been forced to winter in whatever cabins they had been able to throw up for themselves. That meant that they were most likely still there. And if this Tumble Mountain Gorge was as remote as it sounded, chances were good that no other wagon trains loaded with freight and supplies had found their way through from Bannack City far to the west or any other main supply point. If all went well, Bozeman reassured himself, he could lead his wagons through in no more than a day and a half, and it was likely that the market would still be good once he arrived.

With a renewed sense of excitement and anticipation, Bozeman hurried back to his horse and galloped eastward to meet his wagons. That evening in camp, he let his teamsters tap the bung on one of the barrels of whiskey they were transporting and sample its contents. He knew that the celebration was a little premature, but he decided that making it through Indian territory unscathed was worth at least a few belts.

By about ten that evening the fifty-gallon barrel was more than a third empty. Bozeman concluded that he'd better end the flow of whiskey if he planned to make any progress at all the next day. His inebriated crew settled down quickly on their blankets and soon only Bozeman and the usual night guard of ten men remained awake.

Watching the flames of his campfire die down to a bed of coals, Bozeman congratulated himself again for his impending success. Against all odds and all the doomsday predictions of his detractors, he had proved that his trail through the wilderness was no pipe dream. The profits he would soon be carrying back from the sale of his supplies and wagons in Tumble Mountain Gorge would be only the beginning. There was time still left in the year to travel back to Fetterman's Fort and lead yet another wagon train north along his trail before winter snows flew.

He heard the sound of galloping hooves above the snores of the sleeping men around him even before one of the sentries came to him with the news that a rider was approaching.

"It's probably Billy Buffalo," Bozeman told the guard. "Take care of his horse when he gets in and send him straight over to me. I want to share the good news with him."

When Billy Buffalo joined him by the fire, Bozeman informed him, "Too bad you didn't get back earlier, Billy. We've been celebrating tonight. We tapped one of the whiskey barrels, and I would have saved you some if I'd known you were on your way in."

"It's just as well you didn't," Billy responded wearily. "You know how it is with Indians and firewater. I've been drunk twice in my life and both times the whiskey made me so brave I damn near got myself killed. The second time I stayed out for three days and when I finally did come to, I was so beat up that I couldn't hardly move for a week. They told me I tried to take on six troopers from Fort Leavenworth, but I don't remember a bit of it."

"What's kept you out so long, Billy?" Bozeman asked. "I was expecting you back a full day ago."

"Well, I was keeping an eye on your friend back there, making sure she didn't push up any closer than fifteen miles," Billy answered. "And up until about midday today she was keeping her word and everything was fine. But then after their noonday stop, things started getting strange."

At first Bozeman had been listening only casually to

the report of his scout. No longer was he worried about anything Kate Lancaster might decide to do, despite the misleading report she had given him about Buffalo Leap. But there was something about the tone of his scout's voice that made him sit up and begin to pay closer attention. "What was strange?" he asked.

"Well, all of a sudden they veered off our trail. All this time they'd been driving right along in the same wagon ruts we laid down, but this afternoon they started due south, heading straight upstream along Boulder Creek and into the mountains."

Bozeman's brow knit in consternation as he sat silently staring at Billy Buffalo and waited for him to continue.

"For a while I didn't know what to do," the scout admitted. "But I remembered you telling me that the Crow sometimes camped up in those hills so I decided I'd ride down and tell the people what they might be heading toward. I didn't see any harm in it since things have gotten more friendly between you and that woman lately."

Bozeman smirked. "What did she say when you told her?" he asked.

"Oh, she was nice enough about the whole thing, but she assured me that she knew exactly what she was doing. And then she gave me a message to bring to you that I still can't figure out."

"What was that?"

"She said she'd be glad to show you the back way into Tumble Mountain Gorge if you decided you'd like to cut back and pick up her trail."

Chapter 9

Blue Eagle sat on the ground near the blazing campfire. He was surrounded by his regular crowd—a dozen or so young bucks who were always eager to praise him and assure him of what a wise, courageous leader he was. At the moment he was favoring his admirers, as well as everyone else within listening distance of his booming voice, with a retelling of how he had led the siege against the Bozeman wagon train the previous year and turned the "white dogs" back off of Indian land. His narrative was so long-winded that after the first hour of the story, Hank Mandell was seriously considering violating tribal etiquette by leaving in the middle of the tale and going to bed.

In the three months that he had been living with the Sioux, the band led by Blue Eagle had met twice with one led by Red Cloud. Their intent was to feast together on the abundant summer game, to gamble and hold various contests that the Indians so enjoyed, and to hold tribal councils. A festival atmosphere existed in the combined camp during such times, and following the abundant eve-

ning meals, the nighttime hours were generally passed
with the telling of ancient tribal legends and narratives.

With his new basic understanding of the Sioux language, Mandell could understand a good deal of these
accounts. Many of them he found extremely interesting.
The native American Indians, he learned, had a history as
ancient and rich as that of their white rivals. The only
difference was that most of the history of the white race
was recorded in the pages of books, while the Indians
relied on word of mouth and their own memories to pass
the information down from one generation to the next.

But some of the nighttime recitals were boring. And
Mandell had already heard Blue Eagle's yarn. The first
time had been a week before. He had listened with some
interest then because of the particular subject matter. But
he took little pleasure in again hearing how Blue Eagle had
sat atop his horse on a hilltop overlooking the wagon train,
waved his war lance to the four winds and pledged death
to all who dared invade the sacred lands of the Sioux.
After a full day of competing in wrestling matches and
horse races and with his belly full of buffalo stew, Mandell
found himself beginning to nod off.

Because he was near the rear of the group of fifty or
so braves who were listening to Blue Eagle's account, he
thought a quiet departure might not be noticed. But when
he rose and turned away, the Indian broke off his narrative
and called out, "I see the white man among us wants to
hear no more of how his race was shamed that day.
Perhaps he was even among those who showed their yellow tails to the mighty Sioux and went scurrying back to
the safety of their own kind."

Mandell turned and stared for a moment at the faces
of Blue Eagle and his sidekicks where they sat about thirty
feet away. In the tribal councils that Red Cloud had per-

mitted Mandell to sit in on, he had sensed Blue Eagle's resentment of him. But this was the first time the young chief had openly displayed his antagonism.

"I was not at the place you say I was," Mandell replied. "At the time you laid siege to the wagon train, I was fighting in the great war back in the United States."

"Then perhaps you are leaving because you cannot stand to hear your people reviled for the race of cowards that they are," Blue Eagle sneered.

"Just as with the Indians, my people are not all alike," Mandell stated coolly. "We have our cowards and our brave men. And like the Sioux, we also have those who must always proclaim how brave they are because no one else will say it of them."

A dark expression spread over Blue Eagle's face at the obvious insult, but Mandell didn't care. He had no desire to make trouble with this Indian, but if trouble came, he felt no need to back away either. The only way to deal with a loudmouthed bully of any race was to match him growl for growl.

"I've heard your story twice now, Blue Eagle," Mandell went on, "and there's just one thing that bothers me about it." Mandell sucked in his breath sharply. He knew he was making a mistake in saying too much, but couldn't stop himself. "If your siege of the wagon train was such a success last year, then what's this talk I've heard about another train making it all the way through on the Bozeman Trail *this* year? Could it be because this second wagon train was manned by well-armed men, and the great Blue Eagle prefers to shake his spear and shout his threats only at wagons filled with women and children?"

Snarling, Blue Eagle made a grab for the sheath knife at his belt. But before his attacker got it poised for a throw, Mandell had already drawn one of his revolvers.

"I've seen you throw a knife in the contests and I know you're good," Mandell told him, "but don't try it. Bullets are still faster."

There was not a trace of fear in Blue Eagle's steady gaze. He let the knife slide back into its sheath and took his hand away from the hilt. "Unless you kill me now," the young chief hissed, "there will be no peace for you until we fight."

"Then so be it," Mandell replied. Carefully he lowered the cocked hammer of his pistol and returned it to the holster at his side.

The two men sat astride their horses about a hundred yards apart in the long meadow below the Indian camp. To Mandell, who was on the west end staring into the rising sun, it appeared as if the entire tribe must have turned out that morning to witness the confrontation between himself and Blue Eagle. All were trying to crowd in as close as possible around the area where the actual combat would take place. But they had left open a path about twenty feet wide along a direct line that connected the two adversaries.

Mandell was getting anxious for the contest to begin. An old, familiar avalanche of feelings was crashing through him.

But before the fight began, the amenities had to be observed. At that moment, Red Cloud and his medicine man, Angry Dog, were down with Blue Eagle, talking to him in what looked to Mandell like pre-combat ritual. He knew how superstitious the Sioux were. And he guessed that the two might be preparing Blue Eagle for a journey over to the other side in case he didn't emerge the winner.

Looking over the situation as he was, Mandell realized what a great mistake he had made in giving Blue Eagle the choice of weapons and letting him decide the

142

manner in which the fight was to take place. The long, feathered war lance he now held was evidence enough of that cocky miscalculation. Blue Eagle had probably grown up wielding one of these heavy, awkward things. But the nearest thing to it that Mandell had ever carried was a saber, which he'd used only rarely in hand-to-hand combat. Like Blue Eagle, he was stripped to a simple breechcloth and he had slicked his body down with grease so he would be hard to hold on to during close-in fighting. The only other weapon he had with him was a hunting knife. It was sheathed and held by a leather thong tied around his waist. Mounted as he was on his tall, husky saddle horse, he hoped that the extra height might give him a slight edge over Blue Eagle on his short-legged Indian pony.

Red Cloud and Angry Dog turned their horses and rode solemnly down the long open area to Mandell.

"Are you ready?" Red Cloud asked quietly. Mandell looked up at the stolid features of his host and nodded his head. As always, it was hard to read the expression on the chief's face, but Mandell thought he might have detected a glint of concern in Red Cloud's steady gaze. During the past three months they had developed respect for one another.

"Blue Eagle is angry now because of a decision I made on the advice of Angry Dog," Red Cloud declared. "This will not be a fight to the death as he had wanted."

"In the smoke of the holy fire last night the spirits spoke to me and said it must be so," Angry Dog proclaimed in his most dramatic voice.

"Well, I know enough to realize that these things can't always be decided for sure beforehand," Mandell remarked. "But if that's your decision, I'll do my best to spare Blue Eagle's life and save my own at the same time."

"The ways of my people are the ways of violence and honor," Red Cloud explained, "as this day proves. But these are troubled times and we are few compared to the endless waves of white men which pour across the plains. Blue Eagle is an impulsive young man, but as his wisdom grows he will make a good leader. I have no wish to see him die.

"And as for you, Hank Mandell, such men as you who understand our cause and would be our brother are rare. I have no wish to see you killed for the honor of a young chief whose tongue always marches ahead of his reason.

"Nevertheless, according to our custom, Blue Eagle has wagered a prize most precious to him, and so must you, my friend."

"All I have are my horse and my guns," Mandell replied. "If I lose, they will belong to Blue Eagle."

Both Mandell and Red Cloud realized the seriousness of the stakes he was offering. In this country, a man on foot and without weapons was easy prey to any number of human and natural threats.

"It is an honorable wager," Red Cloud responded. "Fight well." With those words he and Angry Dog turned their horses and rode down to their places of distinction at the center of the line where the fight would take place.

No signal marked the beginning of the contest. Blue Eagle simply raised his spear to a horizontal position. With a whoop he dug his bare heels into the flanks of his pony and began to race forward. An instant later Mandell did the same, thinking for a moment how much like the jousting of medieval knights this manner of fighting was.

As the two men closed on one another, Blue Eagle ripped out a savage, high-pitched scream and Mandell could see the violent glint of vengeance in his eye. The expression on the Indian's face said with no mistake that if he was the victor, Mandell would have no need for the horses and weapons he would lose, that despite the wishes of Red Cloud, Mandell would not live to see another day.

The moment their two horses raced past one another, Mandell took a swipe with his sear and partially succeeded in deflecting his opponent's weapon. But despite the fact that Blue Eagle's spear did not penetrate the center of Mandell's chest, where it had been aimed, its razor point still slashed across his upper arm, leaving a deep gash from which blood immediately began to flow.

Again the two turned to face one another and Mandell realized instantly another mistake he had made in choosing to ride his own large horse. Before he had half-completed his turn, Blue Eagle's pony had spun like a cat on its shorter, agile legs and was charging back at him.

Blue Eagle's spear entered Mandell's horse high up on its rib cage. With a squeal of agony, the animal went down. Mandell flung his legs up out of the way and rolled clear of the falling horse, but in the confusion his lance went flying out of his hand and landed more than ten feet away from him. Mandell was stunned, but had the presence of mind to scramble away from his thrashing mount, which was still impaled by Blue Eagle's lance.

In a remarkable display of horsemanship, Blue Eagle spun his pony once more, leaned far down along its side and snatched Mandell's lance up from where it had fallen. Now he enjoyed dual advantage. Not only was he still mounted, he also had possession of the most lethal weapon on the field of battle. On all sides of them the Indian spectators were urging Blue Eagle on with a chorus of uproarious shouts and cheers.

Despite the long odds against him, Mandell resolved that the fight was still a long way from being finished.

Drawing his knife and leaping to his feet, he moved close in beside his downed horse, which was still kicking its legs wildly in a pitiful attempt to get to its feet. By keeping the horse between himself and Blue Eagle, he was able for a while to avoid the vicious slashes from the deadly spear. No matter which direction the young chief tried to ride, Mandell leaped in the opposite direction.

At last, in his frustration, Blue Eagle backed his horse off a few paces, then charged immediately forward, intending to leap his animal over the obstacle and catch his opponent off guard. But that was precisely what Mandell wanted him to do. He had a desperate ploy of his own in mind.

Blue Eagle was holding his lance along the right side of his horse's head. As the animal came hurtling through the air, Mandell jumped to the left side of its head, grabbed the rope bridle tied around its nose and pulled it to the side with all the strength he could muster. The horse stumbled as it started to fall and threw its startled rider off to the side.

When Blue Eagle screamed out in sudden pain, it took Mandell a moment to realize what had happened. As the Indian had fallen to one side, the lance he held had stuck in the ground ahead of him, splintering its shaft. Now, Mandell saw, the young chief staggered clumsily to his feet with one portion of the broken lance stuck in his right shoulder and the jagged point protruding several inches out behind. The features of his face were contorted with pain.

"Will you yield now?" Mandell asked.

In response Blue Eagle reached across with his left hand, ripped the broken lance from his shoulder and hurled it awkwardly in Mandell's direction. Blood immediately began to gush from the wound.

"You fought well," Mandell said. "There would be no dishonor in stopping now."

"White pig!" Blue Eagle sneered. "I'll stop when you lay at my feet with your belly sliced open!" He drew his knife with his left hand and lunged.

As Mandell warded off his opponent's attack with his left hand, he swung his right hand, which held his knife, straight at Blue Eagle's face. But instead of plunging his blade deep within the Indian's skull as he so easily could have, he struck with his fist instead. With the hard hilt of his knife as reinforcement, his knuckles struck with crushing impact, mangling the young chief's nose and mouth. With a throaty grunt and a soft exhalation of air, Blue Eagle wilted to the ground before him.

Hank Mandell did not realize exactly what he had lost in the fight until after the crowd had begun to close in around them and Red Cloud had ridden over to proclaim him the victor. Then the pain started up in his left hand. He looked down and in amazement saw that his little finger and the tip of the one beside it had been severed. Blood was gushing, but the crowd gave no notice to such details. They had a winner in their midst, and though he was not exactly the one they would have chosen, they intended to regale him nonetheless. He was swept up onto a horse beside Red Cloud. Others gathered Blue Eagle up and followed along behind. And the entire party started en masse back toward the center of camp.

Before they had reached the open area in front of the council lodge, Mandell's head began to swim. He knew he'd better try to get his wounds bandaged before he lost much more blood. Turning toward Red Cloud, he intended to say something to that effect, but his tongue had become entirely too lazy to get the words out. His last awareness was of swaying involuntarily to one side and wondering why the ground was suddenly rushing up at him.

Outside the tepee a large campfire was blazing brightly. As many as two or three dozen Indian men were still awake and enjoying the end of the long day's festivities. Inside where he lay, Mandell could hear their voices mingling together faintly as they swapped stories and recounted to one another the details of the day's fight.

He was feeling better after having gorged himself several times during the afternoon and evening on lean red meat. The strength was returning to his body. Angry Dog had prepared poultices, which eased the pain and kept the swelling down in his injured hand and shoulder. And the medicine man reported that Blue Eagle had recovered consciousness and was doing well.

Despite his improvement, Mandell had begged off early during the evening's festivities and come to the tepee to rest. It was one thing to be brave about one's injuries during the heat of a fight, but he had suffered enough wounds to know that afterward the smartest thing a man could do was to be kind to his body and give it the care it needed.

An hour or so earlier, Chief Red Cloud had come by to congratulate him and to issue a word of warning. Blue Eagle was disgruntled over the outcome of the fight, Red Cloud told him, and claimed Mandell had won not because of his superior fighting ability but due to the accident of Blue Eagle's falling on the broken lance. The young chief had already spoken of revenge to his supportive lieutenants, and Red Cloud cautioned Mandell that until the two bands separated, he should be on his guard. Mandell was white, after all, and Blue Eagle and his cronies might not consider him deserving of the Sioux rules of fair fighting.

After the chief left, Mandell lay awake in the tepee, wondering, as he often had in the last three months, why he had stayed on with the Sioux instead of returning to the company of his own kind. He had never come up with a satisfactory answer, but he believed it had something to do with the freedom of Indian life. With the Sioux, a man was restricted only by the boundaries of his own physical prowess and cunning. In addition, the Sioux maintained a respect for both themselves and the land, a respect that too often was lacking among Mandell's own race.

At first when the flap of the tepee swept to the side, Mandell's mind flashed to the warnings that Red Cloud had so recently given him. Stealthily his hand inched out to grasp one of the revolvers that lay on the ground nearby. But then he saw the slender, skirted form in the entrance. It was outlined by the dancing flames behind. And so delicate and unthreatening did it seem that he put the weapon aside and sat up on his pallet.

"Will you let me enter?" a woman's voice asked. The words were phrased as a question, but Mandell thought he detected a note of challenge in them.

"I'm naked against the heat," Mandell told her.

"I don't mind, but if it bothers you, then cover yourself," the woman replied, advancing into the tepee and letting the flap fall closed behind her. "The light is dim in here. Besides, I bathed in the rivers with my boy cousins until I was fifteen."

"Who are you?" Mandell inquired. In the faint light he could tell little about his visitor except her general height, and by the sound of her voice she was young.

"I am Eyes Like The She Wolf," the woman told him.

149

"My father was Many Feathers, who is dead, and my uncle is Chief Red Cloud."

Mandell recalled having Red Cloud's young niece pointed out to him a few days before. He brought to mind the image of a black-haired young beauty of about eighteen who had been by the stream with a group of other Indian women washing fresh vegetable shoots they had gathered for a tribal feast. He was told that Red Cloud had raised his niece from an early age after her father's death, but that now she traveled with the band led by Blue Eagle. None of that explained what she was doing in his tent now, so finally he posed the question to her.

"Hasn't anyone told you?" She was surprised. And as she spoke, she crossed to the opposite side of the tepee, sat down on a heavy, folded buffalo robe there and asked, "Didn't my uncle tell you even after the contest?"

"No one has told me anything," Mandell assured the Indian girl.

"It must be a trick of some sort that they're pulling on you, then." Her brows knit in frustration. "If so, I don't like it. I didn't want to come here in the first place, and now I *know* I don't want to be here." There was a marked impatience in her voice that Mandell found oddly irritating. It had been a long, exhausting day. He had no desire to end it by listening to the prattling complaints of some young Indian shrew, beautiful or not.

"Well leave if you like," he told her, "but first would you explain the mystery?"

"I can't leave!" the Indian girl snapped. "Don't you understand yet? *I'm your prize! I am what Blue Eagle wagered today before the contest began!*"

"And how was it that he was able to bet the niece of a chief?" Mandell asked, still only half believing that anything the girl said was the truth.

"For six months I have been betrothed to Blue Eagle," Eyes Like The She Wolf explained. "My dowry is large because I am the niece of a great chief and the daughter of a famous warrior. But to prove himself worthy of me, Blue Eagle was supposed to perform a courageous deed. The fight today might have been enough in the eyes of Red Cloud and the elders, but Blue Eagle lost and gambled me away. Now all he has left is a flat nose for his troubles. I always knew he was a fool and I'm glad the courtship is ended, but I have to say I am equally unhappy about being here. No one even bothered to tell me until *after* you had won that I was a part of the day's stakes."

"Well then," Mandell replied, "it should be a relief to you to know that you don't have to stay. Beating Blue Eagle and staying alive is reward enough to me."

"I can't go!" Eyes Like The She Wolf turned her fiery eyes on him.

"Well you can't stay, either," Mandell growled. "It's been a long time since I had a woman in my life. When I take another one, it will be one of my own choosing."

It had been a long time indeed, Mandell thought. Now, after more than three years, he didn't think of Liselle quite so often anymore. When she did come to mind, though, the pain and longing were still as sharp and vivid as that day they had parted. There was no telling where she was or even if she was alive. So it was still too soon to cast those painful memories aside, he thought, to forget Liselle and the war and to try to do it in the company of a sharp-tongued squaw.

"I will not leave," Eyes Like The She Wolf announced passionately. She rose from the buffalo rug and moved to stand above Mandell. Her hands were on her hips. She glared down. "After what you did today," she went on, "you may think you're a great man. That may or may not be so. But you're not great enough to shame me before the whole tribe by turning me away. For such a thing I'd cut your heart out and feed it to the camp dogs.''

"Go away, woman," Mandell told her. "I'm tired of listening to you.''

"Well that's too bad because I've only started to tell you what I—''

Mandell swung his left arm out and swept the Indian woman's feet out from under her. Eyes Like The She Wolf landed hard on her back in front of him and the breath rushed from her chest. Mandell watched indifferently as she lay coughing and gasping. When her breathing returned to normal, she was more subdued.

"All right, now that I've got your attention," Mandell grumbled, "maybe you'll stop squawking at me like an angry jay bird long enough to tell me what this is all about. Does Red Cloud know you're here?''

"He sent me," Eyes Like The She Wolf replied.

"And how long is this arrangement supposed to last? Am I supposed to have my fun with you tonight and send you on your way in the morning?''

"I am not a whore, you white-faced fool!" the Indian exclaimed with renewed fury. "By the law I am to be your woman, your Indian wife . . .''

"Good God!''

" . . . and if you turn me out, I will lose face before the entire tribe." Mandell thought he detected a faint note of pleading in her voice. "Anyway," she continued in more controlled tones, "I'm the one who should be disappointed, not you. All my life I've prepared myself to marry the finest brave in the tribe and to raise my sons to be leaders of people. Now look what's happening to me! I don't know what my uncle was thinking when he permitted such a bargain.''

As the moments passed, Mandell was finding the whole situation more and more ironic. Like it or not, the two of them were bound together.

"All right," he muttered regretfully, "you can stay."

"But you must also take me to your bed," Eyes Like The She Wolf told him. "The old woman may want to check me tomorrow to see if I have given as a woman is supposed to give during the first night with her husband."

Again Mandell had mixed feelings. From the first time he'd seen Eyes Like The She Wolf, he'd appreciated her attractive, shapely form—it had matched the loveliness of her features—but at that moment the circumstances were something less than ideal for them to be together. Demanding to stay for the sake of saving face was one thing, but asking him to claim her body for the same reason was quite another. He shivered involuntarily. The situation was too devoid of passion to suit his taste.

While he considered the matter, Eyes Like The She Wolf had already begun to loosen the ties of her beaded buckskin dress. When she'd slipped out of it and was naked, she moved around and lay beside Mandell on the pallet.

"All right, *Husband*," she stated coldly. "Do whatever it is you're supposed to do."

Mandell sat staring at the gently curving form in front of him. For a brief instant he considered picking up the Indian woman and pitching her out the front flap of the tepee with a kick to her bare behind to hurry her along. A few braves were still sitting around the fire outside and such a scene would be fair punishment for her insolence and her insults. But at the sight of her body so close by and so available, other possibilities began to occur to him. . . .

He reached out a hand and moved his palm back and

153

forth across the soft mound of one of her breasts. Despite her previous defiance, the girl's nipple began to harden in response to his touch.

"Do Indian people, uh . . ." he began to ask, but he didn't know the Sioux word for kiss. "Do they do this?" he asked finally, leaning down to brush his lips against hers.

"Yes," she told him, "but most do it better than that."

"I guess I'd better try again, then," Mandell whispered. With the second kiss he pressed his lips more firmly and probed with his tongue until it entered the moist recesses of her mouth. It was a risk, of course. A shrew like the one beside him was likely to bite his tongue just for spite. He tightened his grip on her breast to let her know that he, too, had power.

Disregarding the odd circumstances, Mandell felt himself responding to the soft warm touch of Eyes Like The She Wolf's body. His mouth and hands began to roam farther, sampling and savoring the feel of her flesh. After a few moments, she began reacting gently to his kisses and caresses.

"I didn't know I would like it," she murmured huskily. "Am I supposed to?"

"A man generally hopes so," Mandell answered softly. He felt his body growing eager to claim this young woman. Raising himself up, he parted her legs with his knee, then positioned himself above her.

When she gasped in pain from the first thrust, he considered being more gentle with her. But wasn't he doing what she had insisted that he do, saving her from the harsh judgments of the old Sioux women?

"That hurts!" Eyes Like The She Wolf cried out

sharply as he plunged forward again more forcefully. "Stop it! Something's wrong!"

"What I'm doing will hurt, but only the first time," Mandell whispered hoarsely.

His injured arm was beginning to throb and he figured that the wound had reopened, but at that moment it didn't matter. When his rigid member penetrated through suddenly to the moist recesses of her womanhood, Eyes Like The She Wolf cried out. Her body bucked violently from the sudden pain. Unmercifully she raked her fingernails over his back and her teeth locked without warning onto the muscle of his neck. But immediately Mandell sensed that these were new kinds of responses he was receiving.

"Don't stop," she huffed throatily beneath him.

Their bodies were slick with sweat. Mandell could feel the tender orbs of his partner's breasts sliding against his chest with a rhythm quite separate from the gyrations of her hips.

He began to peak, feeling as if all the energy in his body was pumping from him. At last, with a massive exhalation of air, he collapsed and lay still, panting for air.

"Why do you stop?" the young Indian woman asked. "Do you grow tired so quickly?"

"I've finished," Mandell explained.

"Well what about me? How do I finish?"

With a sigh, Mandell pushed with one hand and rolled slowly to one side. "Just give me a minute to pull myself back together," he requested. "Then I'll do my best to show you."

When he woke at dawn, Mandell felt physically drained. He was more exhausted than he had been the previous evening when he first came to the tepee to relax. Blood seeped from his throbbing shoulder wound and stained the blanket beneath him. In addition, the thick bandage over his wounded hand was encrusted and in need of changing.

At least, he thought smugly, sometime during the night he had shown the young woman who now lay sleeping beside him what it was to "finish." It had taken some doing though. At times he had wondered if the task was more than he could handle in his weakened condition.

But now the gentle smile that spread across his companion's features spoke of a new knowledge the Indian girl had gained. If the old women of the tribe knew half as much about life as old women elsewhere seemed to know, that smile alone should say enough about what had taken place between Eyes Like The She Wolf and the man who had won her in battle.

Chapter 10

May, 1866

John Bozeman finished tamping the dirt around the post he had set in the ground. Then he stepped back to survey his handiwork. The hand-lettered sign nailed to the post announced that this place was, "Bozeman City, Montana Territory."

It did occur to Bozeman that it was a bit pretentious to proclaim a settlement of no more than a dozen log cabins a city, just as it had been pretentious for the founders of Bannack to label their little mountain hamlet a city during its fledgling days. But that kind of flamboyance was part of the Western style. Anywhere that two men built their homes within shouting distance of one another, they soon began to hope that one day they would be known as the founders of a great Western metropolis.

John Bozeman was deeply proud of the small community he had founded. Bozeman City was not sitting on top of any gold deposits, and it had not soared to sudden prominence as had many other mining towns in the region, but Bozeman hoped that one day it might evolve into a bustling center of commerce and trade.

The settlement was located on the eastern fringes of the bustling Montana gold fields at what could well be termed "trail's end" for the Bozeman Trail. Bozeman rationalized that, like Fetterman's Fort, Bozeman City could become a stopping-off place for the people who traveled hard through Indian territory and needed time for rest and repairs before pushing on into the gold fields. At Bozeman City they could resupply and trade for fresh wagon stock.

The plan was a realistic one. Bozeman realized that he was not going to become a wealthy man by guiding travel parties up the Bozeman Trail or by freighting someone else's goods across the plains. Once he had scouted out the original trail and the wheels of his heavy wagons had marked the path for anyone to follow, no other trains of wagons would need his services to get from Fetterman's Fort to the gold fields. Kate Lancaster had proved that two years before.

And Kate Lancaster had also been responsible for Bozeman's decision not to guide wagons loaded with someone else's goods west into the gold regions. After she'd beaten him in the race to Tumble Mountain Gorge, he had been forced to travel nearly one hundred miles west to Virginia City in order to sell his merchandise. And by the time he got there, prices were already plummeting to their summer lows.

The forty wagons of freight had not brought nearly the returns he had expected. By the time he paid his drivers off and dispatched two couriers east with the healthy profits he had promised his backers, his own gains were disappointingly small.

With this new enterprise in mind, he had kept about

two hundred of the best oxen and horses from his wagon teams and persuaded some of the teamsters to come to this place with him. They had spent the fall building their cabins and stockpiling hay for their winter feed, and by the time the first isolating snowfall struck, they had been ready to face the long winter.

The next year, during the summer of 1865, Bozeman and his men had done fairly well. Enough parties had made it through along the trail to keep his stock trade alive. With the profits he had purchased supplies of food, ammunition and other essentials to sell in the small store he'd set up.

Indian disturbances along the trail were increasing. From the time they left Fetterman's Fort until they crossed the Yellowstone far to the northwest, no traveler felt safe. But by late that summer an encouraging piece of news had reached the southwest Montana area. The pleas for protection had finally been heard back East. With the Civil War at last concluded, more troops would be available to quell the scattered, violent Indian disturbances. In particular, plans were in the works to establish a string of forts along the Bozeman Trail so that the route would be a safe one for travel.

All this John Bozeman had taken as an encouraging sign that his business would soon begin to flourish. But now in the spring of 1866 he was again beginning to have his doubts. The troops had come as promised and begun the construction of their forts along the Powder River, a tributary of the Tongue River. They set up along the Bighorn River, too. But from the start, the military effort had been a disaster of mismanagement. Too few troops had been sent to do the job they were assigned, and those who had been sent were either raw, poorly equipped recruits, or war veterans disgruntled over the fact that they had been shipped west to fight Indians. During that first winter the soldiers nearly starved at their isolated, incomplete forts. Mutinies were commonplace.

Rather than being intimidated by the presence of troops sent to subdue them, the Indians in the area were outraged over the blatant treaty violation. There was talk of a great Indian confederation that would drive both the soldiers and the civilian travelers off Indian land.

The first groups to set out along the Bozeman Trail that spring found themselves subject to immediate, vicious attack by parties of Sioux, Crow and Cheyenne. The summer was promising to be a violent one, and John Bozeman, situated where he was, anticipated seeing the trail he and John Jacobs had discovered turned into a bloody battle ground.

His chore completed, Bozeman hefted his shovel onto his shoulder and turned to start back toward his cabin, the nearest building in a long, neat row of log cabins that comprised the main, and only, street of Bozeman City. To the rear of the cabins a couple of men were at work with hoes in one of the settlement's large vegetable gardens. Off to the right half a dozen more workers were putting the roof on a large livery barn they had begun construction of that same year.

When Bozeman saw the workmen on the barn roof begin, one by one, to pause in their work and stare off to the east, he too turned and looked in that direction. In a moment he had spotted the distant shapes of a man and horse racing toward him across the long meadow.

It didn't take Bozeman long to recognize the rider as Billy Buffalo. The young Shawnee had a distinctive style. Billy claimed he could speak in a secret tribal tongue to horses, and that when he needed the maximum effort from his mount, he could make the animal *want* to give it to him. As he watched man and horse shooting across the plains with grace and speed, Bozeman could easily believe that story.

From all sides, men dropped what they were doing and converged on the center of the settlement. It was as if each one of them sensed that Billy's message would be important. Billy reached the grassy area in front of the cabins and swung one leg over the saddle. His feet were on the ground before his horse had even come to a complete stop.

"There's big trouble out on the trail, Mr. Bozeman," he announced excitedly. "The train I've just come from is about fifty miles west of here. They're not sure they'll be able to make it to the Yellowstone before they're attacked and wiped out."

"How many wagons?" Bozeman asked.

"Just fourteen," Billy reported. "And since it left Fort Smith eight days ago, that wagon train has lost three men and nine head of oxen. They've been hit three times by small bands of Indians—Cheyenne, they think."

The story was becoming a familiar one. The people in the party had left Fetterman's Fort a month before, believing that because the United States Army was in the area, the Indians would begin to quake in fear and cease all harassment of the wagon trains headed northwest. They had learned differently about one hundred miles into their journey. It was at that point they were attacked on the portion of the trail between Fort Reno and Fort Kearny. After surviving the initial fracas with a small band of Sioux, they had decided to press on and begun to travel with a column of forty soldiers who were headed northwest to Fort C.F. Smith with dispatches, mail and supplies. During that stretch of trail, they were not bothered. But once they'd left their military escort behind, their problems began again.

"I'd say those people have real trouble out there," Billy declared. "So far they've only been hit by ten or fifteen Indians at a time, but I scouted out one Cheyenne camp nearby with at least two hundred people in it, counting women and children. If the braves from that camp all decided to attack, there's no question that the people in the train are goners."

Bozeman pursed his lips and nodded solemnly as he listened to his scout's account. Initially he had thought it a good idea to keep Billy Buffalo out on the trail as much as possible, advising the travelers on the road ahead of them and steering them toward the goods and services available in Bozeman City.

But each time the scout returned after days in the field, his accounts were filled with reports of roving bands of Indians and attacks on various groups of travelers. It was becoming increasingly apparent that the northern portion of the Bozeman Trail was no longer the "safe" area it once had been. Travelers could no longer count on any semblance of safety until they had crossed the Yellowstone River about forty miles west of Bozeman City and entered the fringes of the mining district.

After hearing Billy's account, Bozeman glanced around at the row of log cabins. He surveyed the trim, spacious gardens and the corrals filled with livestock for sale or trade. "Damn," he muttered to himself.

There were twenty-six men living in Bozeman City, including Bozeman and Billy, fourteen men who worked for Bozeman and ten others who had settled in to operate various business enterprises. The town was by no means a Virginia City, but within its boundaries a pretty comfortable life could be had, and it was true they had not experienced even one Indian scare in the two years of the settlement's existence. Yet trouble was close at hand. Bozeman knew what, in good conscience, they had to do.

He didn't have to announce his intentions. The others realized as well as he did what was required of them.

"All right, we can't all go," Bozeman told them. "If six stay behind to watch over things while we're gone, that will leave twenty to ride out and see if we can help."

"Are you talking about going against two hundred Cheyenne?" one man, named Paul Grimly, asked.

"We'll travel light on the fastest horses here," Bozeman answered. "That way, if we make contact and decide it's not a good time to fight, we can run like hell instead."

They camped that first night on the northern banks of the Yellowstone. During the early hours of morning the pickets stationed around camp engaged in a brief gunfight with a party of unidentified Indians who tried to steal some horses. None of Bozeman's men were hurt, but in the morning there were signs that at least one Indian had been killed or wounded and taken away by his comrades.

The following day, shortly after they crossed the Yellowstone, Billy Buffalo returned from scouting and reported seeing about fifteen Cheyenne traveling in the same direction as Bozeman's group about three miles ahead. He also reported spotting tracks. They had been made, Billy said, by close to fifty unshod Indian horses sometime the previous day.

Bozeman and the men with him were beginning to feel pretty nervous by that time. Were they about to take on a bigger job than they could handle? During the noon break there was considerable talk about turning back. But Bozeman reminded the grumblers that they had agreed to save the lives of the women and children in that fourteen-wagon train, and that without help the entire train was doomed. Reluctantly the men consented to push on. And again Billy forged ahead to investigate the country that lay before them.

If it still existed, the wagon train was close by. But Bozeman knew that wish was by no means guaranteed. It had been over two days since Billy had left the train to ride for help. During that time they should have been able to push north at least to the Yellowstone. But in the ten miles that Bozeman's group had covered since they left the river, they had not seen a single sign of the white travelers. What Bozeman hoped was that the wagon train either had been delayed by breakdowns or had held up in some secure spot to wait for help.

No more than thirty minutes after Billy had ridden out following the noon stop, he came racing back with startling news.

"We got big trouble now," the scout rasped breathlessly. "There's about fifty Cheyenne only a couple of miles up ahead. They all are braves and they all are headed in this direction. My guess is they know we're here and they're coming for us."

"What about the wagon train?"

Billy grimaced and shook his head. That was all that needed to be said about the fate of the travelers in the fourteen wagons. But now that they were known to be dead, the most immediate concern of Bozeman and his men was their own survival. They were more than fifty miles from Bozeman City. The ride back would be long and perilous.

"What do you think, Billy?" Bozeman asked his scout. "You know this country better than any of us."

"The most important thing is not to head back the same way we came," Billy warned. "By now most of the

Indians in the area probably know we're here. I'd guess they'll be waiting for us somewhere along the trail. We're all well mounted and we can go places that wagons can't, so I think we should make for the edge of the mountains and then strike out overland back to Bozeman City. None of the Indians will expect us to take that route."

"All right, then," Bozeman agreed. "That's what we'll do."

He turned his horse to the west and spurred it to a ground-eating gallop. All of the mounts maintained that speed for at least two hours. By dusk they were well into the foothills of the northern portion of the Absaroka Range, and before full darkness, Billy had located a sheltered ravine in which they could make their camp. On its lower end the entrance to the ravine was only about twenty feet wide and littered with boulders of varying size. Half a dozen men positioned there with repeating rifles could withstand a charge by a hundred Indians, and the upper end of the ravine was so steep and ragged that the possibilities of being attacked from that direction were remote.

After an uneventful night, the men began to gain new hope that they would make it back to Bozeman City without a fight. The sentries on the last shift woke the others before dawn and everyone hurriedly began building breakfast fires so that they could be in the saddle by first light. Billy Buffalo slugged back a quick cup of coffee, stuffed his shirt pockets full of the first biscuits to come off the fire, and was heading out of the ravine by the time the first streaks of grey light were beginning to show up in the eastern sky.

He had ridden out no more than a hundred yards beyond the entrance to the ravine when a shot roared out. Billy's horse squealed in pain and began to fall. But with amazing agility the young Indian drew his rifle from the saddle boot and leaped clear before the animal hit the ground. Immediately he began racing back toward the gorge, running in a zigzag pattern. No other shots were fired.

As the other men picked up their weapons and took positions near the mouth of the gorge, Bozeman eased over to where Billy knelt on the ground behind a three-foot boulder.

"Did you get a look at any of them?" Bozeman asked. "Is it the Cheyenne who were following us before?"

"I don't know," Billy answered. "I didn't see anything, but I think the shot came from that aspen grove off to the left there. Whoever fired at me was at least a couple of hundred feet away."

The sky slowly began to lighten and Bozeman moved from man to man, instructing each one not to fire his weapon unless their group was openly attacked. Within a quarter of an hour there was enough light for everyone to see scattered figures moving through the trees. It was impossible to tell how many Indians were there or even what tribe they belonged to, but Bozeman and his men knew there was nothing for them to do at that moment but sit and wait.

The minutes dragged. By the position of the sun, Bozeman could tell that no more than an hour had passed when at last a single mounted figure emerged from the trees and started slowly in their direction. The sights of twenty rifles were trained on him instantly, even though the rider carried a stick with a red flag tied on it—the Indian sign for truce.

When the man approached to within a hundred yards and was passing by the spot where Billy Buffalo's downed horse lay, one of the riflemen closest to the entrance of the gorge turned his head back to the others and exclaimed, "Good God A'might! It's a white man!"

*   *   *

As he rode forward, Hank Mandell could practically *feel* the sights of rifles trained on his chest. All it would take to finish him, he knew, was one squeeze by a trigger-happy hothead. The braves he was with had told him that it was a crazy thing to do, riding out to try and talk to a band of men who were tensed and ready for a fight, but Mandell had convinced them that it was something he must try, that it was the only way to prevent a bloody battle.

Mandell stopped his horse about a hundred feet away from the first man and just sat there for a moment, letting everyone get a good look at him. He knew he must look strange. He had let his hair grow long and wore it as the Indians did, tied back with a wind band. The skin of his bare, husky chest and arms was tanned bronze. He wore a pair of buckskin pants, and there were beaded moccasins on his feet.

Mandell stared at the men staring at him. After spending the past two years never glimpsing the face of another white man, these men up ahead looked somehow odd and unfamiliar to him, too. They were men of his own race, but because of the life he had been leading for so long, he felt estranged from them.

"I need to talk to you men," he called out at last. "It's very important that we get things worked out before the top blows off this powder keg we're all sitting on."

"Who are you?" a voice challenged. "And what in the ever-loving hell are you doing out there with all those redskins?"

"I'll explain everything as soon as you let me ride in and meet with the person in charge," Mandell promised.

"All right. Come ahead," the same voice allowed.

Mandell wound his way through the rocks and into

the ravine. Then he stepped to the ground just as a man left his place behind a large rock and came over to greet him. "The name's John Bozeman," the man told him.

"Are you the Bozeman that the trail's named after?"

"That's right, and you're . . .?"

"Hank Mandell."

"Well, Mr. Mandell, I'd sure be interested in knowing what you're doing out there with all those Indians. But first and most important, maybe you can tell us what sort of mess we've gotten ourselves into."

"If things don't go just right," Mandell replied frankly, "I'd say you and your men have bought yourselves a whole lot of trouble. I'm with a hunting party of about a dozen Sioux who are over in those trees. But your real headache is just over the crest of that hill to the right. A war party of about seventy-five Cheyenne braves are just itching to charge in here and take your scalps. They wiped out a wagon train down the trail the day before yesterday and their blood's still racing over the victory. Now they want to follow up that coup by wiping out you and your men."

"We knew they were after us, but we didn't know there were quite so many," Bozeman said.

"Well, just what in the hell are you doing out here anyway?" Mandell asked. "Surely you must have known that there was Indian trouble afoot in this area."

"We knew it, but we came to try and help that train," Bozeman explained. "Obviously we didn't make it in time and now we're just trying to make it out alive."

"You might be able to if you do things like I tell you," Mandell advised. "But if just one of your men gets trigger-happy and decides he'd like to notch his gun for killing an Indian, you all might as well start wishing you'd made out your wills."

"First I'll listen, Mandell, and then I'll decide whether you know what you're talking about."

"Fair enough," Mandell smiled, and he went on to explain to Bozeman that he and the Sioux braves had been out on a simple hunting trip when they'd come across the Cheyenne camp the night before. The Cheyenne had been celebrating and feasting on the food they had taken from the wagons. Frequently they tortured the last two men they had taken prisoner during the fight. But when it was all over, the Cheyenne had one last prisoner tied up and tucked away at the edge of camp.

"When I found out they had captured themselves a white woman from the wagon train," Mandell continued, "I started right off trying to trade them out of her. I offered them my horse and gun, but they thought the woman worth a whole lot more than that. Then another thought occurred to me. I told them that since they were on your trail anyway, they could probably get a high price for the woman from you."

Bozeman's eyes narrowed upon hearing that. "It doesn't seem like we're exactly in an ideal bargaining position here," he answered dourly.

"Maybe and maybe not," Mandell returned. "You're forted up pretty good and I've already told the Cheyenne that me and the braves I'm with don't want to throw our lives away trying to blast you out of here. We're hunting right now and a camp of nearly a hundred people is waiting for the meat we're supposed to be bringing back. Anyway, the Cheyenne know what kind of losses they would suffer if they attacked." Mandell paused and glanced at the faces of the men around him. He knew that his next statement would arouse their suspicions more than anything he had told them so far. "What they really want is your horses," he explained, "and I told them how they could get their hands on some of them without having to lose a single man doing it.''

"I think I know what you're getting at, Mandell," Bozeman responded darkly. "You want us to trade horses for that woman they have. Is that it?"

"That's exactly it," Mandell affirmed. "I had a chance to talk to the woman for a minute last night. She's in pretty bad shape—sick with fever even before the Cheyenne got their hands on her. And it's been pure hell for her ever since. She told me that only the leader of the group and a few of his henchmen had gotten to her so far, but that it was only a matter of time until the whole blasted bunch got a crack at her. I don't think she'll survive that." Mandell paused again. Then he looked John Bozeman straight in the eye and declared, "Ten horses will buy her life."

"Ten horses!" Bozeman exclaimed. "We've only got nineteen horses for twenty men as it is, thanks to one of your people. . . ."

"I know, and I'm sorry about that," Mandell apologized. "It was one of our young mavericks that shot your man's horse out from under him."

"And if we turned ten more horses over to you," Bozeman went on, "that would only leave nine. We'd never make it out of this country alive."

"I told the Cheyenne that if you made the trade, you'd have my safe conduct out of here," Mandell put in. "The Yellowstone is only about fifteen more miles in the direction you were traveling, and me and my men would travel with you that far."

"You're trying to tell me we'd have Sioux Indians protecting us from Cheyenne?" Bozeman scoffed. "Isn't that something like letting the cat guard the canary?"

"Some of my men don't like the notion either, but if

I seal the bargain with my word, they'll stand behind me all the way."

"I'm going to have to talk this over with my men," Bozeman remarked after considering the matter. "Their lives are at stake here and it wouldn't be fair for me to choose for them." As Mandell stood slightly apart from the rest of the men, they gathered and talked among themselves about what he was proposing.

When Bozeman at last approached Mandell, his face was drawn with concern. "We all agree on one thing, Mandell," Bozeman announced. "Even if you're playing it straight with us right down the line, what you're suggesting is plumb crazy. Still, one fact made us swing the other way. We know what we're facing if we stay here and it doesn't look good. But if we go along with you, there's at least a chance we might make it out of this thing alive. You tell your conniving friends out there to bring the woman on and they'll have their horses."

It took Mandell a long time to make the arrangements. First he had to persuade the Cheyenne to stand by their agreement of the night before. Then he had to convince the men in his own group that out of loyalty to him they should help him enforce the safe conduct he had promised.

Not too surprisingly, the second task proved more difficult than the first. During a heated discussion, two of the Sioux braves questioned Mandell's loyalties. Nevertheless, Mandell was at last able to enforce his will among the others.

His problems were not over, however—and he knew that. Somewhere down the line, the steps he had taken that day would come back to haunt him.

* * *

Seeing their ten horses tied in single file and ready to be led out and handed over to the Indians incensed several of Bozeman's men. They threatened to rebel and refuse to let him make the exchange.

The thought of being on foot in such wild country, perhaps at the mercy of roving bands of mounted Indians who wanted nothing more than to slit their throats and steal their scalps, was incredibly frightening. At the last moment some of the men speculated irrationally that it would be wiser to make a run for it than to trust their lives to a bargain made by a white man that not a single one of them knew.

Bozeman knew that he might be throwing away his own life and the lives of all of his men by agreeing to do what Hank Mandell suggested. Every word Mandell had spoken could have been a lie. He could have been setting them up for massacre.

But Bozeman knew that if he and his men did try to make a run for it, they would have to ride past the Sioux in the aspens and straight through the Cheyenne camp over the rise to reach the open country beyond. That would be a race right into the jaws of certain death, and the prospects if they stayed in the ravine didn't seem much better. In that case the Cheyenne could still charge in and kill them all. Or the Indians could simply sit back and starve them out.

The only way any of his men stood a chance, Bozeman knew, was to trust Mandell and make the trade.

After a wait of nearly an hour, he spotted Mandell and a couple of Indians top the rise and start in the direction of the ravine. Behind his horse, Mandell was pulling an improvised travois on which a blanket-wrapped figure was lying. That would be the woman, Bozeman thought, if there was truly a woman. He waited another moment, mounted his own horse and took up the lead rope of the horses that were being traded.

Beside him, Billy Buffalo looked up. "Watch their eyes, my friend," he cautioned. "Sometimes a man's eyes will tell you what he's going to do before he does it."

Bozeman rode out slowly, wanting to make the exchange as close within the range of his own men's rifles as possible. Of course that would not save his life, Bozeman knew. Rifle sights were undoubtedly trained on him from the aspen grove to the left. But at least if this all was a ruse, one of his men would probably be able to drop Mandell out of the saddle before he could dash to cover.

The two men with Mandell were both Cheyenne. They were lean, handsome Indians whose dark eyes readily communicated all the chilling hatred they felt for the white race. It was obvious that only the thinnest thread of reserve and respect for Mandell kept them from pulling their weapons that instant and killing Bozeman before any exchange could be made.

When they met, Bozeman leaned to the side and glanced around the rump of Mandell's horse. It was true. A white woman truly did lie atop the travois. A threadbare blanket lay over her nearly to her shoulders and she appeared to be naked beneath it. From what little he could see of the woman's bruised shoulder and the battered cheek on one side of her face, it looked as if her experiences with the Cheyenne had been every bit as horrible as Mandell had reported.

"All right, turn the string over to Three Bows here," Mandell instructed, "and then I'll ride on back with you. My braves will meet us in front of the ravine as soon as your men are ready to leave."

"That's fine, but first I want to check something," Bozeman said, stepping to the ground and starting around the side of Mandell's horse. "I want to make sure we're buying a live woman instead of a dead one."

When he reached the woman's side, he could tell by the slight rising and falling of her chest that she was still alive. But she seemed to be unconscious.

Bozeman stared down intently at her for a moment. Then his mouth sagged open in amazement. One of her eyes was swollen nearly shut and her features were battered and gashed from the abuse the Indians had given her, but still there was no doubt about who she was.

Atop his horse, Mandell turned to Bozeman. "She told me her name is Kate . . ."

"Kate Lancaster," Bozeman interrupted. "Yes, I've made the lady's acquaintance in the past. And it seems like every time I come across her she costs me more than I can afford to lose."

Chapter 11

Her dreams consisted of a prolonged series of brief, painful flashbacks. It was as if a nightmare world was trying to keep its grip on her as she struggled to escape it.

In the throes of the fever, she had barely the strength to pull herself up off the pallet and crawl toward the rear of the wagon to escape. The boiling heat of the burning canvas canopy stretched above her. All around the screams of dying men and women mingled with the roar of gunfire and the victorious cries of the Cheyenne as they overran the wagon train.

She knew that she was about to die. The illness had left her weak. There was no strength to fight back, to flee, or to even keep herself from tumbling clumsily to the ground when she reached the back of the wagon. She was more afraid than she had ever been before.

As her eyes fluttered open briefly, she saw through blurred vision that log walls surrounded her. Sunlight splashed across the room through an open window to her side, hurting her eyes and forcing her to close them once more. But a cool breeze drifted deliciously in and caressed her body.

Three Bows had quickly overcome her, beating her into submission with his fists. The violence had exhilarated him and increased his sexual excitement. By the time he'd collapsed roughly down on top of her, he was breathing heavily and mumbling words in his own language. She was sure they'd been derisions and Indian obscenities.

The pain of being raped was not as bad as the pounding she'd endured on every part of her.

The whole thing had lasted only a short time . . . but then others came.

Somewhere outside two men were talking. Though she could scarcely grasp what they were saying, she realized that the words were English. The conversation had something to do with radishes and corn. Though it made no sense, the mere fact that it was white men who were talking sent a rush of joy through her.

Then a wagon rumbled by outside and the monotonous squeak of heavy, ungreased axles reminded her of a similar but much more horrifying sound.

She had never realized before how much torment and desperation could be communicated in the screams of a dying man. The sound had a quality that penetrated deep into the human soul and filled it with terror.

She knew the Indians must be torturing at least two of the men they had captured from the wagon train, but she did not want to know which ones. All she really wanted was the unconsciousness. It came and went all through the

*long night like tides. What she hoped was that it would
claim her fully so she would no longer have to listen to the
screams.*

The bed was lumpy and crackled softly beneath her
whenever she moved even slightly. It was made of cornhusks
that had been stuffed into a canvas cover, she decided. But
to be on a bed of any kind was comforting to her aching,
bruised body. Every movement caused her some amount
of pain. She felt as if she were a leaden thing, devoid of
the power to move herself without great effort. She knew
she was naked and exposed, but the simple task of pulling
up the sheet which lay at her feet seemed impossible.

She focused her attention on the sound of footsteps
crunching on the dry ground outside the window. Two
men were approaching. When they got closer, she was
able to hear what they were saying.

"Yes, I'm just going to check on her now."

"Is she doing better?"

"I think so. The fever wasn't so bad last night and
she seemed to rest easier. But I'm beginning to wonder if
she's ever going to come to. It's been three days."

"She'll pull through. She's a strong young woman,
strong enough to chase the devils from her body."

In a moment the footsteps approached the door of the
room where she was lying. The door swung open.

It took her a moment to recognize the features of the
bearded man who stood there gazing at her. Then finally a
puzzled look came onto her face and she said weakly,
"You?"

"Me." John Bozeman grinned back at her.

Suddenly she realized that she was utterly naked. She
struggled to sit up and reach for the sheet, but the effort
was too much for her.

177

"Are you going to let me lie here uncovered like this while you're in the room?" she asked with as much defiance as she could muster.

Bozeman merely chuckled. "How do you think Billy Buffalo and I have been seeing you for the past three days?" he asked. "I hate to say it, Kate, but you no longer have many secrets from us as far as your body is concerned." But he relented and came over to pull the sheet up over her. "For the first couple of days," he continued, "you were burning up with fever and we had to keep dousing you with water day and night to try and bring your temperature down. Billy went out in the hills to gather herbs to treat your cuts. That one right below your left breast and another on your thigh were the worst, but they've closed now and started to heal."

Kate knew she should be grateful. Bozeman and his friend obviously had devoted a lot of time and effort to saving her life. But the thought of two men hovering over her, completely at liberty to look and touch wherever they wanted, was humiliating. In spite of herself, she still felt resentment toward Bozeman.

"Your stomach's bound to feel like it's about to cave in," Bozeman remarked. "We were able to get some water down your throat once in a while, but it's been at least three days since you've had any solid food. Would you like to try to eat?"

"I guess so," Kate replied. She did not feel exactly hungry, but knew that she would not start getting her strength back until she began to eat.

Bozeman left the room and a moment later returned carrying a wooden bowl and a spoon. "It's potato soup and it's not very hot," he apologized, "but right now it will probably be the best thing for you." As he helped her sit up in the bed, Kate was struck by his gentleness and solicitude. There must be more to this man than she thought, for him to treat her so nicely after the dealings they'd had.

"I don't guess you remember anything about how we got you back here, do you?" Bozeman asked as he raised the first spoonful of soup to her mouth.

"I remember a man coming to me in the Indian camp, but it wasn't you," Kate replied. "He talked to me for a while and told me he would try to help me."

"That man was Hank Mandell. He lives with the Sioux," Bozeman told her. Briefly he explained how she had been bought from her captors for ten horses and how Mandell miraculously had arranged for all of them to be escorted to safety by some of the very Indians who would have preferred to kill them.

"But what really has me puzzled," Bozeman admitted at last, "is what you were doing in a wagon train loaded with homesteaders. I've wondered about it ever since we brought you here."

"I was on my way to Virginia City," Kate explained, "and then I thought I might go on up to Helena later. I figured with the ten thousand dollars I had just made—" She broke off suddenly. "My God! The money!" she exclaimed as a horrified look twisted onto her face.

"You didn't have it on you when you came into my hands," Bozeman let her know. "You didn't have anything on you, not even clothes."

"I had ten thousand dollars in greenbacks and government promissory notes hidden behind a board of the wagon I was in," Kate moaned. "But the wagon was on fire when I crawled out of it. Oh, God. . . ."

For a moment she lapsed into a dazed silence, but Bozeman forced her out of it by shoveling another spoonful of soup in her mouth. "At least you're still alive," he reasoned. "You can earn yourself another ten thousand dollars. With the tactics you employ,'' he added grimly, ''I'm sure of it.''

When she'd resigned herself to the loss, Kate gave Bozeman some answers explaining precisely how she had come to be where she was when the Cheyenne attacked the wagon train.

Early in the spring, she had secured a government contract in Omaha to bring a shipment of supplies west to the new forts that were being established along the Bozeman Trail. Unlike some of the other contractors who dragged their feet and seemed in no hurry to fulfill their obligations, she had hurriedly bought her supplies and wagons and was pushing west as soon as the Nebraska winter weather began to subside.

Hers was the first wagon train of the year to start up the Bozeman Trail, and she found the soldiers at Fort Reno, Fort Kearny and Fort Smith eager to receive the food and supplies she carried. When she had delivered the last of her goods at Fort Smith, the commander there made her an offer for her wagons and teams. After she had paid off the teamsters who worked for her, she still had ten thousand dollars to show for little more than three months' work.

A small wagon train arrived at Fort Smith from the south a week later and she paid one of the families to let her travel along with them. With so much ready cash in hand she decided it was time to make investments, and she learned that certain mining stock in the Virginia City area was bringing good returns.

She planned only to eat and sleep with the family because she had a good saddle horse to ride. But the fourth day out on the trail she began to grow feverish and was soon flat on her back in the wagon. While there, she had pried loose one of the planks and hidden her money in a small empty space behind it.

Indians began to harass the train a short time later. Before it reached the Yellowstone River, enough Cheyenne had banded together to complete the devastating work.

Kate did not talk about what had happened to her after the wagons were sacked and burned, and Bozeman did not press her for details. Like the physical injuries she had suffered at the hands of the Indians, the mental wounds were still fresh and painful, and the chances were great that they would remain that way long after the last bruise had disappeared from her skin and the last cut had closed and healed.

By the time the bowl of soup was empty, Kate was exhausted and ready to rest again. Before he left, Bozeman took the sheet from her so that she would sleep cooler. And as her mind drifted drowsily, one of Kate's last thoughts was how safe she felt in the capable hands of this man.

"John, I'd like to take a real bath," Kate announced as she served up two bowls of venison stew from the pot over the fire and carried them to the table. "For three weeks I've been rinsing myself down with water from a tin dishpan and that's just not the same as being wet all over."

"Well, the nearest bathtub I know of is one I heard they imported from the States for one of the fancy cathouses in Virginia City," Bozeman chuckled, "but I'm not sure you're quite up to making the trip yet."

"I'm not going to be *that* choosy," Kate laughed. "I've heard some of the men talk about a place close by called Clearwater Falls where they go to swim. Why couldn't I go there?"

181

"The falls are about three miles up into the hills and it is pretty up there," Bozeman conceded, "but I don't know . . ."

"Damn it, John!" Kate snapped. "I don't need your permission. I can go by myself."

"Now you just hold your horses a minute, lady," Bozeman barked back. "I've invested a lot of time and energy into getting you patched together. I didn't do it all so you could go running off to do something stupid. You know as well as the rest of us that the Crow have started crossing the Yellowstone in small groups to see what sort of mischief they can get into. And you also know we've had to start posting guards around the cabins and the herds every night. Why are you so all-fired anxious to get taken again by the Indians?"

Kate calmed a bit. "You're right, I guess," she relented. "It's just that I'm feeling cooped up. You know the kind of wandering life I've always led. But since I've been here I don't think I've walked a hundred yards from the door of this cabin."

"Well," Bozeman reminded her, "it hasn't been that long that you've been able to walk a hundred yards in *any* direction."

"But I'm better now, John. I'm getting my strength back and I'm ready to quit playing invalid. Look at the amount of work I've done around here during the past few days. I've cleaned this cabin from top to bottom till it looks more like a home than a pigsty. And I've cooked practically every bit of food that's gone in your mouth for the past week. I think I'm ready for some sort of excursion, and I *know* I'm ready for a real bath."

Surprisingly, Bozeman found himself slightly regretful that Kate was recovering so fast and so completely. It had felt good to him taking care of her and seeing to her simple needs. The feeling was one of balance and completeness.

But Kate's lifelong need for independence was returning to her. Once again she was regaining her ability to face the world alone.

"All right, Kate, you shall have your outing and your bath," Bozeman promised. "When do you want to go?"

"In the morning," she told him. "I'll pack a picnic lunch and borrow a rifle from one of the men. We'll make a day of it at Clearwater Falls."

The circumstances were going to be a little awkward, Bozeman decided as he gazed out toward the pool at the base of Clearwater Falls. He wanted to be far enough away to give Kate privacy while she bathed. Yet he needed to be fairly close, too, in case trouble sprang out at them. Kate quickly settled the question for him.

As soon as they reached the edge of the pool, she slid down from her horse and dived into the water wearing her clothes. When she surfaced a moment later she was out near the center of the pool, treading as she wrestled out of them.

"I just couldn't wait!" she exclaimed as she hurled a soggy shirt at Bozeman, dunking herself in the process. She did a roll and thrashed around below the surface for a moment. When she came up again, in her hand she held the trousers she had been wearing. "Bathing out of a dishpan could never feel this good!" she laughed.

Her spirits had been high all morning during the ride to the falls. She had chatted gaily most of the way, commenting on the details of the wildlife they were passing and pointing out how lovely the forested hills ahead looked in the bright morning light. And when they finally reached their destination, the beauty of the falls themselves made her breath catch in her throat.

The water cascaded down from a ledge above in a glistening sheet ten feet wide and fifty feet long. The clear, oval pool below was about thirty feet across and ten feet deep in its center, and its bottom was lined with a thick blanket of sand. The falls were located in a sheltered, horseshoe-shaped depression in the side of a hill that was carpeted with lush, green summer grass.

Bozeman spread Kate's clothes out in the sun to dry. Then he turned to tend to their horses. He ground-reined them so they could graze, then carried his and Kate's rifles and the sack containing their lunch over to the grass near the water's edge. In an instant all his noble plans were lost in the pleasure of watching her cavort unabashedly in the water.

He remembered how after she'd regained consciousness Kate had been forced to grow accustomed to his intimate attentions to her body. Then she had needed the care he was giving her. But as he stared at her swimming in front of him, he could make no pretense of looking at her with an eye to her health and well-being. Her fever was long past and the cuts on her body had diminished to thin red scars that time eventually would erase. Now it was impossible to gaze at her without simple appreciation for her loveliness. Her full, youthful figure inspired thoughts that had nothing to do with medical matters.

Kate dived deep into the center of the pool, only to resurface directly beneath the pounding water of the falls. There she found some firm footing and stepped up until only her feet and ankles were visible in the churning water. For an instant the scene seemed frozen in time. Bozeman knew that this moment would be recorded indelibly in his mind. Kate's face was concealed behind the cascading sheet of water. But the water parted at her shoulders to stream in shimmering rivulets across her breasts, stomach and thighs. The morning sunlight made her body glisten like porcelain. Arching her body forward, she dived, lancing into the water like a creature conceived in its depths and returning to the womb.

When her initial rush of enthusiasm was past, Kate swam to the edge of the pool near Bozeman and waded out of the water. With some effort, he tore his eyes away from her body and stared toward a miniature rainbow that had risen from the base of the falls. "I need my soap so I can get the job done right," she explained. And she delved into the sack of food for the bar of homemade soap she had brought along.

"Maybe I should scout around a bit," Bozeman remarked, rising nervously.

Kate paused at the water's edge and turned to look at him. The strangeness in his voice alerted her that something odd was going on. Her eyes caught his in the act of lingering over the shape of her breasts. And when at last their gazes met, she realized in an instant how uncomfortable he must be feeling.

But her reaction was not one he expected. Her face grew sad. For a moment she looked near tears. "That might be a good idea," she murmured. "I'll be finished in a few minutes."

For the next quarter of an hour Bozeman roamed aimlessly, wrestling within himself, trying to decipher the confusing mix of emotions at work inside him. A faceless guilt nagged at him. It was as if by his lustful thoughts he had violated an unspoken trust that Kate Lancaster had put in him. She had come there that day merely to relax and bathe, but in that one instant of wordless interaction they shared, she appeared to recognize that innocence no longer existed between them.

On the other hand, he thought, was that how things *really* were? Surely a woman could not undress and display herself so openly in front of a man without realizing what thoughts would enter his mind. Kate Lancaster was no child. Perhaps the message she was sending him was much more in line with what he'd been thinking than he realized. Eagerly he turned and started back toward the pool.

Kate was sitting on a rock at its edge. She had put her shirt on. Only her feet were submerged in the water she had been enjoying so thoroughly just moments before. Without hesitating, Bozeman began peeling out of his clothes. "I think it's time *I* took a bath," he announced.

With her head lowered, Kate's long brown hair completely hid her face, and she asked without looking up, "Then shall I take a walk?"

"Not unless you want to," Bozeman answered, picking up the soap and wading out into the water. For a while he paid no attention to her as he scrubbed, but when at last he did turn and glance back in her direction, he saw that she was gazing intently at him. Her face bore a pained, almost stricken, look. And he knew that the moisture which glistened on her cheeks was not water from the pool.

"What is it, Kate?" he was compelled to ask. "What's happened to ruin your day so suddenly?"

"I'm afraid, John," she breathed quietly. "Will you hold me, please? Just for a minute?"

Bozeman held out his hand, and slowly she rose and waded to him in the waist-deep water. He enveloped her in his arms and she laid her head against his chest, trembling slightly as she submitted to the inexplicable wave of emotion she was feeling.

"I thought this day would be so wonderful," she told him in a voice barely above a whisper. "I was almost desperate to be happy and free for a while from all the dark memories that keep swirling around in my head.

"I don't know what I expected to happen out here today," she went on, "but I do know that I longed for every second to be good." She hesitated. "But when you gave me that look a few minutes ago," she continued, "and then left, I knew it couldn't be that way. If I scrubbed my skin until it bled, I would never be able to wash away the filth of what happened to me out there. And after all that, what decent man would ever want to—"

"Is that what you think?" Bozeman exclaimed, interrupting her.

"I know the kind of reputation a woman carries once she's been taken off by the Indians and they've done their worst to her."

"I don't know about all of that," Bozeman returned, "but I do know what I was thinking while I watched you swimming. I thought you were the loveliest woman I had seen in as long as I can remember."

"Then it wasn't revulsion that made you turn away?" Kate raised her head to look at him at last. Though the tears still lingered in the corners of her eyes, she was beginning, tentatively, to smile.

"My God, Kate! I just couldn't trust myself to watch you any longer. I didn't think you were ready yet for what I had in mind, but I knew that if I stayed much longer looking at you . . ."

"Maybe I *am* ready, John."

Their first kiss was a brief one. When it was over, Kate pressed herself even more tightly against Bozeman and drew a deep sigh. "Perhaps the best way to get rid of ugly experiences is to replace them with good ones," she suggested softly. "What do you think of that idea, John Bozeman?"

"I think, Kate Lancaster," he answered, leaning away from her slightly so that he could go to work on the buttons of her shirt, "that we're about to test the truth of what you said."

The shirt slid easily from Kate's shoulders. As it floated gently away toward where the pool overflowed into a rippling stream, the two lovers were too wrapped in one another's arms to notice.

Bozeman awoke to Kate waving a chicken leg under his nose, enticing him to the lunch she had spread out on the ground.

"Sleeping in the morning is a sign of sloth," she teased. "That was a saying my mama used to have. She had hundreds of them. I recall another was, 'A whistling girl and a crowing hen, both will come to no good end.' "

"You tired me out, lady," Bozeman smiled, "but I'm glad you woke me up. I'm starving."

"I've been thinking," Kate told him as they went to work on the meal of fried chicken and fresh green vegetables, "about what I should start doing with myself now that I'm well again."

Bozeman looked up from his food, but said nothing.

"As I see it," she continued, "there are three different directions I can go in—back east to Omaha, on to Virginia City or south to Salt Lake City. It might be easiest to get back to business in Salt Lake City because the Mormons know me there and would extend me credit, but their goods are expensive and—''

''Are you so eager to leave, Kate?''

She lowered her eyes and her voice became tentative as she said, ''I didn't want you to think I was so terribly eager to stay, John. It's too early to tell what this morning might mean to either of us. I just didn't want you to think that it meant you would go on being stuck with me. . . . I'm not used to having anybody or depending on anybody and the idea frightens me more than a little.''

''Kate, if you're an honorable woman, you'll stay until I give you permission to go.''

Her eyes flared angrily and her expression became fiery and defiant. ''Are you trying to tell me,'' she snapped, ''that because we had ourselves a romantic little roll in the grass, the only course for both of us is to get married or something? I never took you for such a stickler, John.''

''I'm no stickler, Kate, but you're a businesswoman, aren't you? Surely you must realize that with the debt you owe me—''

''Debt?'' she exclaimed. ''What debt?''

''Well, Kate, there's this matter of the ten horses you cost me to get you back from the Cheyenne. You see, I'm not sure I want to let you get away from me until we figure out the terms of your repayment. It could take weeks . . .''

''. . . or even months, John,'' Kate finished for him, letting an understanding smile begin to creep across her face.

''Perhaps it could take years,'' he smiled back at her. ''And of course, along the way, we might find a moment or two to deal with any silly romantic notions that this day might have put in our heads. This is serious business, Kate.''

"It sounds like monkey business to me," she quipped. Then with an exaggerated sigh of resignation she added, ''But I suppose you leave me no choice—as an honorable woman, that is.''

Chapter 12

Across the tepee, Eyes Like The She Wolf was rocking gently forward and back, crooning a soft Indian lullaby as she nursed her infant daughter, Raven. Her breasts were swollen with the milk they contained and her nipples were elongated from suckling the child. On the ground in front of her, young Swift Otter—now barely a year old—lay sleeping on a blanket, his round face beaded with dots of perspiration from the late-August heat.

Gazing at his family, Hank Mandell felt a rush of bittersweet emotion. In the course of two short years, his wife and children had become his whole world.

Thinking back, Mandell could recall that relations had not always been harmonious between himself and Eyes Like The She Wolf. Twice he had beaten her. The first time had been over a tongue-lashing she had tried to give him in front of his hunting companions. It was after he had given away both hindquarters of a deer he killed. The second whipping was for chasing him out of their tepee at knife-point after he'd refused to trade six horses—part of her dowry from Red Cloud—for a new and larger tepee that would have raised their residential status in the tribal community.

It had often been a strain for Mandell to live with this quick-tempered and sharp-tongued young woman, but he had never once doubted that the good times they shared far outweighed the periods of strain and conflict. Many a heated confrontation had lapsed into an interlude of eager lovemaking once the fury was past, and Mandell realized that deep within, Eyes Like The She Wolf was proud to have a man who was strong enough to dominate her. She could not have loved any other as deeply and as fully.

Life among the Sioux had continued to be satisfying. Mandell knew that despite his white skin, his courage and skill had earned him a unique position of respect among the Indians. Though he could never be elevated to chieftain's status, he often found himself taking on a leadership role. Sometimes he was chosen to be in charge of hunting expeditions, and twice he had led retaliatory forays against parties of Blackfoot who had tried to encroach too deeply into Sioux territory. Among the Indians he had eventually come to be known as White Wolf. For a white man to carry that name signified special distinction in that the Indians considered any albino creature as a sacred manifestation of their gods.

But Mandell was slowly realizing that time and circumstances were beginning to work against him, steadily eroding the foundations of the life he led. That fact had been revealed to him weeks before when he had engineered both the rescue of Kate Lancaster and the escape of John Bozeman and his men from disputed territory. Since that day, the attitude of the Indians around him had begun gradually to change.

For one thing he'd been tactfully excluded from the

meetings that Red Cloud and Angry Dog were holding more frequently. They took place with emissaries of various tribes in the area and were evidence that the famous Sioux chief was working to forge a strong confederation of all the local tribes.

Before, Mandell had often been invited to the council meetings that had been held to decide tribal matters, and his opinion was usually seriously regarded by the chiefs and elders. But Red Cloud was aware of what an impossible position these new and grave tribal concerns would put Mandell in, so the tradition of inviting him to council had quietly ceased. In addition, when parties of braves rode out and he was not asked to go along, Mandell knew that their mission was to hunt and kill not game, but human beings.

Thus far, Eyes Like The She Wolf had stood faithfully by his side during this growing isolation. Mandell knew that such loyalty was no small sacrifice to a woman whose status among her peers was important. They talked very little of the changes that were taking place in their lives, but Mandell was gratified by the many small ways in which Eyes Like The She Wolf showed her continuing support and love for him.

That morning he realized he was being shut out again. Earlier, representatives of the Crow, Cheyenne and Blackfoot tribes had begun to arrive at Red Cloud's large camp deep in the central portion of the Bighorn Mountains. They had met in council throughout much of the day, and on the few occasions that Mandell had ventured from his tepee, he had been treated with cold reservation by even the members of the tribe who had once been his staunchest friends. Something major was afoot, and it was obvious that the secret was shared by everyone in the camp except Mandell and Eyes Like The She Wolf.

"White Wolf. I would speak with you." The words came from directly outside the entrance flap to the tepee. Neither Mandell nor Eyes Like The She Wolf needed to be told who was speaking. It was easy to recognize the solemn voice of Red Cloud.

Mandell walked to the entrance. "Please enter, my chief," he offered, inviting Red Cloud to take the seat of honor. The Sioux leader sat cross-legged on a portion of a buffalo robe spread on the ground nearby.

Lines of concern showed on Red Cloud's features. They seemed to have aged the chief beyond his forty-two winters and imparted to his face a certain stoic sadness. Serious matters were brewing—that much was clear.

"Perhaps you realize why I am here, White Wolf," Red Cloud began.

Mandell nodded that he understood.

"It is a mark of my respect for you and my love for Eyes Like The She Wolf that I have chosen to come here myself to say these words," the chief went on. "For two years now you have lived among us as a brother. Never have you given me cause to doubt that you were a true and faithful ally to the Sioux people. But the time has come for you to go."

Mandell's glance shifted to his wife, but Eyes Like The She Wolf had diverted her gaze down to the face of their baby girl and was silently cradling the child to her. Mandell knew she understood that this was not a time for defiance. Nor was there any hope of appeal.

"You cannot be two men at once in a time of war," Red Cloud intoned. "I know you for a man of honor and I would never ask you to turn from your own race and fight alongside us against them. In my heart I see you would prefer death to that.

"You were mentioned in council," he went on, "and

the Blackfoot leaders asked me for your life as a token of our unity with them. I told them that no such bargain could be struck. But I promised that when the sun rose over the land tomorrow, there would be no white man living among us. It is my will and my decision for the sake of the Sioux nation.''

"Then we must leave immediately?" Eyes Like The She Wolf asked. She had raised her head at last. By her steady gaze, Mandell could tell that she had mustered her strength and was forcing herself to face this tragedy bravely.

Red Cloud did not answer the question immediately, but the look he gave his niece communicated the regret that he was feeling in his heart.

"You are a Sioux woman and your place is with the Sioux," he told her at last. "In times past I have seen our women go away with white men. I know that away from us they are treated as slaves and dogs. They are scorned and rejected, and their half-breed children are considered less than human beings, worthy only of abuse."

"But with Mandell it would be different!" Eyes Like The She Wolf pleaded desperately. "With him—"

"It would not be different," Mandell interrupted. "You are my wife and I cherish you above all else, but you must believe that outside among my people you would live in misery. You would be the red-skinned whore that I had taken to my bed. Never again would you be able to hold your head up as the proud Sioux princess that you are."

"No! Noooooooooo!" Eyes Like The She Wolf's voice took on the wail of an Indian woman in mourning. A look of anguish swept over her features.

Mandell moved across the tepee to his wife's side. Laying the baby gently aside, he took her in his arms and held her tightly against him. Only the sounds of her ragged sobs broke the stillness. Her tears flowed, staining her cheeks and moistening his chest. She dug her fingernails into the flesh of his back as she had done so many times during the intensity of lovemaking, only now she was clinging to the man she loved to prevent him from leaving her.

"You must face this bravely for my sake and our children's," Mandell told her softly. "And for your own sake, too. We knew this day was coming, that there was no way to prevent it. It is the way of things."

When at last Eyes Like The She Wolf began to calm, Mandell let her go and turned away, unable to bear the pain of seeing her in torment. Across the tepee lay a stack of his belongings. He moved to it, deciding to travel light and leave behind practically everything they had owned together. He put on a buckskin shirt, then strapped a gunbelt and knife around his waist. As he began thumbing cartridges into the magazine of his rifle, he said as steadily as his sorrow would permit, "It is best that I go quickly. When I leave this camp, I will be a dead man, and you will go on with your life among your people."

"That is as it should be," Red Cloud agreed quietly.

When his simple preparations had been made, Mandell knew that he must leave quickly before his courage failed him. At the entrance to the tepee, he and the chief bade one another farewell with a final firm handshake. Then he turned for one last treasured look at his wife and their two infant children.

The tears and grief were gone now from the features of Eyes Like The She Wolf, and a peculiar sort of light shined in her eyes. When Mandell saw that look, he knew that she would have courage enough to face this loss.

"You are not dead," she told him. "You will not be

as long as I can remember a single moment of our life together.''

A knot of emotion collected in Mandell's throat. He did not trust himself to speak. Instead he turned from the tepee and fled.

John Bozeman stood at the window of his cabin, gazing thoughtfully down the long meadow to where his horse herds were placidly grazing. On a small rise above where they fed, a solitary figure sat staring into the distance. In a moment, Kate came up beside him and looked out, too.

"It's almost eerie the way he just sits there," she whispered. "I've watched him off and on for over two hours and I've never seen him move a muscle."

"His mind isn't inside his body right now," Bozeman explained. "It's far away in another place with other people."

"I wish I could do something for him. Anything at all."

"You can't. What he's going through right now can't be shared, Kate. All we can do is leave him alone and let this thing run its course, no matter how long that takes."

Bozeman knew only a scant few details about what was troubling Hank Mandell so deeply. In the days since Mandell had showed up at Bozeman City a week before, he had offered hardly any explanation about why he had left the Sioux or what it was that now ate at his soul. He had mentioned once that the Bozeman Trail was likely to be more dangerous than ever before. And another time he had, in passing, spoken of a woman.

But most of Mandell's time was spent as he was now spending it, out among the horses. It seemed to be the only

197

place that he could find even a semblance of peace, and so Bozeman had permitted him free access to the herds, to wander among and commune with them as he wished.

Mandell's brooding presence had made some of the other men uneasy. They often referred to him as "the squaw man," but only behind his back. And they distrusted him because of his long and close association with the Sioux. Some speculated that he might be a spy sent down from the mountains to check out the settlement in preparation for an Indian attack. Others suggested that the Indians had done something to his head to make him crazy.

But both John Bozeman and Kate Lancaster were unswerving in their defense of Mandell, never forgetting what courage he had shown in saving them from death at the hands of the Cheyenne. He was a haunted man perhaps, Bozeman told the others, but not a crazy one, and as long as he decided to stay at Bozeman City he was welcome to remain.

At last Bozeman turned away from the window. He passed through the living quarters of his log home to the larger storeroom beyond. Billy Buffalo had ridden in early that morning with news that a contingent of troops was coming up from Fort Smith on a supply-buying trip. With the furies of winter only a short two months away, the army was hastily purchasing all the merchandise that would be needed in preparation for the long period of isolation the men would soon be facing at their remote wilderness forts.

Bozeman was hoping that he could sell them most of the goods that he had procured over the summer from Fort Benton to the north and Salt Lake City to the south. All day he had been taking inventory so he would know exactly what he had for sale when the quartermaster wagons arrived.

That happened shortly before noon, and Bozeman was surprised to see a civilian leading the thirty mounted troops that rode along as an escort. He was a grizzled old character, dressed in an odd combination of white men's clothing and Indian garb. His greasy buckskin jacket appeared to have served far too many seasons and his wool trousers and shirt were hardly in better shape. A short, wiry growth of whiskers sprouted out from the lower half of his face, and on his head he wore a flat-crowned hat with a wide, round brim.

It was the man's eyes, however, that stirred the most immediate interest from John Bozeman, reminding him oddly of his former friend and partner, John Jacobs. Like Jacobs', these were the wizened, cunning eyes of a man who knew the ways of the wilderness intimately and feared nothing he might face. Judging by his age, which was about sixty, and by the fact that he was traveling with a troop of soldiers, Bozeman believed this man must certainly be Jim Bridger, the legendary military scout and frontiersman.

That fact was confirmed moments later as the soldiers began to dismount and their civilian leader came over to shake Bozeman's hand. John Bozeman introduced himself and welcomed his guest to the "city" that bore his name.

"An' me," the other man responded, "I'm Jim Bridger an' I'm right glad to make your acquaintance. Seein' as how there's so much real estate in these parts that bears your name, I'm surprised we hadn't met up before today."

"I feel like I know you, Mr. Bridger," Bozeman responded. "Ever since I crossed the Mississippi River six years ago on my way west, it seemed like every place I went there was at least one fellow spinning a yarn about how one time he and Jim Bridger did thus and such, or how once he saw Jim Bridger do this and that.''

"Well, whatever you heard 'bout me," Bridger grinned, "it's all jus' a pack of ugly lies started by my enemies to ruin my reputation.'' He turned his head and skillfully ejected a stream of tobacco juice that splattered across the back of a large beetle scurrying by in the dust.

"Say, Bozeman," Bridger continued. "We heard tell how you might have some staples for sale here an' we thought we might jus' take 'em off your hands for the gov'ment afore some of these local redskins decide to ride in here an' help themselves.''

"You heard right," Bozeman told him. "I do happen to have some goods for sale.''

"Wellsir, then it sounds like we're about to do ourselves a piece of business," the scout winked. "But if you've heard any truth 'bout me a'tall, then you know I'd just as soon do my parlayin' over a drink of whiskey.''

"I think I can fix you up in that department, too. It's a long ride up here from Fort Smith. You and your men look like you could use a belt.''

"It's a doggoned fact that we could, son," Bridger grinned.

The famous scout slugged back his first glass of whiskey greedily, but was inclined to savor his second. Bozeman joined him, but did not try to keep up the thirsty pace.

"On the way here," Bridger commented, "I spotted this queer-actin' fellow sitting on a hummock out amongst your horses. Seein' him like that called to mind a buzzard waitin' for somethin' to die.''

"The man's name is Hank Mandell," Bozeman explained. "From all I can gather, he's been living among the Sioux for the past two years. About a week ago, though, he showed up here and asked if I could put him up. I owed him a big favor so I told him to stay as long as he wanted."

"Mandell, you say?" Bridger asked. "Might he be the man that the redskins call White Wolf?"

"That's him," Bozeman confirmed.

"Why sure," the scout spoke out, "I've heard plenty about White Wolf. The Crows say he's a big man amongst the Sioux—even took himself a Sioux wife, so they tell me, an' had a couple of whelps by her. I wonder what he's doing here?"

"So far he hasn't said and I haven't asked."

"He musta lost his medicine," Bridger speculated.

"His what?"

"His medicine. His good luck. As long as the Indians believe a man like that brings them luck, they treat him fine. But when they decide his medicine's gone, then they're likely either to kill him or run him off. I'd say your friend out there's mighty damn fortunate they chose to do the latter."

"I suppose," Bozeman responded, "but right now he doesn't act like a man who considers himself very fortunate. He doesn't do much of anything but sit and brood. Sometimes being around him is like sitting on a keg of powder with the fuse lit and wondering when it's going to go off."

"Mebbe he wanted to stay Indian and go on keepin' house with his squaw," Bridger judged. "I've seen it happen before."

When the conversation eventually turned to other matters, Bozeman realized that Bridger would not be the one to actually handle the supply transactions. A young lieutenant had come along on one of the wagons to take care of that. When the army man joined the two men a short time

201

later, the talk turned to business matters. Eventually Bridger wandered out of the log building, carrying half a bottle of Bozeman's whiskey with him when he went.

When Mandell saw the grizzled old character approaching him past the fringes of the horse herd, he turned his head away, communicating with his icy silence his desire to be left alone. But the determined intruder came on, nonetheless, climbing up the slight hill Mandell was sitting on.

"The man who always looks back cannot see the joy that lies in front of him," the stranger sermonized, stopping close to Mandell.

It was an old Indian proverb. On hearing it, Mandell snapped his head around. The stranger had recited in nearly perfect Sioux.

"Who are you?" Mandell asked in English. His tone was guarded, though he was beginning to sense a soul connection with this man.

"The name's Jim Bridger," the stranger reported. "You don't need to tell me you've heard of me—I know that everybody in these parts has. And you're White Wolf."

"I was White Wolf when I lived out there," Mandell responded, indicating with a toss of his head the spacious stretches of open country before him. "But now I've gone back to being Hank Mandell again. Sit if you like, Bridger."

As Bridger squatted on the ground nearby, he held out the bottle he carried. "Drink?" he offered.

"I guess I could use one," Mandell admitted, "but the idea scares me. I'm so close to being crazy now that I don't know what I'd do if I had some liquor in me. I'm afraid somebody would look crossways at me and I'd have them killed before I knew what I was doing."

"Well, I take some serious killin'," Bridger grinned,

holding out the bottle a second time. "I'm willin' to take the risk if you are."

Mandell accepted the bottle at last. Taking a generous swallow of its amber contents, he handed it back over to Bridger.

"How about it, Mandell?" Bridger asked lightly. "You feel any urges to let some blood?"

"I guess not," Mandell replied, letting a trace of a smile flash across his face.

The bottle went back and forth between them a couple of times. In the muggy August heat, the alcohol coursed through Mandell's body, easing the tensions that had been his constant companion since the moment he rode out of Red Cloud's camp several days before.

"I gather by you bein' here, Mandell," Bridger noted at last, "that the Sioux have disowned you. Is it because of the trouble that's brewing in these parts?"

"Red Cloud knew I could never join them in a war against my own people," Mandell answered. "Besides that, his allies were starting to ask for my scalp. It was time for me to go, but *damn*, it was a hard thing to do! Somewhere out there I've got a wife and two babies and I'd almost as soon have gone on the warpath with the Sioux as to leave them behind."

"But you couldn't."

"No," Mandell murmured bitterly. "But if ever a man was tempted to say to hell with the race that spawned him . . ." He accepted the bottle and took another long pull. Then he threw it empty on the ground.

"So have you given any thought to what you'll do now?" Bridger asked.

"Not much. I'll drift, I guess, and maybe pick up enough work here and there to keep food in my belly and lead in my guns. It doesn't matter much to me."

"It sounds like a hell of a rotten life," the scout drawled, "an' you, my friend, sound like a man whose jaw's dropped so low it's commencin' to drag in the dust. I guess right now you jus' figger on spendin' the rest of your life moonin' over the Indian squaw you shared blankets with for a year."

"It was two years," Mandell snapped. "And what do you know about it anyway? If all you came up here for was to give me a hard time, Bridger, I may as well tell you straight out that I'm in no mood to take any shit from you."

"Well, I've been through three squaws in my time," Bridger came back, "an' loved every one of 'em. So mebbe I do know enough about it to tell you that this kind of thing's as common on the frontier as buffalo chips. What happened to you ain't no sort of special tragedy that makes your life stand out like something out of Shakespeare. It's a part of the West that plenty of us have lived through. If you want to jus' sit out here on this rise an' brood till your butt roots, that's your concern. But it makes you less a man than I took you for."

"Now you just hold on a goddamn minute, Bridger!"

"On the other side of things," Bridger went on, "if you think it's time to be somebody an' start doin' somethin' again, then there's a good chance I got an offer for you."

An instant before, Mandell had been ready to bring the conversation to a violent conclusion. The dark mood he had been in for days made him almost relish the thought of slamming his fist into somebody, even if it had to be a Rocky Mountain institution like the great Jim Bridger. But before he could poise himself to strike, he realized that the scout's last words had sparked his interest.

"The thought comes to mind," Bridger continued, hardly appearing to care he'd almost had a fight on his hands, "that if you've lived with the Sioux for two years, then you must know the country hereabouts tolerably well an' be a fair hand at gettin' along in it."

"You could say that, I guess," Mandell conceded.

"As you might know," Bridger told him, "a few months ago I hired on as chief of scouts for the three army posts along the Bozeman Trail. Well, a part of my job is to line up other qualified men to scout for them. I've got a job for you, Mandell, if you decide it's time for you to get up off your ass and walk down from this hill."

"You want me to scout for the army against the Indians?" Mandell asked incredulously. "You must be out of your mind, Bridger! I wouldn't join the Sioux in a war against the U.S. Army, and I'll be damned if I'll join the U.S. Army in a war against the Sioux."

"Did I say anything about a war, son?" Bridger chuckled. "If I did, it was 'cause my tongue got in front of my eyetooth—I hope to hell it never comes to that. General Connor, who's in charge of the paleface side of this shivaree, has maybe a tenth of the men that Red Cloud can muster with this confederation he's trying to put together. . . ."

"You've heard about that?" Mandell asked.

"Why sure. The Crow got big mouths and two faces. An' if it comes to a fight, there'll be white men's bodies scattered on the ground all the way from Fetterman's Fort to the Yellowstone. In all my days, I've never seen a more poorly trained, disorganized and disaffected military outfit. You'd think after the great rebellion back East the army would have a little better sense about how a war's supposed to be fought, but I don't see many signs that all the generals who are supposed to be in charge of this campaign are using brains enough to fill a good-sized hoofprint.

"So y'see," Bridger went on, "I see my job more as

205

one of keepin' these yahoos alive for as long as I can. They don't seem to realize that they're up against some of the finest light cavalry in the world, but soon they'll learn. Yessir, pretty soon ol' Red Cloud will start to teach them that lesson in spades!''

"But that still doesn't explain why you'd believe I'd want to be a part of such a disorganized rabble.''

"Mebbe for the same reason I'm here,'' Bridger replied simply.

"And what might that reason be?''

"To try to keep as many hotheads alive on both sides as I can,'' the scout asserted. "Even with things the way they are, there's still plenty of young fools in this outfit who think that any time they want they can ride out and give the redskins a good thrashing to teach them a lesson they deserve. They see the Crow and the Cheyenne and even the Sioux as just a bunch of whining, shifty savages that would turn tail and run at the first sign they had a real fight on their hands.''

"Then they *are* fools,'' Mandell confirmed, "and I agree with you. They need all the help they can get.''

"But the Indians need some friends on this side of the fence, too,'' Bridger put in. "I know they've got to make a stand now and then so they don't let themselves get shoved onto some wasteland reservation, but the less blood they let in the doin', the better it'll go for them in the long run.''

"I can't ever see the Indians getting pushed around,'' Mandell disagreed. "The Sioux are too proud and too strong to be turned into reservation Indians.''

"Now, mebbe, but the years ahead are going to be tough ones for the plains tribes like the Sioux. Right now they've got numbers an' every kind of strategic advantage on their side in the fight to control this trail, but time an' might are on the side of the palefaces. It's been that way ever since the first white pilgrim stepped ashore on Plymouth Rock.''

Mandell stared reflectively over the open green country and the distant forested mountain slopes. It was hard to deny the truth in what Bridger was predicting, but it was equally hard to admit the inevitability of it. A pang of grief stabbed at him as he pictured his wife and children starving on a barren, sun-scorched reservation, banished forever from the open country that they loved. He would do anything in his power, he decided, to prevent that from happening, or at least he would try to delay it as long as possible. If it meant going to work for the U.S. Army and trying to serve as a buffer between it and the angry leaders of the Indian nations, then it was something he should do.

"All right, Bridger," he announced at last. "You've got yourself a scout. But I might as well tell you right up front that I won't lead troops on offensive operations against any of the plains tribes. And I won't stick my neck out too far to try to save the lives of any damn fools who are determined to throw them away on the trail to glory.''

Chapter 13

The powdery, foot-deep snow churned up in small, swirling clouds behind the thudding hooves of Mandell's horse. He was racing toward the gates of Fort Kearny. A sentry had spotted him riding at top speed back toward the fort, so the wide front gates were partially open to admit him. The post commander, Colonel Henry B. Carrington, was waiting just inside to receive his message.

"The wood wagons have circled and are under attack," Mandell announced abruptly. "Lieutenant Francis sent me back with word that he needs some relief—pronto!"

"How many Indians?" Carrington asked.

"There's no way to tell in dense woods like that," Mandell replied. "There could be fifty or five hundred. I didn't have the chance to scout around and check things out before the shooting started, and then I was barely able to break through without getting shot."

"Can you give me any idea about how bad it looks to you?" Carrington inquired.

In the three months that Mandell had been assigned as

scout at Fort Kearny, the forty-two-year-old commander of the fort had come to depend on his advice and judgment in critical situations. Though it was not apparent to his superiors back East, Carrington was beginning to realize that he was facing a capable, determined enemy whose vastly superior numbers gave them every advantage on the battlefield.

"Our men got the wagons circled without losing anyone," Mandell told him, "and the way they're forted up now, it will be costly to the Indians if they intend to attack. I'd say the situation isn't critical yet, but there's no telling when it might get that way. The best thing to do would be to send a rescue party out and get everyone back here as quickly as possible."

As if to emphasize his words, the sounds of distant gunfire drifted toward the fort, borne on the west wind blowing down from the mountains. Carrington squinted and peered through the partially open gates. But the fight was taking place off to the left and beyond a distant rise, so none of it could be seen even by the sentries in the fort's guard towers.

"All right," the army man decided suddenly. "I'll muster as many men as I can spare. You stay here, Mandell. That way you can guide the relief party out to the wagons."

"Colonel!" Mandell barked out, letting a note of defiance sound in his voice.

Carrington spun around, impatient to get the relief effort started but aware that first he would have to deal with his scout. "I know," the colonel snapped, "that you've said you will not lead troops on any offensive operation against the Indians. But this is a relief mission, Mandell, and one that you recommended yourself, I might add.

"I'm not fool enough to send out only a few dozen men with orders to draw sabers and charge against an enemy force of undetermined size. But we have to get our woodcutters back. Will you go?"

"I'll lead them out to where the wood wagons are," Mandell assured his superior, "but if any of these firebrand junior-grade officers that you've got under you decide to carry matters any further than that, they'll have to do it without my services."

"My orders will be for them, under no circumstances, to cross beyond the Lodge Trail Ridge," Carrington promised as he turned again and marched away.

While waiting for the relief troops to hurry to the stables and saddle their horses, Mandell glanced around the interior of the fort, wondering how well this place would stand up to an all-out attack by Red Cloud and his combined forces, or more precisely, how long it would take for the fort to fall.

Fort Kearny had been built in two sections. Though most of the construction had been completed the previous fall, now in late December some work was still going on. To his right was the large parade ground. It was surrounded on its four sides by the row of headquarters buildings that provided quarters for the officers and enlisted men of the command as well as various other billets. Immediately to his left were the cavalry yard and buildings that served as billets for the noncommissioned officers and teamsters. There were also stables, mess halls and a hospital.

In a large open area to the far left, hay for the horses and wood for the fort's cooking and heating needs were stored. The entire fort was surrounded by a high wall consisting of heavy logs placed side by side in a deep trench. Several guard towers had been placed at equidistant locations around the perimeter. Six gates opened through the walls for varying purposes. Two were on the north, one was on the west and three were on the south. At the southeast corner of the fort, Little Piney Creek flowed close to the log wall and a gate there provided the occupants of the fort with ready access to fresh water.

It took the troops only a short time to prepare their mounts and assemble in the nearby cavalry yard. But as their officers began to get them lined out in formation, Mandell realized with a sinking feeling who would be in charge of the relief party.

Captain William J. Fetterman was one of the "firebrands" Mandell had referred to in his earlier conversation with Colonel Carrington. Displaying overenthusiastic zeal for most of his duties, in many ways Fetterman reminded Mandell of Blue Eagle, the young Sioux chief he had been forced to fight two years before.

Fetterman believed utterly in the superior fighting ability of the United States Army. Consistently he was eager to risk his own life and the lives of his men to prove it. His claims about what damage he and a mere handful of seasoned U.S. troops could inflict on the Indians usually were outrageous exaggerations. And once in a private conversation Carrington had mentioned to Mandell that he considered Fetterman as his "main problem child."

Somehow Fetterman had conspired to assume command of this group. But even as he was receiving his explicit orders from Colonel Carrington, Mandell feared the worst about what this impractical hothead might decide to do on his own.

He waited patiently on his horse until the soldiers were lined out and ready. Then, as two men swung the big gates open, he turned his mount and rode out.

There had been gunfire off and on all the time he had been inside the walls, but from the sound of things over the last few minutes, it seemed that the action had died down to an occasional flurry of sniping. That was encouraging. As Mandell led the column off to the left, following the double line of ruts the wagons had formed in the snow earlier that morning, he permitted himself to hope that they might get everybody back to safety without a major confrontation.

All through the fall and early winter while he was scouting for the army, the troops had experienced repeated small clashes with the Indians. The casualty rate had been low but constant. And often the Indians had committed atrocities on the bodies of their victims as an unceasing reminder to the American troops of what a ruthless foe they faced.

During this time it was the soldiers' opinion that no major attack had taken place because the Indians were too few in number to consider such a tactic feasible in the face of the superior weaponry of the Americans. When Mandell heard such talk, he usually kept his contradictory opinions to himself, even though he knew who the troops were truly up against.

From all indications, Red Cloud was now in direct command of the Sioux and Cheyenne forces fighting in the area. Mandell guessed that the chief might at that moment have as many as three or four thousand braves he could commit at will to any action.

But, wise leader that he was, Red Cloud was conservative with his manpower even when his numbers were great. He could easily have attacked any of the three forts along the trail and destroyed it along with all the people it contained, but the cost in Indian lives would have been too great. It was far easier and nearly as effective to wait in the forests and the hills nearby and mount attacks at those times when the white men had no sturdy walls around them for protection. Like a cunning, patient hunter, Red

Cloud was waiting for his prey to make only a single major mistake. When that happened, he would make his play with lethal finesse.

As soon as the rescue party topped the distant hill and started down the gradual incline on the other side, they spotted the line of wood wagons just beginning to emerge from the forest. The empty wagons were jolting along at a hurried pace as the jittery men in their mounted escort rode along beside with their rifles ready.

The two groups converged and Lieutenant Frances, who was in charge of the wood-cutting expedition, explained that when the firing had begun to die down a few minutes earlier, he and his men had decided to make a run for the fort. They had come nearly half a mile with only an occasional shot fired at them from the depths of the forest. But they were nonetheless glad to join up with the reinforcements that had been sent from the fort.

"Did you ever determine exactly how many hostiles you were up against?" Captain Fetterman asked the lieutenant.

"I don't suppose there were ever more than twenty-five firing at us at any one time," Frances reported.

"And faced with that small number you circled your wagons and went on the defensive?" Fetterman chided. "You have nearly forty mounted men under your command. Didn't you believe they were enough to deal with a threat from only twenty-five hostiles?"

"Sir," Frances snapped, spitting out the word, "my orders, issued by Colonel Carrington himself this morning, included no mention of taking aggressive action against the Indians. We might have gone charging out into the woods after twenty-five snipers and run into a thousand just beyond them."

"Hogwash!" Fetterman exclaimed. "If there were a

thousand Indians out there, they all would have attacked you and we would be loading your bodies into the backs of those wagons right now."

Mandell kept quiet during the exchange, though he soundly agreed with the judgment of Lieutenant Frances. Once again Captain Fetterman was in the process of proving that he was more bold than intelligent, but Mandell realized that it would be senseless to speak up. Fetterman wasn't the sort of man to let anything so trivial as the truth have an effect on his preposterous notions of glory.

"Lieutenant," the captain went on at last, "you might be hesitant to give pursuit to those hostiles with the forty troops under you, but my command is eighty strong and I have no such reservations. I see this situation as the opportunity to teach these bedraggled savages a severe lesson."

Lieutenant Frances' eyes communicated all he had to say about the subject and Mandell realized that it was time for him to speak up.

"Cap'n, I wasn't twenty feet away when the colonel gave you your orders, and they didn't include a damn thing about giving pursuit to the Indians who attacked the wood wagons. You were told to relieve the wagons and escort them back to the fort—and that's all!"

"I am making a field decision based on the situation at hand," Fetterman shrilled, "and I assume full responsibility for any consequences resulting from my action."

"I'm sure glad you feel that way," Mandell growled, "because it's a sure bet nobody else would want to lay claim to such a stupid notion! This thing stinks like buffalo chips in a hot fire . . . and if you've got a lick of sense about you, you'll stop and *think* before you go galloping off into the woods after the Indians that attacked this wood train!"

"Mr. Mandell, I am well aware of your supposed

neutrality in this campaign," the captain sneered. "But may I remind you that our charge from the United States government and the Department of the Army is to seek out these savages and punish them for their hostile acts? In this snow, those twenty-five Indians should be easy enough to track. Besides, our mounts are probably much fresher than theirs. This is a perfect opportunity to run them into the ground. I'm sure if Colonel Carrington were here at this moment, he would agree."

"He'd agree your head's so empty that the swallows could nest between your ears," Mandell snapped.

Despite the angry insult, Fetterman remained calm. "Your services will not be needed from this point on," he told Mandell. "Now get out of the way and let me and my men get on with the job we were sent out to do!"

Mandell and Lieutenant Frances sat on their horses watching Fetterman lead his men deeper into the woods to the west. "Good God!" the lieutenant muttered, "he's really going to do it!"

"I never doubted that he would, not from the minute we rode out the gates of the fort," Mandell responded.

"Maybe I should take my men and go along," Frances speculated nervously.

"You should if there's none of them that you'd care to see go on living," Mandell replied.

"But what can I do?" Frances asked.

"You can take your men and wagons and go on back to the fort like any sensible officer would," the scout told him. "Then tell Colonel Carrington what's going on out here. Maybe he can get a dispatch rider out to order Fetterman back before anything serious happens." As the last of Fetterman's men rode by, Mandell gazed after them. Then, with a resigned sigh, he announced, "I'm going to circle around in front of that blasted fool and try to reach the crest of Lodge Trail Ridge ahead of him. If I can get far enough in the lead and take a look at what he's up against, then maybe I can at least give his men fair warning."

As the lieutenant issued the orders for the wagons to move out, Mandell turned his horse to the left and began weaving a hasty course through the forest. He knew how vulnerable he was making himself by separating from the rest of the troops and proceeding so noisily through the trees, but at that moment the necessity for haste demanded that he take the risk. He rode due south for nearly a quarter of a mile. Then he cut back to the right, following the path of a frozen creek bed steeply upward toward the crest of Lodge Trail Ridge.

When he neared the top of the ridge, Mandell entered an area where boulders and ragged outcroppings of rock made riding next to impossible. So he left his horse behind and moved carefully forward on foot to a point where he could see down into the snow-blanketed valley beyond. From that vantage point he realized that his own ascension had taken longer than he thought. Far to the left, the row of blue-clad, mounted figures was just beginning to top the crest of the ridge and descend on the opposite side. Ahead of the soldiers lay a broad, open meadow that swept in a gentle arc to the southwest, following the contours of the valley. And on either side were thick forests similar to the one he had just passed through.

It took Mandell only an instant to spot the locations where the Indians lay in wait and to realize how brilliant a trap had been set for the troops. To Fetterman's left and slightly ahead of him about a hundred mounted Indians had concealed themselves in a ravine. Once the trap was set in motion, they would be the ones to slam the back door closed and cut off all possibility of escape. But the real threat lay directly ahead, scattered among the trees on either side of the meadow Fetterman was heading toward.

No doubt, Mandell realized, Fetterman was still following the trail of the twenty-five or so decoys who had attacked the wood wagons. By the time he got into the meadow and realized his mistake, it would be too late.

There wasn't time to ride over and warn the soldiers. And the sound of a shout would not carry that far.

But a shot would!

Mandell reached for his revolver. But before he could get the muzzle up and pull the trigger, the back of his head exploded with pain and he tumbled forward off his horse.

For a time he saw only a swirling blur as he struggled to hang on to the remaining threads of consciousness left to him. At last, with great effort, he was able to raise up onto one elbow. What he saw when he looked around was a pair of moccasins and buckskin leggings.

"Red Cloud refused to believe it, but our spies told us that it was you who now scouted for the horse soldiers at Fort Kearny. Tonight when I return to camp your head will hang from my saddle as proof that you, like all the rest of your breed, were a man of two faces."

A leering grin of triumph was spread across the features of Blue Eagle as he stood above Mandell. In one hand he held the rifle he had apparently used on his victim. In the other he held the twin revolvers that only recently had been in Mandell's holsters.

"But before you died," the Indian continued, "I wanted you to see this and to know that your treachery has been useless."

Mandell's sensibilities began to return. He was at last able to sit up on the snow-covered ground but still did not have strength enough to even consider trying to take on Blue Eagle with his bare hands.

By that time Fetterman and his command had advanced into the meadow and the jaws of the Indian trap. They were still lined out in their orderly column of twos, unaware of the trouble awaiting them.

Mandell wondered why Blue Eagle was on the ridge instead of down among the Indians who lay in wait. But that question was answered a moment later when the Sioux chief cut loose with an earsplitting war cry and fired three shots from his rifle into the air. Apparently Red Cloud had delegated to Blue Eagle the responsibility, and the honor, of signaling for the day's attack to begin.

Within seconds after the signal, a fusillade of shots roared out from the trees. Several soldiers tumbled immediately from their saddles and the unexpected assault brought chaos to the troops. While some of them swung their horses about in confusion, trying to determine from which direction they were being attacked, several others turned their mounts and bolted back toward the incline of Lodge Trail Ridge.

But it was too late for any of them. Hordes of mounted Indians converged from all directions.

Mandell realized for the first time what a great force Red Cloud had brought together to accomplish the ambush. In the confusion it was impossible to guess their numbers, but he thought two thousand would probably be a conservative figure.

The soldiers were slaughtered with startling swiftness, and all through the brief battle the triumphant sneer never left Blue Eagle's features. Though he apparently was preparing to take credit for the day's massacre, Mandell knew that Blue Eagle was not yet the kind of leader who was capable of organizing such a smoothly executed coup.

The Indians below began to dismount and pounce on

the last few soldiers, quickly stripping them of their clothing, equipment, and of course their scalps.

"Your horse soldiers die like dogs before the panther, and soon our people—" he began.

But Hank Mandell was not prepared to become another of the day's casualties, especially at the hands of his old rival, Blue Eagle. With a quickness that caught the Indian completely off guard, he wrapped his legs around those of Blue Eagle and rolled to the side, throwing the Indian off balance by slamming him to the ground. Mandell's revolvers went clattering out of reach of both of them, but Blue Eagle still clutched his rifle.

As the Indian pulled his legs under him and started to rise, he brought the stock of the rifle up, intending to once more use it as a club. But Mandell swung his leg toward his opponent's face, catching him across the chin with the heel of his boot. Caught off balance, Blue Eagle flipped backward. For an instant before he disappeared over the edge of a nearby precipice, Mandell glimpsed the horror in his eyes.

He had no idea how far Blue Eagle had fallen, so he approached the edge of the overhang carefully, not wanting to be shot in the face as soon as his head appeared over the rim. When at last he raised his head and gazed down, he saw that Blue Eagle lay on a rocky ledge about ten feet below.

The Indian moved sluggishly, as if he was only half conscious. His right arm twisted unnaturally beneath him and a small rivulet of blood dribbled down the side of the rock beneath his head where his skull had struck the stone. His rifle lay a few feet away. Its stock was shattered.

The urge was strong in Hank Mandell to locate one of his weapons and finish Blue Eagle off. If the Indian did manage to survive and return to the tribe, Mandell soon would be branded as a mortal enemy of the Sioux. The Indians would have no understanding of his reasons for working for the army. Even Eyes Like The She Wolf probably would renounce him as a traitor. Besides all that, Blue Eagle had been his personal enemy and it went against all his instincts to leave him alive to strike again some other time.

But if he took Blue Eagle's life, Mandell reasoned, wouldn't that make him more of a traitor to his Indian friends than anything else he had done? What would be left then of all his grand notions of saving the lives of both red men and white and somehow serving as a buffer between the two factions?

He turned away at last and searched among the rocks until he had found his pistols. Then he started back through the rocks toward the place where he had left his horse. There was a long ride ahead and urgent, tragic news to be delivered.

A furious, unexpected snowstorm struck late in the afternoon, hampering efforts to retrieve the bodies of Captain Fetterman and his slaughtered troops. But Colonel Carrington was obsessed with the notion of not letting a single one of the dead men go unburied, so he himself led the patrol and the wagons that went out to retrieve the corpses.

Mandell thought that venturing out so soon after the battle was an unwise move. But he also realized that the morale of the one hundred twenty survivors at Fort Kearny demanded that it be completed. Many of the men in the command were already fearful that the dead bodies would be defiled and mutilated by the Indians, then left unburied to become meat for scavengers.

Carrington ordered Mandell to organize several men

as scouts and outriders for the body detail. By dark the wagons had penetrated to the meadow beyond Lodge Trail Ridge, performed their grisly mission and returned safely to the fort. Already the remaining troops were bringing out dress uniforms to clothe the mangled corpses of their fallen comrades. And the work of building eighty-one coffins and digging the same number of graves would go on for at least two or three more days.

Amidst such a tragedy, those who remained alive at Fort Kearny still had to worry about the risk of an open assault on the fort. Everyone sensed that the Indians were off somewhere in the Bighorns celebrating their victory. But it was also believed that the Indians must be considering how much easier it would be to overpower an under-manned Fort Kearny and make the annihilation complete.

Somebody, Carrington decided, would have to ride through to the outside with news of the massacre and a plea for reinforcements. So when an aide came to Mandell's quarters late in the evening and said that Colonel Carrington wanted to see him, Mandell realized instantly who that somebody would be.

The Christmas Day Ball was the event of the year for the officers and their wives at Fort Laramie. The annual fête was this year being hosted by General Innis Palmer, commander of the garrison, and was being held in Old Bedlam, the bachelor officers' quarters. For weeks, preparations had been underway to insure that the fête would be a gala event. Dozens of lamps illuminated the resplendent crepe decorations that hung on the walls and ceiling, and all evening the post band had performed a succession of waltzes and lively dance tunes. The ladies of the post had each striven to outdo one another in the selection of their gowns, and their mates and escorts had hauled their best dress uniforms out of storage and had them pressed for the affair. Outside, one of the worst blizzards of the year raged on, but no one seemed to care. The air was warm inside and the atmosphere was lively and gay.

Lieutenant Marshal Heaton was indignant when he spotted a ragged, rough-looking man enter the makeshift ballroom by a side door and stand there, gazing about darkly. Heaton's first impulse was to order the intruder to leave immediately. But there was something about the man's looks that made the lieutenant curb his tongue.

The new arrival was cloaked in a heavy, buffalo-skin coat that reached to the floor. The brim of his felt hat was held down over his ears by a grimy kerchief tied beneath his chin. Icicles clung to his mustache and week-old growth of beard. And on the side of his face his whiskers were dotted with beads of water that moments before had been snowflakes. As the man's nose warmed, it became a livid shade of red, and his eyes narrowed until only slivers of them were visible. When he turned and started over toward Heaton, he stopped wearily.

"They told me the general was in here someplace," the man mumbled hoarsely.

"He is here," Heaton confirmed. "But who in the devil are you?"

"The name's Mandell."

"Well, if you'll wait somewhere else, Mr. Mandell," Heaton suggested coolly, "perhaps the general might have time to speak with you later in the evening."

A sleeve of the buffalo robe rose up toward Lieutenant Heaton and a rawhide-gloved hand gathered up a wad of uniform tunic and shirt in the vicinity of the officer's throat. The top button of the lieutenant's collar popped loose from the strain, and in an instant the startled young man found his face only inches away from that of the stranger.

"Listen, you pompous young whelp!" a steady, angry voice told him. "I don't care if your general's out back on the two-holer with his pants down around his ankles or rolling around between the blankets with the first sergeant's old lady. I've just come over two hundred miles from Fort Kearny through one of the worst blizzards of the winter and I need to see General Palmer *right now*!"

A further display of force proved unnecessary. The brief fracas had thoroughly disrupted the entire ball. In a moment the general came working his way through the ring of officers who had instantly gathered around Mandell.

"What is going on over here?" the general demanded angrily. "Tonight of all nights we could use some peace—"

"I've got a dispatch for you from Colonel Carrington up at Fort Kearny," Mandell interrupted, producing from inside his coat a folded piece of paper wrapped in oilskin.

A frown of puzzlement knitted the general's brow, but he opened the dispatch and quickly read over it. When he reached a certain portion of the message, Palmer muttered quietly under his breath, "Eighty-one dead. My God!" When he had finished, he looked back up at Mandell. "How did you get a hold of this? Is the information in it verified?"

"I took the dispatch from Colonel Carrington's own hand," Mandell explained, "and rode it through myself. I know everything he says in it is God's own truth because I was there."

"But this dispatch says the battle took place on the twenty-first and today is only the twenty-fifth," the general read incredulously. "Are you trying to tell me that you covered that much distance through a storm like this in a little under four days?"

"The only thing I'm *trying* to do," Mandell growled impatiently, "is to get some help started on its way to Kearny before it's too late."

"I'll want to have a complete account from you later," the general told Mandell. "But right now there are urgent matters that must be seen to.

"Tyler, get a wire off to Omaha immediately requesting emergency authorization to dispatch two companies of cavalry and four of infantry for the relief of Fort Kearny. And Marcus, you get over to the NCO barracks and . . ."

As the general moved off, he was surrounded by a host of aides. Seeing the general suddenly galvanized into action, Mandell slumped into a chair along the wall. The rest of the men had begun to huddle about in small groups to discuss the encounter, and for a moment Mandell found himself alone.

But soon a hesitant figure approached him. He glanced up at the curious face of the young lieutenant he had collared only a short time earlier.

"After such an exhausting ride," Heaton began, "I bet you could use a good hot meal and about a gallon of coffee on the side. And we have a real bathtub in the back of the barracks. I could get a man to stoke up a fire and start some water heating."

"First things first, Lieutenant," Mandell told him. "If there's an unused bunk anywhere on this post, I'd be much obliged to borrow it. Then in the morning I'll take you up on that hot meal and bath."

"No problem, Mr. Mandell. Just follow me." The lieutenant led the exhausted scout toward a stairway that went to the second floor of the barracks. "And if there's anything else you might need . . ."

"I'll need a good horse when I start back tomorrow,"

Mandell interrupted as he followed the army man single file. ''I started out from Kearny riding the best thoroughbred on the post, but the trip was too much for him. About a hundred feet inside your gates, he dropped stone-cold dead underneath me.''

Chapter 14

July, 1867

A smile spread automatically across Kate Lancaster's face when she stopped her horse at a high place on the trail and paused to look over Bozeman City. A couple of new cabins had sprung up while she'd been away. And another was under construction on the north side of the settlement along a wide dirt pathway that was now being called Main Street. That would bring the total number of buildings to about thirty, she estimated, more than twice what had been there when she was first brought to Bozeman City the year before.

In times of constantly shifting fortunes the place had not only survived but grown. And Kate knew that no small share of the credit for that was due to John Bozeman.

During the year they had been together, her respect for Bozeman had continued to grow at the same time her love for him was deepening. Sometimes his far-fetched plans and impractical dreams made him seem too much of a visionary. But the man retained one quality that made him remarkable. Even in the face of the most disappointing failures—such as his inability to ever turn any great profits from the establishment of the Bozeman Trail—he never lost his faith and drive. Instead, he turned his energies and abilities to some new enterprise.

The previous spring he had resigned himself to the fact that Bozeman City might never become the trail's-end resupply point he had envisioned. So homesteading and ranching in the area became his primary concern. And after he encouraged a few farming families and small cattle growers to settle in the fertile regions nearby, he began to gear his own business toward meeting their particular needs. The wagonloads of goods that were shipped south to him from Fort Benton that year included plowshares and cultivators, scythes and pitchforks, fencing wire and seed assortments.

Early in the summer, Bozeman had also taken men out to construct a ferry across the Gallatin River, and less than a month later he sold the ferry for several times the sum it had cost him to build. A steam-powered sawmill was on order from a dealer in the East. If it arrived on schedule that summer, by fall it was likely that a few frame houses would begin cropping up in and around Bozeman City. Bozeman had promised Kate that the first boards produced by his new sawmill would go into the white frame house he had vowed to build her someday.

But Kate Lancaster had never been one to sit idly by watching things go on around her. She was proud of the part she had played in Bozeman's current successes. Following the dictates of her wanderlust and her trader's profession, she had made several trips away from Bozeman City on behalf of the various ventures that they shared.

During the first few weeks of spring, she had traveled alone north to Fort Benton to dispatch, by boat, their supply and equipment orders to the States. She'd traveled to Salt Lake City to purchase food staples and other necessities from the Mormons there and had seen to their quick delivery. Her latest adventure—the one from which she was just now returning—had been to sell a portion of their thriving horse and mule herds in the bustling mining center of Virginia City.

Kate smiled contentedly. Such trips were enjoyable to her. They gave her the sense she was a part of things. But after each one, it felt good to return home again.

Home!

After nearly fifteen years of living such a rambling, rootless existence, the word had an odd ring to her. Not since her family had been killed many years before had there been any place that Kate had considered home. But now that rude cabin where Bozeman had nursed her back to health a year before had become a place that she cherished and wanted.

Kate tapped the sides of her horse after a long and satisfying look at Bozeman City. The animal clicked into motion as if it, too, wanted very much to be back home again.

John Bozeman stretched his arms straight above his head on the broad, soft bed, then yawned contentedly. The narrow, cornhusk mattress on which he had started out his bachelor housekeeping had since given way to a large feather bed of Kate's design. The previous fall, she had kept Billy Buffalo out for nearly two solid weeks hunting migrating ducks and geese. And though the men in Bozeman City eventually tired of a steady diet of waterfowl,

229

she had finally accumulated enough feathers to have her mattress. Bozeman smiled, thinking of Kate's determination and strength.

They had just finished the most enjoyable part of their reunion. In the calm afterthrill, they were feeling lazy and content. Bozeman studied the smooth contours of Kate's body, softly revealed in the pale moonlight that came in through a curtained window. He could not resist reaching out to trace the curve of her form from throat to belly. For once the touch simply felt pleasant to Kate and didn't stir a surge of sexual excitement as it would have an hour or so earlier.

"John, I've been thinking about it all the way back from Virginia City," she announced unexpectedly, "and I've decided that it's time for you to make an honest woman of me."

Bozeman raised up on one elbow and smiled. Despite its abruptness, the declaration did not surprise him. "Judging by the sorts of business practices you were employed in before we came together," he returned, "that might not be an easy chore. I'll never know when you might decide to pull another Buffalo Leap stunt on me and try to trick me out of all my worldly goods."

"The suggestion does have its own particular appeal," Kate replied, "but you know what I'm talking about."

"Sure. You've decided that you'd rather have the best of both worlds. Me and my vast business empire."

"John, you really can be such a pompous ass sometimes," Kate snapped. "It's hard enough for me to be the one to do this proposing. If you're going to go out of your way to make it even harder for me, maybe we should just forget the whole thing!"

"I swear, Kate, I've never met a woman who could

get her hackles up so fast over so little," Bozeman chuckled. "I've never been opposed to the idea of marriage—I've made that plain enough in the past. But don't you remember the talks we had over the winter on the subject? And don't you recall telling me you had never craved 'the ties that bind'? Back then you were full of a lot of talk about always wanting to be your own person and never wanting to be dependent on anyone.''

"I still want to be my own woman," Kate declared, "but that doesn't mean I can't be married to someone while I'm doing it. And besides, John, it's unfair to hold each other to everything we said back then. When the deep snows came, I came down with a terrible case of cabin fever. And remember how we used to fight? After the first couple of months I got sick to death of the sight of you."

"God, how I remember!" Bozeman agreed. "We were lucky there were ten-foot drifts outside the door. They were what forced us to stay together and work things out. Otherwise, one or the other of us would have been long gone."

Kate rose from the bed and padded into the other room to pour a cup of coffee. When she came back to the bedroom, she shared it with Bozeman. He fumbled for his tobacco and pipe, then smoked as they both sat cross-legged on the bed.

"Taking these long trips has given me plenty of time alone to think things out," Kate continued. "I've come to the conclusion that overall things are pretty damn good between us.

"You know, John, you're not the first man that's ever been interested in me. But the others' ideas of marriage always boiled down to the same basic presumption. Each wanted a woman to cook his food and tend his house

231

and have his babies. And of course it was appealing to have a soft, warm somebody close at hand when a person was feeling randy . . ."

"I love it when you talk dirty, Kate," Bozeman teased, reaching out to give her breast a light pinch.

"I've been too many places and done too many things to ever want to end up like that," she continued, ignoring him. "But it's different between you and me, John. You want me to be who I am and do what I'm capable of doing. With you I don't picture myself chained to a cabin with a squawling baby under each arm, seeing only to *your* needs and *your* desires."

"Well, I've seen from the start," Bozeman responded, "that the best way to run you off would be to try to take a firm hold on you and hang on for dear life. So far what you've decided to give me of your own free will has been plenty good enough."

"That's why I think a marriage would work between us."

Bozeman took a contemplative puff on his pipe. For a moment, the cloud of smoke he exhaled hung between them. "I love you, Kate," he said quietly and seriously, "and I do want to marry you, but not until I'm sure we both realize that marriage *is* a tie that binds. Remember, the winter snows will come again."

"But so will the spring thaws," Kate reminded him, "and in the long run, that's what it's all about, isn't it, John? Surviving the winters to enjoy the spring? So shall we do it?"

"Why the hell not?" Bozeman replied, grinning once more as he reached out and pulled her to him. "Why the hell not!"

*　　*　　*

Hank Mandell settled the sights of his rifle on a spot midway between the Indian's shoulder blades. Then he took a deep breath to calm his racing nerves and squeezed the trigger. The brave's body bucked from the impact of the round, but he didn't fall immediately. Instead, he turned his head slowly around. Even across the hundred yards that separated him from Mandell, his eyes communicated all the fear and amazement of a man who is so suddenly confronted with his own mortality. Then his body crumpled slowly to the ground.

The skirmish had been going for thirty minutes or so. Indians and white men alike, trying to kill one another.

Mandell and Jim Bridger had been separated the instant the fight began. Now Mandell had no idea where his traveling companion was or even if he was still alive. But he did know that if Bridger remained among the living, he was without his clothes or any rifle to defend himself.

The two scouts had been on their way north, carrying supply requisitions from the commander at Fort Smith and expecting to deliver them to a government procurement agent in Helena. The post commander at Fort Smith, Lieutenant Colonel Luther P. Bradley, had decided not to send the usual contingent of troops along because Indian activity had been especially heavy in the area recently and he could not spare the men.

Bridger had assured the colonel that by staying off the established trails and traveling mostly by night, he could get through safely.

The day before Bridger left, Mandell had ridden up from Fort Kearny delivering mail and dispatches from the States. When he learned of Bridger's supply mission, he volunteered to go along. Except for his one brief trip to Fort Laramie the previous winter, which hardly counted as entertainment, it had been nearly a year since Mandell had visited any place except the three isolated forts along the Bozeman Trail. Again he was yearning to see what the world outside looked like.

Along the first leg of their journey, the two men had done fine. In fact, by the time they reached the banks of the Yellowstone River shortly before dawn on the morning of their third day out, they were beginning to believe that they might make the entire trip through hostile territory without encountering a single Indian.

They decided to hole up for the day under a wide, rocky overhang at the base of a bluff that overlooked the Yellowstone. The location was ideal, they believed, because it kept them and their mounts out of the line of sight of any enemies from above. In addition, it provided them with a clear field of vision, for they could see over the tumbled mass of stone jutting up between them and the river.

Bridger had decided to take a swim in the river before spreading his blankets and resting. In the faint light of early dawn, he worked his way across the rocks to the bank and dived straight into the swift waters of the Yellowstone. The first round was fired just as he surfaced, about fifteen feet out from the bank and slightly downstream from where he had left his things.

When the bullet ricocheted off the surface of the water about a foot from his head, Bridger bobbed immediately back below the surface. He did not move toward the bank, knowing this would make him an easy target.

Mandell spotted Bridger from the bank only one more time. That was when he surfaced briefly about a hundred feet downstream to catch a breath of air.

That first shot had come from off to the left on the

cliffs above. For a while Mandell remained where he was, rifle in hand and pondering the situation. He assumed the bullet had been fired by an Indian, but he had no idea how many more of them might be up there or whether they knew where *he* was, too. Finally he decided that the Indians probably were aware of the location of the camp, because Bridger had walked directly down from the spot to the river. If that was so, then they might want to come down and check out what Bridger had left behind, Mandell thought.

Carrying his rifle and all his spare ammunition, Mandell worked his way along the base of the bluff and tried to stay out of sight as he searched for a good vantage point from which to turn and watch the camp. Initially he wanted to get some idea of how many Indians there were. After doing that, there would be time to decide whether to take off in search of Bridger or to stand and fight.

When a shower of small stones and gravel rained down nearby, Mandell cautiously stepped out and looked up. What he saw was an Indian scaling his way down the steep side of the bluff. From the Indian's manner of dress, he appeared to be a Blackfoot, and a foolish one at that for exposing himself so stupidly.

For the time being, Mandell decided, all bets were off as far as his loyalty to the plains Indians was concerned. He had never cared much for the Blackfoot Indians anyway. Besides, this fight was more of a personal life-or-death struggle than anything else. In addition to that, these Indians had fired at his good friend and in fact might have killed him. That alone turned the whole affair into a personal grudge match.

Mandell plucked the Indian off the side of the cliff with a single shot. When the body bounced off the jagged rocks a few times and landed practically at his feet, Mandell confirmed that he was a Blackfoot and cut out at a quick trot along the base of the bluffs. He didn't want to make the same mistake the Indians had and be open to gunfire.

From then on, Mandell saw only occasional indications that the Indians were still in the area, but he gathered that there must not be more than three or four of them still alive. They were probably playing it cautious, he concluded, not knowing themselves how many white men they were up against. Using what cover he could find, he made his way toward the water, hoping to find some indication of what had happened to Bridger.

A lot of time was spent slithering on his belly while every once in a while an occasional round zinged startlingly close. There appeared to be one sniper remaining. Or, if there were others, Mandell told himself, they'd most likely climbed down to level ground.

The second Indian he spotted was being considerably more cautious than the first, but not quite cautious enough to keep himself alive. Mandell had seen the warrior easing along the base of the bluffs, then had waited for just the right moment to settle his sights on the man and bring him down.

Two Blackfoot were dead and one still was alive on top of the bluffs, not to mention others likely scattered among the quarter-mile stretch of rocks and boulders at the river's edge. Mandell sighed deeply. He knew that with Bridger still unaccounted for, his own life was in even more jeopardy.

A bullet zinged off a nearby rock, scaling from the rock a sliver of stone that embedded itself in his thigh.

Mandell gritted his teeth to stop from crying out. Then he moved away from the spot to be better protected from the marksman above. Blood was gushing from his leg wound, but he knew that for the moment he did not have time to tend it. The time had come, he decided, to settle things with the Indian on the bluff—one way or the other.

Revealing himself long enough to attract another round, Mandell saw where the Indian was firing from. He braced his rifle against a boulder. Then he settled his sights on the top rim of the rock when he was sure the Indian was hiding behind it. The next time his attacker popped up to take another shot . . .

But Mandell soon became aware that something strange was going on above him. He thought it must be a fight, because he caught an occasional glimpse of various human parts flailing in midair. Then a rifle sailed out over the rim of the bluff, followed by a man who staggered to the brink, clutching a knife that protruded from his belly. At last the man tumbled over the edge, his shrill scream chopped off abruptly as his body was dashed against the rocks a hundred feet below.

All was quiet for a while. Mandell hunkered close beside the boulder he was hiding behind and hastily tended to his wound. Cutting a slit in his leather trousers, he peeled back the material, then yanked the offending piece of stone from his flesh. The remaining cut was only about two inches wide, but it was equally as deep and blood was pulsing from it in a steady flow. Unknotting the kerchief from around his neck, Mandell folded it over a few times, then tied it tightly around the wound to curb the bleeding.

As he finished, he heard a voice call out. "Hello down there. Are you still alive?" The voice didn't sound like Bridger's, but Mandell was aware that the rocks could work strange changes on such things as the way a man sounds. He looked up and saw a figure standing where the mysterious fight had taken place earlier. The man calling out obviously wasn't Bridger—he was fully dressed—but even across the distance that separated them, Mandell thought there was something familiar about him. He was scanning the rocks below, looking for signs of life. In a moment he raised his hands to his mouth and called out again, "Hello! Are you still alive?"

"Yeah, I'm all right," Mandell called back.

"Good. You're safe now," the other man assured him. "The last two Blackfoot rode away a few minutes ago. Guess they'd had enough."

"Thanks, but who are you?"

"Billy Buffalo. Just stay there and I'll be down in a few minutes."

As he waited for the young Shawnee to ride the long route around the end of the bluff, Mandell headed back to where he and Bridger had been camped beneath the rocky overhang. He was relieved to find that their horses were still tied securely and that all their belongings were safe.

By the time Billy Buffalo reached him, Mandell had completed re-dressing the cut in his leg and the first words to come out of his mouth were, "Have you seen anything of Jim Bridger? He was traveling with me."

"Bridger's tucked away under some bushes about a half a mile downriver," Billy reported. "He's banged up considerably and embarrassed about being caught with his pants down like he was, but he'll be all right, I think."

Billy went on to explain that he had been riding along the south bank of the Yellowstone about half a mile downstream when he'd heard shots being fired. He'd dismounted immediately and was about to begin working his way forward on foot to see what was going on when he saw an

238

odd shape tossing and tumbling in the current a couple of dozen feet out from shore.

During one of his dives, Bridger had become entangled in the branches of a waterlogged tree that, with its rolling and tossing in the swift current, was keeping him submerged too much of the time. By the time Billy had succeeded in looping a rope around one of the branches and then hauled it, along with Bridger, to the shore, the aging scout was half drowned and nearly exhausted from his struggle to stay afloat.

"I think a few of his ribs were busted by that tree," Billy went on, "and he's got a bullet crease right across the flat of his butt, but it takes a lot more than that to finish off an old mountain grizzly like Jim Bridger. I left him under some bushes back there, still spitting up river water and cussing himself for getting ambushed in the open. Afterward I came on down here to give you a hand."

"Well, I'm sure obliged to you," Mandell told him, "but what in the hell are you doing out here alone anyway? Surely you're not still looking for wagon trains to lead into Bozeman City."

"No, but I do a lot of scouting for Mr. Bozeman," Billy explained. "He keeps me out patrolling the river, looking for signs that any large bands of Indians have crossed over to attack the settlements on the north side. Usually I don't get this far west along the Yellowstone, but I was looking for signs of survivors from two boats that cracked up a few miles upriver a couple of days ago. I thought maybe a few people had caught hold of some debris and floated downstream—I didn't find anything."

The two men kept their conversation brief. Each realized that the two Indians who had ridden off might soon return with more of their comrades. Mandell saddled his and Bridger's horses. Then he and Billy set off down the river to where Bridger was waiting.

"This brings to mind the time I run across Dr. Marcus Whitman at the '36 Rendezvous, or maybe it was the '37 Rendezvous," Jim Bridger said. "Well anyway I had this here arrowhead stuck in my shoulder, an' it'd been in there so long that the meat an' gristle had grown plumb around it." Bridger was lying on his stomach across a table in John Bozeman's cabin. His pants were down around his knees as Bozeman worked to clean and close the six-inch bullet crease across his backside.

"Wellsir, Dr. Whitman was just a young man then, fresh to his calling an' new to the crazy kinds of afflictions you run across in the wilderness. He had to dig all around inside my shoulder to find that blamed arrowhead an' get it out, an' I swear I think the whole thing bothered him a sight more than it hurt me. Howsomever, he got over bein' bothered by much of anything later, an' he did himself a world of good works out in the Oregon Country a'fore them sneakin' Cayuse killed him an' that pretty wife of his back in '47."

"Well, I'm no doctor, Jim," Bozeman interjected, still at work on the scout's injury, "but I do think I can get this thing taken care of good enough that it will heal on its own."

"It'll be a joy to be able to sit a saddle again," Bridger chuckled. "Me'n Hank still got ourselves plenty of territory to cover a'fore we get this supply business taken care of, an' I don't fancy havin' to stand up in the stirrups the whole way."

"So things are really pretty bad out there, are they?"

"If you can think of a word that's worser than 'miserable,' " Bridger quipped, "then you could use it to describe what them bluebellies are goin' through right now."

"Small attacks against haying and wood parties are practically an everyday occurrence now," Mandell added, "and every group of travelers that's tried to use the trail this year either has been badly shot up or massacred. But the worst part is the supply situation, and only part of that problem can be blamed on the Indians."

"If I could get to 'em," Bridger bristled, "I'd sure like to wring me a few gov'ment contractors' necks. Word is that some of the food an' arms shipments that were requisitioned this spring haven't even left Omaha an' Independence yet, an' here it is nearly August. The dispatches that come through always say that everything will be on its way soon, but that don't put no bread in the oven."

Bozeman finished caring for Bridger's injuries and the scout rose from the table and arranged his clothing.

"I guess things are worst at Fort Kearny right now," Mandell went on. "They're so short of ammunition that the troops don't even fire target practice anymore, and I swear some of those greenhorns there need it. It really looks bad, John. If Red Cloud had any idea how critical the situation really is, he'd probably start knocking those forts off like ninepins."

As the two men talked, John Bozeman could not help feeling that he shared responsibility for the trouble. Chances were good that someone else might have scouted and established a new trail if he had not done so, but he had been the one to explore it and encourage its use. And it followed that if men were suffering for lack of provisions and dying for lack of ammunition along the trail that bore his name, it should also be partly his responsibility to do something about it. A plan began taking shape in his mind.

"We figure it'll take at least another four days to get to Helena an' three more to get the supplies bought an' ready to go," Bridger reasoned. "Then the trip back will take mebbe two weeks. It's a long time for them to have to wait, but if they tried to hold out for the stuff to get through from back East, they could find themselves snowed in for another winter without nothin'. Then Red Cloud wouldn't have to do much but jus' sit back an' watch everybody starve to death."

"How would it be, Jim," Bozeman asked, "if there was a way to get a shipment of supplies through in one week instead of three or four? I've got an idea in mind. . . ."

When Kate returned late that afternoon from a visit to one of the nearby farms, she was amazed to see nearly every wagon in the settlement assembled around the building where Bozeman kept his supplies warehoused. At least twenty men were at work carrying crates, sacks and boxes out and loading them on the wagons. To one side, Bozeman stood keeping a careful account of it all. Kate tied her horse to the rail in front of their cabin, then walked over to where John and the others were at work.

"I'm almost afraid to ask what's going on," she broke in, half smiling.

"Jim Bridger and Hank Mandell rode in earlier this afternoon on their way to Helena," Bozeman told her.

"Now I *know* I'm not going to like what I'm about to hear," she said.

"Probably you won't," Bozeman agreed. "They said the forts down along the trail are in desperate need of resupplying because their shipments haven't reached them from back East."

"So you plan to take them what you've got stored here?"

"That's right. It's sort of an unauthorized loan. Bridger left a little while ago to continue his trip to Helena. He assured me he would replace all this when he comes back through with his supply wagons a couple of weeks from now. Hank Mandell stayed behind to scout for us and I've already got twenty-five volunteers to drive the wagons and ride along."

"It all sounds very noble," Kate commented, "but isn't there one flaw in your plans? What about those three or four thousand angry Indians who are supposed to be roaming around the Bighorn Mountains and the Bozeman Trail? Don't you think they might have something to say about all of this? And don't you think they might decide to express their feelings with bullets and arrows?"

"You're right," Bozeman agreed, sensing Kate's frustration and concern. "It's likely we will run into trouble, Kate. But somebody has to do something, and since we're the closest ones to the situation, it looks like the responsibility falls on us."

"Does that responsibility include dying with a Sioux arrow in your heart?" Kate asked. "The whole idea is crazy, John! *Just plain crazy!*"

"*Easy*, Kate," Bozemen urged. "You're going to stir up this camp even more with your hot temper. Let's go inside if you've got to blow off steam.

"Look," he told her once they were alone. "I *know* this is a crazy idea and I *know* we're all risking our necks going out there, but is it any more crazy than those first trips that you and I made three years ago up that trail? Those were wild ideas, too. We were both risking our fool necks exclusively for the sake of profit. At least now me and those men out there will be taking a risk for the sake of saving lives.''

With that, Kate's anger began to drain away. She stepped close to Bozeman and put her arms around him for a hug. ''You're right, John,'' she relented. ''I guess my reactions are so strong because you and I have much more to lose now. Three years ago my life was all adventure. Sometimes I found myself actually relishing the danger that came my way. But things are different now. We have each other and the thought of losing you makes the future look like a pretty ugly place.

''But I know this has to be done,'' she went on. ''I knew it even when I was arguing against it, and I promise I'll stand behind you all the way. When are you planning for us to leave?''

The words, *You're not going*, were right on the tip of Bozeman's tongue. But he sensed how useless it would be for him to utter them, as useless as if Kate had tried to say the same thing to him. If she was determined to make this trip with him—and that apparently was the case—then there was nothing he could do to stop her short of tying her up and leaving her behind in the cabin.

But accompanying that thought was the resolve that he would never fire the final round from his rifle. One bullet must always remain. That bullet would be for Kate in case a situation became so desperate that there was no chance of escape.

''The moon will be full tonight and the sky promises to be clear,'' Bozeman said. ''There will be light enough

to set out this evening as soon as the wagons are loaded.''
He kissed Kate tenderly. Then with a sudden smile he
added, ''And there might be one good thing to come out of
this piece of business after all. Hank told me there's a
Methodist minister and his family stalled at Fort Smith,
waiting for a safe means to make it on through to Virginia
City. If you have any final reservations about becoming
Mrs. John Bozeman, you'd better speak up pretty soon or
you'll be married before you can say, 'Happy Honeymoon'!''

Chapter 15

Bozeman awakened early. For a time he lay quietly beneath the wagon, gazing at Kate's features as she slept.

"My wife," he whispered, feeling a spontaneous smile spread across his features. Even sleeping underneath a wagon and still fully dressed in her coarse, trail clothes, Kate looked lovely, Bozeman thought. He stirred, picturing the soft, pliant body that dwelled beneath the heavy cotton shirt and denim trousers.

Then he shook his head disbelievingly. This was a hell of a place for a man to be taking his bride on their honeymoon.

After persuading the Methodist minister to perform their wedding ceremony five days before, he and Kate had struck out almost immediately from Fort Smith and headed for Fort Kearny, the next outpost down the line. They passed the days counting the tedious miles roll away beneath the steel-rimmed wagon wheels. And the nights were spent sleeping beneath a wagon that offered only an improvised canvas skirt to give them privacy from the twenty-five other men in the party. Twice they had skirmished with the Indians, but both groups of attackers had been small and the travelers had hardly slowed their pace as they drove the red men away.

Though their luck had held thus far, Mandell and Billy Buffalo still stayed out constantly, scouting the land on all sides for indications that a large group of Indians had spotted the wagon train of supplies and intended to attack it.

Kate had not uttered a single complaint the entire way, which was no particular surprise to her new husband. She was as used to this sort of dangerous travel as any man in the group. She even insisted on assuming her share of guard and livestock duties.

Their biggest disappointment so far had been the refusal of Colonel Luther Bradley, the commander of the garrison at Fort Smith, to provide them with any troops to escort them on to Fort Kearny. He had accepted his portion of the supplies readily enough, but when it came time to see to it that the other forts would get theirs, his "no" had been firm. His own scouts and a party of neutral Crow Indians passing through the area had warned that large numbers of Sioux were in the mountains massing for attack. Bradley had explained that his first obligation was to protect his own post and the lives of the men, women and children who lived within its walls.

In his anger, Mandell had come close to assaulting the Fort Smith commander with his bare hands. But Bozeman had talked him out of the notion and they had pushed on alone.

At that moment they were less than a day's travel from Fort Kearny. Mandell assured Bozeman that the new commander there, General Henry Wessels, would be much more understanding when it came to providing an escort for the supply train along the third and final leg of its journey on south to Fort Reno.

When he heard the men beginning to stir in the grey light of dawn, Bozeman woke Kate with a gentle kiss on the cheek. "We've just got one more day on the trail," he told her. "By tonight I promise that we'll be sleeping on a real bed with real sheets, even if I have to whip the orneriest officer at Fort Kearny to borrow his quarters from him."

"You provide the bed and I'll help make sure it gets put to good use," Kate smiled back, raising a hand to sift her fingers through her husband's red beard.

It took only half an hour to prepare a hurried breakfast, hitch the stock to their traces and be on their way. Kate acted in the place of one of the drivers who had burned his hand the day before and took up the reins of one of the heavy freight wagons midway down the line. Meanwhile, Bozeman rode on to the front to be on hand in case the lead driver needed any special instructions.

After they had been on the trail for no more than two hours, Hank Mandell came galloping across the open country from the southwest and found Bozeman to make his report.

"I checked the trail almost all the way to Kearny," he reported. "It looks clear the whole way but there's trouble brewing over in the hills to the west of the fort."

"What's going on over there?" Bozeman asked.

"I saw signs that some big bands of Indians are moving through the area. It looks like they're starting to converge on a wood camp about six miles northwest of the fort.

"It appeared to me," Mandell explained, "like several hundred Cheyenne have come down recently from the north and a few hundred more Sioux have arrived from the south and west. I'm not positive what's going on because I scouted in a wide circle, well clear of where the Indians are camped, but my guess is they intend to take the wood camp.''

"How soon?''

"Probably today from the looks of things.''

"And how many men are there in the camp?''

"Including civilians and their military guards, there's generally about thirty or thirty-five men out there. Even before I left they were fending off one or two small attacks practically every day. By now they know how to fort up fast . . .''

"Yeah,'' Bozeman interjected, "but no matter how hard they fight, they won't be able to hold off a large number of Indians for very long.''

"You're right,'' Mandell agreed, "and like I told you before, ammunition's a real problem right now.''

"Well, what do you suggest, Hank? Do you think the Indians know about us yet?''

"I guess not, but it's only a matter of time before one of their scouts spots the train. The only thing I can suggest is to push as hard as you can on toward the fort. And it might not be such a bad idea to send someone ahead with news that you're on your way. The general might decide to send a welcoming committee out to meet you and lead you on in.''

"All right, that's what we'll do, then,'' Bozeman decided. "I'm expecting Billy back about any time. When he gets here I'll start him on his way to the fort. About how far is it?''

"No more than six or seven miles, and the road's in

good shape from here on with only one creek to ford. You should be traveling no more than four hours."

The two men rode along in silence for a moment, both gazing out toward the rolling hills and patches of forest to the west. Somewhere out in those hills, men were probably fighting and dying at that very moment. And it was a stirring thought to realize that at practically any time the hills could come alive with hundreds of Indians bent on killing every white person in sight. The situation was quickly reaching the crisis stage. Bozeman could only pray that their luck would hold out a little longer.

"I'm going back out, John," Mandell announced after a while.

"I don't see that it's necessary," Bozeman told him. "Why not swing out to the side and ride as one of the flankers for the train? Or you could just as easily carry word on ahead to Fort Kearny. That's what Billy would be doing if he were here to get the order. Why go back out there with the hills crawling with Sioux and Cheyenne? You're good, Hank, but you're not bulletproof."

"I've got good friends at that wood camp," Mandell explained, "men that I've come to know and like a lot over the past year. If they're under attack and need help, I want to try to get some for them."

They rode on without speaking for a moment more. Then Bozeman said, "It's hard for you, isn't it, Hank? I mean, because it's the Sioux out there on one side and your friends on the other."

"It's hard to figure quite what's right," Mandell admitted. "I swore when I took on this job that I wouldn't do anything to bring any grief down on the Sioux. But when a man's right in the middle of a war, it's damn near impossible for him not to pull for one side or the other.

"I guess last year after the Fetterman fight, my think-

251

ing started turning around. Somewhere along the way I became a white man again. I don't know. The only thing I'm sure about right now is that I can't just stand aside while over thirty men get massacred—especially when there's a chance that I might be able to do something about it.''

"I don't have any advice to offer you,'' Bozeman told him sympathetically. "The only thing I can say is that I guess you'll just have to let your conscience guide you and then hope for the best from then on.''

Mandell nodded agreement. "Right now,'' he sighed, "my conscience is telling me that I've got to head over toward that wood camp and see what's going on.'' Wheeling his horse around, he headed out at a gallop across the open country to the west of the wagon train. He turned once to wave. But in a couple of minutes he had disappeared into the distant line of trees.

Bozeman spurred his horse back to the front of the wagon train and advised the lead driver to pick up the pace. Then he turned and worked his way back slowly along the line of wagons, spreading the word about what was happening near the wood camp and explaining how close they now were to the second objective of their journey.

When he came alongside the wagon Kate was driving and told her about the scout's report, he could sense her struggle to keep the lines of worry and fear from showing on her face. After what she had been through the year before at the hands of the Cheyenne, Bozeman knew it was difficult for her not to feel terror over the prospects of what might lie ahead.

"I was wondering,'' she told him, mustering a smile, "if we would have any excitement to break the monotony of this trip.''

252

"It looks like you'll have an answer to that question within the next four hours, but I have to admit I'd rather be bored," Bozeman chuckled. "They tell me that in these parts too much excitement can be bad for the health."

"We'll deal with whatever comes along when it comes," Kate declared. "That's what I told my drivers the first time we started up this cursed trail, and I guess the rule still applies."

"It's the way we've always done things, I suppose," Bozeman smiled. Then, after leaning far out of the saddle to give Kate a kiss, he turned his horse and moved on to the next wagon.

By the time Bozeman had worked his way nearly to the rear of the train, he spotted Billy Buffalo coming up their back trail to catch up with the wagons. Billy sighted no Indians sneaking up behind the train.

"At least that's one good piece of news for the day," Bozeman told the scout. "I just wish things were as peaceful up ahead right now."

He quickly related to Billy what Mandell had seen and gave him his instructions about riding ahead to the fort. Within another minute the young Shawnee had put the spurs to his horse and was galloping on ahead.

They were little more than five miles from the fort now, Bozeman estimated. If Billy made it on through safely and the general mustered his men without delay, they could be moving along with an armed escort within two hours. But two hours was an eternity in this wild country. Bozeman knew that if any of those hundreds of Indians Mandell had seen earlier decided to turn aside and attack the train, the troops that Billy Buffalo led back to them might find only burning wreckage and mangled corpses when they arrived. There would be no real safety for any of them until they were within the walls of the fort itself.

253

When Hank Mandell returned again, the grave look on his face and the lathered condition of his horse spoke of the urgency of the news he carried.

"They're in some deep trouble over there at the wood camp," he announced hurriedly to Bozeman. "I couldn't work my way in very close, but I did get near enough to see the Indians hitting them from two sides at once."

The camp, he explained, was located in a large, open meadow within a quarter of a mile of the forest. It had been constructed of heavy boxes taken from several of the wagons and placed in a circle to form a corral and camp-site inside.

From a distant hilltop, Mandell said, he had watched hundreds of Indians race toward the wood camp from the direction of the woods to the west and along the length of the meadow to the east. The men behind the wagons had countered the assault and turned it back at last, but that charge would hardly be the last of the day.

"I know how much ammunition was designated for that camp," Mandell went on, "and I know my friends are bound to be running out by now. If help from the fort isn't on the way right this minute, it's probably too late for them. But it might not be too late to get through with some of the ammunition you've got in these wagons. That's the only way I can see for any of those men out there to have a chance."

"Whew!" Bozeman sighed and shook his head. "That's a tall order. Do you have any idea how you might get through?"

"There's a dry creek bed that winds its way west into the hills near there," Mandell informed the train leader. "It's deep enough to conceal a man on horseback—that is, if the Indians aren't using it themselves—and plays out about a quarter-mile from the camp. From there on it would be plain hard riding over open country.''

"The whole thing sounds pretty damn risky to me,'' Bozeman remarked sourly.

"Hell, yes, it's risky,'' Mandell snapped. "But do you have any better ideas?''

"I can't say that I do.''

"Well, then,'' Mandell concluded, "my idea will have to do, that is if you'll cut loose with the ammunition I'll need to take along. They're using mostly breech-loading Springfields and some Henrys, but it wouldn't hurt to bring some Winchester rounds and Colt .45 slugs, too.''

"I'll get the men to load up four horses while you change mounts,'' Bozeman assured him. "The one you're on looks pretty well spent.''

"I won't be able to handle but a couple of horses besides the one I'm riding.''

"Good enough,'' Bozeman announced. "I'll take care of the other two.'' A tight grin spread across his face. "You didn't think I was going to let you hog all of the day's glory, did you, Hank? Besides, if there's two of us and a lucky shot happens to take one of us out, then the other would still have a chance of getting the job done.''

Mandell made no protest. "You're right, John, and I can't say as how I'd mind the company either. This is going to be a hairy one.''

Mandell rode off toward the nearby remuda of spare horses to change mounts and Bozeman called a temporary halt to the train. After instructing some of the men to begin loading the necessary ammunition on four pack horses, he rode down the line of wagons until he came to the one Kate was driving.

"What's up?'' she asked, slipping to the ground beside the wagon to stretch her legs.

255

Bozeman dismounted. "Mandell says the Indians are attacking the wood camp," he reported. "They're going to need some more ammunition out there, Kate, if they have any hopes of holding out until help can get to them from the fort. Mandell thinks he knows a way to reach the camp. He's going to try it . . . and I'm going with him."

A stricken look washed over Kate's face. Bozeman knew instantly that her every impulse was to protest and plead with him not to go, but her only response was to whisper hoarsely, "Oh, John . . ."

"I couldn't in good conscience ask any other man to go if I wasn't willing to go myself," Bozeman told her. "Someone has to go with Mandell. Doing that will double the odds that at least some of the ammunition will get through." He hesitated. "If I sent another man, Kate, and he got killed . . . I'd feel like I was his murderer. It has to be me."

"I *hate* it, John," Kate responded, near tears. "But I do understand." She wound her arms around him and held herself tightly against him, communicating with that gesture all she could not find words to say.

"I guess now's the moment I'm supposed to tell you not to worry and that I'll be fine," Bozeman put in, "but right now those seem like pretty empty assurances. Just know that whatever happens, Kate, I love you. Before we came together, I never knew that one human heart was capable of feeling so much love for another person."

"And I love you just as much, John," Kate whispered.

For a moment they stood holding one another. Tenderly Bozeman stroked his wife's hair and for an instant felt that he could not bear to leave her for any reason, let alone for one as dangerous as this one. The two of them should not be on this trail at all. They should be back at home in their cabin or in any other place where they could continue to enjoy their lives together.

"Ready, John?" Mandell had ridden up and was sitting atop his fresh horse a few feet away. It was obvious he was uncomfortable about interrupting but anxious that they be on their way.

Bozeman raised Kate's chin with his hand and gazed into her tear-reddened eyes. Then he kissed her lips and turned away.

Putting his foot in the stirrup, he mounted up, wheeled his horse and whooped, "Let's do it!"

Chapter 16

Bozeman raised his head cautiously over the rim of the ditch and gazed out at the meadow beyond. A faint smell of gunsmoke hung in the air, though the clouds of smoke that must have boiled up during the most recent round of fighting had long since been borne away by an early afternoon breeze.

Off to the right in the midst of the battle scene lay the scattered carcasses of perhaps two dozen Indian horses. Evidence of Indian corpses was scarce, however. Most braves considered it a matter of honor to remove the bodies of their wounded and dead comrades from the battlefield before they withdrew, even at considerable risk to their own lives. But a few bloodied bodies did remain, lying twisted and fly-covered where the white men had taken a stand against their aggressors.

Bozeman amd Mandell studied the battlefield briefly, for the most part to make certain that no surviving Indians lay nearby in hiding. Afterward, Bozeman turned his attention to the fortifications the wood camp men were using to shield themselves. The scene was pretty much as Mandell had described it to him. The wooden wagon boxes were laid out end to end in a circular shape that formed a barricade about four feet high and seventy-five feet in diameter. The boxes' one-inch boards were not thick enough to stop a bullet, but they provided the soldiers and civilians inside with protection enough to allow them to hide and move around freely.

It had been no easy chore, Bozeman realized, to reach this point safely with their four laden pack horses. In fact, though Mandell knew the countryside well, he was still amazed that they accomplished it without being spotted by a single hostile.

Riding the ravine had been a singularly unnerving experience. Its near to fourteen-foot depth, while keeping them out of sight, had also made them blind to anyone who might be approaching from either side. And the steep, crumbling banks would have made it practically impossible for a horse to scramble onto level ground in most places.

But Mandell had timed the ride perfectly. They had waited in a thicket far from the wood camp while the Indians mounted yet another charge against the wagon box fortifications. After that charge was held off, the Indians had turned aside and headed for some nearby hills.

Mandell reasoned they would regroup, tend their wounded, renew their prayers and receive instructions from their leaders. That, he told Bozeman, woudl leave the meadow east of the wood camp clear of all Indians for a time, and it was then they should start out along the ravine, which wound a ragged course along one edge of the meadow.

At the present time they were stopped at a point where the ravine passed closest to the fortifications before turning sharply to the southwest and playing out. Mandell pushed on ahead to check out the spot where they would lead their horses up out of the depression. Bozeman was waiting. Almost half an hour had passed. Bozeman sat atop his mount, impatiently holding the leads of the four pack animals and wondering ever since the first five minutes had passed what was taking his companion so long.

When Mandell finally did return, his arrival was preceded by the hurried clatter of shod hooves on hard rock. He'd whipped his horse around a curve in the ravine ahead and only paused long enough to wave at Bozeman and shout a hurried "Come on!" before spinning his mount around and racing back in the opposite direction.

Bozeman loosened the lead ropes of both pairs of pack horses from the horn of his saddle. Then he gave them a firm tug as he spurred his own horse into motion. He had no idea what was going on, but figured by the urgency of Mandell's summons that there was no time to waste. Riding hurriedly past the curve ahead, he then proceeded another hundred yards up the ravine before finding the spot where Mandell had scrambled his horse up to level ground and was standing on the edge of the ravine waiting to assist him.

"Dismount and then send the horses up one by one," Mandell instructed him. "I'll catch their reins when they get to the top. It's steep, but I think they can make it all right. Anyway, we haven't got time to find a better place."

"Why, what's going on?"

"I guess you couldn't see them from where you were," Mandell replied, "but the lower end of the meadow's alive with Indians. There must be four or five hundred of them at least and they'll be along any minute."

It took them only a minute to get the horses out of the ravine. But by the time Bozeman scrambled up after the last animal, he was hearing the distant war cries of the attacking Indians. He swung up into the saddle. Then he squandered an instant to gaze down.

About a half mile away down the meadow the Indians had already begun their charge. They were advancing along a front at least two hundred yards wide as they made for the white men's wagon box fortifications.

Mandell had wasted no time in waiting for his companion. Snatching up the lead ropes of his two pack animals, he'd started his horse across the meadow at a dead run. Bozeman was not far behind.

The first bullets began to whine past them long before they reached the circle of wagon boxes. But the Indians were firing wildly from their racing mounts and neither the men nor their horses were hit. In camp, two men lowered a wooden barricade to admit them, and Mandell and Bozeman did not slow their pace until they were inside.

The scene inside the ring of wooden wagon boxes was one of chaos and devastation. At one time nearly fifty horses and mules had been tied off to two long picket ropes, but at that moment practically all were down from various bullet and arrow wounds. The bodies of four dead men lay side by side along one edge of the circle. In another spot a half dozen wounded men were caring for their own and each other's injuries as best they could. Twenty men still remained in their firing positions around the ring, even though some of *those* men, too, were suffering from various minor wounds.

"We've got ammunition!" Mandell called out to the surprised survivors. Hastily he began slashing the pack ropes with his knife and lowering the packs to the ground. "Who needs some?"

The response was immediate and at once Bozeman and Mandell snatched up armloads of cartridge boxes and distributed them to the defenders. With renewed hope, the men began to fire their bolt-action Springfields and lever-action Henry rifles, devastating the foremost ranks of the attackers.

About two hundred yards from the fortifications, the Indian ranks split as if a wedge had been driven through their formation, and they began to ride in a wide circle around the wagon boxes. None dared swing in too closely. They had seen the effectiveness of the white men's repeating rifles and knew that death awaited the foolhardy braves who advanced too far. But they kept up a heavy fire at their enemy and repeatedly they perforated the one-inch planks of the wagon boxes by raining arrows down on the men inside.

After Bozeman and Mandell had distributed the necessary ammunition around the camp, they too took up their rifles and began to fire at the Indian warriors. The attack lasted a full twenty minutes. When at last it was over, a few dozen Indian stragglers raced across the open meadow, using the thick clouds of gunsmoke for cover as they rescued their wounded comrades and recovered as many of the dead as they could. Some of the men in camp continued firing while this was going on, but Bozeman laid his overheated rifle aside and just stared.

"I've never seen such fine riding," he commented to a man who was leaning against the barricade nearby. "Did you see the way those two Indians over there leaned down and snatched that brave up off the ground without ever breaking the stride of their horses?"

When the man didn't answer, Bozeman looked closer and saw that a steel-tipped arrow had entered his body from behind, passing completely through his chest before lodging in the wood plank of the wagon box in front of him. He lifted the man under his arms to support his weight and managed to dislodge the arrow from the board. Then he dragged his grisly burden to the spot where other casualties lay. There were more in a moment. And on the faces of those who brought them over—as well as on those of the other survivors—was a fear that deepened as the number of seriously wounded multiplied.

Bozeman glanced across the enclosure and saw Mandell putting together a hasty bandage for a young soldier with a shoulder wound. He walked over to join the two men. Even as Mandell continued to work, the young soldier held out his right hand to shake Bozeman's and introduced himself. "Mr. Bozeman, I'm Lieutenant Frances—the man in charge of what's left of this outfit. I want to thank you for risking your life to bring us this ammunition. When you broke through, I bet there weren't a hundred rifle cartridges left among the lot of us."

"Hank said the situation was bound to be critical out here," Bozeman replied.

"I just wish that now there was some way for the two of you to get back out," Frances said. "It looks like it's only a matter of time before they overrun us. I took a head count a minute ago. Out of the thirty men we had, only thirteen are still in any shape to aim a rifle and pull a trigger."

"Counting John and me, it's fifteen," Mandell put in. "That's enough to throw a bunch of lead back out. And from what I can tell, those Indians must be suffering three or four times the number of casualties that you are."

"Yeah, but Red Cloud seems determined to take this camp at any cost," the lieutenant responded. "This is the fourth charge they've made today and it's still only early afternoon."

"Are you sure it's Red Cloud who's in charge here?" Mandell asked.

"Pretty sure. Off and on all day, there's been one chief who keeps appearing on that hilltop off to the right of the meadow. Look, he's back up there right now."

Mandell turned and saw the distant figure. Picking up a pair of field glasses from the ground nearby, he squinted for a better look.

Atop a fine, sleek Indian pony, Red Cloud looked powerful in his flowing, feathered headdress and fierce war paint. In his right hand, as he gazed with calm intensity at the wood camp, he held a symbolic feathered lance. It was a weapon Mandell had seen hanging in the council lodge many times. Seeing it, an odd feeling swept over him. He felt almost as if the chief knew at that very moment that his old comrade was gazing up at him through the field glasses.

For the first time, ridiculous as it seemed to him, Mandell began to feel the full burden of his decision to bring the ammunition to these besieged men. A pang of grief stabbed at him as he realized that at last his final ties to the people he had lived among for two years was broken. With hardly any thought to what he was doing, he had taken up a rifle and helped these men fight off the Indian attack. In addition, he had killed two men that he clearly recognized as Sioux warriors. There could be no going back later—not to his wife and children or to the happy life he had led as White Wolf.

"Lieutenant, sir, we're in bad need of water," announced a tall man who had just approached them. Mandell looked up and recognized the face of Sergeant O'Shannon, the platoon sergeant under the lieutenant's command. "Some of the wounded men especially need it to wet their throats and wash their wounds."

"What happened to the water we had in the horse trough?" Frances asked.

"It caught a bullet during the last attack and leaked out before anybody noticed."

"Hell, Sergeant! I don't know what to tell you. If there's no water, then there's no water!"

"Well, sir, I thought about taking a couple of men and making a dash to Little Dusty Creek. I've got a man gathering up all the canteens he can find now, but I thought I'd better get your okay first."

"That's risky, Sergeant," the lieutenant returned doubtfully. "It's at least two hundred yards over to the creek, and once you get down in the creek bed, you'll be out of sight of camp. No one here will be able to give you fire support if you get jumped."

"But we need the water bad, sir," O'Shannon insisted.

Frances sighed in resignation. "Go ahead and try it, Sergeant. I don't suppose it will be much more dangerous for you out there than it will be for all of us in here when those redskins decide to hit us again."

As the sergeant started away, Mandell picked up his rifle. "I'm going out with them," he announced. "They'll all have their hands full of canteens. If there are any Indians in the tall grass out toward the creek your men will need somebody close by to do their shooting for them."

Mandell checked the loads in his rifle and twin revolvers before going out and Bozeman took a position nearby with a couple of other men to give covering fire to the water detail.

When Mandell, O'Shannon and two other men squeezed through a gap between two wagons and started cautiously toward the creek, they were not challenged. After crossing about eighty yards of open area and passing through a wide patch of thick grass, they dropped down out of sight in the creek bed itself.

Two or three long minutes passed. The men behind

the barricades waited, knowing that if their comrades ran into trouble at that point, there was nothing any of them could do to help. But everything seemed peaceful enough. And every moment, Bozeman kept expecting to see the men reappear and start back with their full canteens of water.

Then a shrill war cry split the air. It was followed by a scream and a staccato of shots. Moments later, Sergeant O'Shannon and one of the other men scrambled out of the creek bed and broke into a run toward the wagon boxes. Each had several canteens slung over his shoulder. But the left sleeve of the sergeant's tunic was crimson with blood from the elbow down. Rounds were still being fired behind them in the creek. However, no Indian targets appeared to give the men behind the barricades something to fire at.

Then Hank Mandell burst into sight. He was firing in back of him with a revolver, his one remaining weapon. As he broke away, a shot from behind caught him in the left leg and he tumbled down out of sight in the tall grass. Bozeman held his breath till an instant later Mandell was back on his feet and hobbling clumsily toward safety.

"They was waiting for us down there," O'Shannon announced breathlessly as he squeezed back through to the protection of the barricades. "A minute after we got down by the water, a dozen of them rushed us from both directions. They split Johnson's skull with a tomahawk before any of us knew what was going on, and then ever-loving hell broke loose all around. Mandell told us to come on ahead with the water while he covered us."

By then Mandell had made it to the edge of the grasses. But he was staggering and it was obvious that the wounded leg would not carry him for very long. Behind him the deep grass was beginning to wave and rustle as the Indians eased up over the edge of the rim of the creek.

267

"They're coming along through the grass on their bellies!" Bozeman exclaimed. "Lay down some fire behind Mandell while I go out and help him in!"

Before anyone had a chance to stop him, Bozeman put his rifle aside, drew his pistol and started out to meet his friend.

"You damned fool! Go back!" Mandell shouted. "Get the hell out of here!" He was still making some progress, but the features of his face were contorted with pain and it looked as if his bad leg would fail him at any moment.

Bozeman reached his side and snapped off a couple of shots blindly into the grass. Then he looped one of Mandell's arms around his neck and started forward with him. From behind the barricades, several men were pouring out a continuous fire into the grass as the Indians still managed to get off a few shots of their own.

When they reached the wagon boxes, Bozeman shoved Mandell ahead where other hands waited to help him in. While Bozeman waited, he turned his head and glanced behind him. He saw the young brave stand up in the midst of the grass and raise his rifle to his shoulder, and though he knew the range was too great for his handgun, he still raised his own pistol.

The two weapons sounded simultaneously, and a fraction of a second later Bozemen felt something slap hard against the right side of his chest and spin him around. He slammed against the side of one of the wagon boxes, then clutched desperately at the boards to keep from falling. The Indian went down a moment later as several rifles from behind the barricades fired on him.

The way to safety was right in front of him, but Bozeman's legs went rubbery. His head swam and he let go of the side of the wagon box. As he tried to take a step, he fell just as able hands caught him and dragged him inside.

The Indians began to mass on the far end of the meadow to the east. In the woods to the west they gathered as well. Meanwhile, several of the men around Mandell had begun to remove the laces from their boots. Each solemnly tied one lace around the toe of one boot. If need be, every man would tie the other end of the lace to the trigger of his rifle and then use his foot to pull the trigger and kill himself. In the event that the camp was overrun, this was a preferable alternative to being captured alive and tortured by the Indians. But Mandell left his laces in place. He still had one of his pistols with him. That would serve the purpose if the time came.

He had rigged a crude splint for his wounded leg so that he could stand beside the barricades and shoot when the attack began. Scarcely a man among them was not suffering from some sort of wound. But even some of the most seriously wounded had figured out ways to be of use during the coming onslaught. There was little talk now, but a mood of grim determination permeated the air. No man in camp expected to be alive in half an hour, but each had resolved that when the day's bloody business was concluded, the Indians would have paid a high price for their victory.

After a brief interlude, Red Cloud had returned to his place on the distant hilltop. Mandell suspected he was meeting with his chiefs and encouraging them to make this upcoming attack the final one. No doubt, Mandell thought, the day's losses were weighing heavily on his mind, and even if that night the Indians found themselves celebrating the death of the last white man in the wood camp, the mighty head of the Indian confederation would know deep within him that the cost of the victory had been much too dear. The wails of the widows and orphaned children in the Sioux and Cheyenne camps would drown out the cries of victory from the surviving warriors.

From the woods west of the wagon box camp to the farthest end of the meadow to the east, anxious eyes were focused on that single mounted figure whose signal would launch hundreds of men forward to complete the annihilation of less than twenty others. But though the afternoon was cloudless, a distant boom rolled up the long meadow like a clap of thunder. The sound was manmade. A miniature geyser of dirt erupted in the midst of the distant congregation of Indians, at once pitching fractured human bodies skyward and tossing horses about like discarded toys.

"Hot damn!" one of the men behind the barricade exclaimed. "If the howitzer from Fort Kearny didn't do that, then I'll eat every one of these here damn Springfield bullets!"

The first round from the howitzer caused considerable confusion among the Indians massed at the lower end of the meadow, and when it boomed out a second time, they began to scatter. The small, portable howitzer was hated more than any other weapon in the Fort Kearny arsenal. The cannon was a horrible equalizer, lending disproportionate power to a small number of men. The plains Indians feared its roar as they feared the wrath of their own deities.

Red Cloud remained for a while longer on his hilltop. There still would be time to attack the wood camp and annihilate the white men there before reinforcements arrived to save them, but the effort would be wasted. It was clear that the army of Indian warriors had been transformed into a scattered rabble, fleeing at the sound of the white man's thunder gun.

The men behind the wagon box barricades were too exhausted to cheer, even when Red Cloud turned his horse west toward the mountains—his home. A few sagged to the ground as the Indians began to scatter. The rest remained in their firing positions with their weapons ready, hardly able to believe what they were seeing.

Moments later, as the contingent of reinforcements appeared at the far end of the meadow, their spirits soared. About fifty mounted cavalry led the formation, spread out in a broad skirmish line. And behind them marched the main body of troops—about two hundred infantrymen. Next came the brass howitzer, drawn by a matched pair of horses. A dozen ambulances and empty wagons brought up the rear.

As they drew nearer, Mandell saw that General Wessels himself was leading the rescue party. He was riding behind the skirmish line but ahead of the columns of infantry. The sight was a splendid one, but the joy of the moment began to fade for Mandell when he saw Kate riding alongside the general. Within a short time it would be his grim task to inform her that, although she had been a bride for less than a week, already she was a widow.

"I want to see him, Hank." Kate spoke quietly but firmly, still in the initial state of shock that precedes the onset of a deep, pervading grief.

"I just don't think it would be a good idea," Mandell told her. "I don't know how you'd handle it, seeing John in the condition he's in right now. Maybe it would be better if you waited a little while and sort of let the whole thing soak in first."

*   *   *

Mandell shuddered involuntarily, remembering how he'd gone out with the others to meet the reinforcements. He'd searched for Kate amid the throng of men and horses. When he found her amidst the survivors sharing their jubilation, it had not even been necessary to speak the dreaded words he had prepared himself to say.

"Is he dead?" she'd asked, and his face had told it all.

Kate dismounted then. Forgetting about the horse she was riding, she walked alongside Mandell to where the ring of wagon boxes stood. Her steps were plodding and her eyes took in nothing of what passed in front of her. She didn't speak, and Mandell respected her wishes not to. But when they reached the edge of the camp, he took her by the arm and stopped her before she could pass through to the inside of the circle.

"I'm no stranger to the sight of death, Hank," she said, anticipating his words of protest. "When I was twelve years old I had to dig four graves and bury my father, mother and two brothers after they had been hacked to death by the Cayuse. If I could handle that, I think I can handle this, too. I just want to see him, that's all—right now."

John Bozeman's body lay a slight distance apart from those of the other dead men. Mandell had covered him with a piece of canvas that he'd cut from one of the wood camp tents. In the vicinity of where Bozeman had been shot in the chest, a six-inch circle of blood had saturated his coarse white shirt, but Kate took no notice of the wound.

"Oh, John . . ." she whispered, her voice catching in her throat as she knelt beside him and spoke his name.

"He died good, Kate," Mandell told her quietly.

272

"He got it saving my life and he didn't last but about five minutes afterward. He was never afraid, not for a minute, and we talked mostly about you until he finally went."

For a moment Mandell was silent, feeling his own emotions welling up inside him. But it was a time for strength. Kate would need a strong ally nearby when her own grief began to rise.

"He wanted me to tell you that he loved you, even though he knew there had never been any doubt in your mind about that. And he told me to let you know he considered you the most remarkable woman he had ever met. It was the damnedest thing, Kate, but there near the end, just thinking about you and talking about you seemed to give him the courage he needed to pass over with dignity."

Kate reached out her fingers and brushed a wisp of hair up from her dead husband's brow. Then she leaned down to place the tenderest of kisses on his lips. Sensing that at that moment no more words were necessary, Mandell turned away quietly. When he glanced back an instant later, he saw Kate sitting on the ground beside Bozeman. She was quietly talking to him.

Chapter 17

The flames that were consuming the buildings and stout log walls of Fort Kearny brightly illuminated the hot summer night. Hank Mandell and Jim Bridger sat watching the whole spectacular sight from a hilltop a mile away from the fort. The Indians had spent a couple of hours late that afternoon ransacking the buildings and stockade for anything that might be of value to them. Afterward, they had quickly put the torch to the entire fort.

There was something mesmerizing about the distant ball of dancing yellowish light on the nighttime landscape. The flames were not only consuming the physical remains of the fort, they were also nullifying all the hard work and determination it had taken the pioneers to build and maintain it. Red Cloud and his confederation of the plains Indian tribes had won their war. The Bozeman Trail was being closed forever.

"I've seen a sight of plumb amazin' things in my

sixty-four years," Bridger drawled with almost studied calm, "but Hank, I confess it, this is a first for even me. I ain't never seen a whole fort go up in smoke all at one time this way!"

"In the backs of our minds, I guess we all knew this day had to come," Mandell reasoned. "But it still seems like a tragedy to me. I can't stop thinking about all the men who died on both sides over the past few years."

After several bloody but indecisive clashes over the previous fall and winter, including the attack in which John Bozeman had been killed, the United States Army had decided that it was no longer worth the effort to keep the Bozeman Trail or any of the three forts along it open.

The past spring, the army had attempted to hold two peace conferences at Fort Laramie to work out the terms of their withdrawal, but Red Cloud and the leaders of most of the hostile plains tribes refused to enter into any sort of negotiations until the forts were closed. Only a few of the more passive Crow leaders showed up to make their mark on the treaty. And their main interest leaned more toward the government handouts than the treaty itself.

In late summer of 1868, orders came through to the commanders of Fort Smith and Fort Kearny to begin making preparations to evacuate their forts. By August, everything was in readiness. Some of the government property at the forts was sold, some was loaded on wagons to be taken along, and what remained was abandoned when the entire garrisons moved out en masse down the Bozeman Trail. Their destination was Fort Russell, which was located in the southeast corner of Wyoming, well south of the disputed territory.

Even before Red Cloud and the other chiefs abandoned their fall hunts to sign the white men's paper, they already had much of what they had fought to gain. The Indians would be guaranteed exclusive control of all the territories they claimed north of the North Platte River and east of the Bighorn Mountains. The three forts along the Bozeman Trail would be abandoned and the trail itself would be forever closed.

Other provisions of the treaty allowed for cattle, clothing and farming implements to be provided to the Indians so that they could settle down to a life of farming and raising livestock. But the Indians, as well as those white men who knew them intimately, scoffed at the notion that the plains tribes would ever willingly give up their nomadic existence to follow "the white man's road." Still, there was no need to roam, the Indians reasoned, because there would always be enough buffalo, elk, deer and bear on the lands they owned to support them and their descendants indefinitely.

Bridger and Mandell had stayed on in their scouting jobs until the end. But that day as the garrison of Fort Kearny started south, both had agreed that their duties were finished. It was time for them to be on their way. The former occupants of Fort Kearny were spending the night on the trail no more than fifteen miles from the fort.

So it was only out of curiosity that Bridger and Mandell had decided to ride back and see what the Indians would do with the place. That night's fire, though a fascinating sight, was no big surprise to either of them. The Sioux and Cheyenne had a habit of burning places, as well as people, that they no longer cared to have around.

"So where does your trail lead from here, Jim?" Mandell asked.

"Over toward the Grand Teton country, I figure," Bridger told him. "I'm pretty much tired out of these military goin's-on for a spell—an' I don't s'pose I'll be none too popular with the Indians in these parts for a long time—so the best thing to do is to move on out an' park my bones in some new surroundin's for the winter season.

"I recall when I wintered in the Teton Range back in '42—maybe it was '46—they was grizzlies over there so mean they'd chaw down a growed man in no more'n four bites an' then snatch up his rifle for to pick their teeth with. Why, they had elk over there so big they'd uproot a fifty-foot oak tree jus' trying to scratch their back against it. I shot myself one of them one time an' me'n my squaw ate for a whole winter off of it. Then in the spring we took the hide an' made ourselves a canoe an' still had enough left over for a good-sized tepee an' 'leven pairs of moccasins."

Mandell chuckled at the yarn. "Seems like the last time I heard you tell about that elk, the leftovers went into the making of a ground-length sleeping robe and six pairs of leggings."

"Well, you know how it is inside an old man's head," Bridger grinned. "Mebbe sometimes I don't recollect so well as I used to. But I catch your point anyway. I guess that elk story's grown just a shade too tall over the years, ain't it?"

"A man could stand on it and top out a redwood tree," Mandell teased.

"Anyway, it's the Teton country for me," Bridger sighed, "an' you're welcome to come along if you're of a mind."

"I kind of have my sights set in another direction," Mandell told him, "though I'm grateful for the invitation. I've been in touch with John Bozeman's widow up north in Bozeman City. She asked me to come up and visit and she even said I could have a job there with her if I wanted it.''

"How's things worked out for her since her man got killed last year?''

"Well, she says things won't ever be quite the same without him," Mandell replied, "but she's letting her life go on just the same. From all I could ever tell about her, Kate's that type. She's got a shrewd head for business, too, and from all I've heard, she's made a pretty good go of the things she and John got started before he died.''

"Sounds like you could do a lot worse than to take her up on that job offer.''

"I might after a while, but right now I've got a feeling it'll take some time before I can get myself nailed down to any one place on a steady basis. I guess I'm in pretty much the same shape I was in when I first came west. I'm looking, but I haven't yet figured out what it is I'm looking for. There was only one time there for a while that I was sure what my life was all about. But that's part of the past now.''

"Well, my friend," Bridger said at last. "Wherever the search takes you, I hope it goes well.''

"You too, Jim. And watch out for those man-eating grizzlies.''

The two friends parted with a final handshake. Then Bridger turned his mount and headed back south along the trail. Mandell took a final moment to gaze down at the flames of the burning fort below. He recalled how troubled and dangerous his past two years there had been. He wouldn't be sorry to go, that was certain, and he doubted he would ever have the desire to return in later years. Like so much of his past, he was satisfied to let his time at Fort Kearny become a closed chapter.

*　　*　　*

John Bozeman

There were a few things Mandell was certain about, concerning the three men who were tracking him. They were Sioux, and they were good, and they had extra horses, making the task of eluding them next to impossible.

He had been aware of them on his back trail for the past half day, but he knew they had probably been back there much longer, perhaps ever since he'd ridden wide around the flaming remains of Fort Kearny and started north the night before last.

But their movements puzzled him. Why would three Indians devote this much time and effort to doggedly pursuing him when there was sure to be so much celebrating going on back in their base camps? There had to be more to their tracking him than the desire to hang another white man's scalp on a war belt. Perhaps they knew who he was and had some specific plans in mind for him when they took him prisoner. Mandell shivered. That thought carried chilling implications.

Mandell knew it would not be long before they did catch him. His horse was nearly exhausted from the strenuous pace he was setting for it, but the Indians kept changing theirs so that none of their animals ever got completely fatigued.

By late afternoon Mandell realized that he soon would have to stop and make a stand. He had only caught occasional glimpses of his pursuers over the past two hours, but knew they had closed the distance to less than a quarter of a mile.

As he paused on a knoll and took a moment to glance around once again, the sight that confronted him increased his worries considerably. Instead of the three Indians, there were only two behind him now, and neither one was leading an extra mount. Mandell immediately recognized

280

the old Indian tactic. In an appropriate situation, it was usually effective.

It was probable that the third Indian had struck out on his own, taking all three spare horses with him. He would ride the mount he was on at breakneck speed until it could run no more. Then he would quickly turn it loose and switch to the back of a fresh animal and repeat the process. Following that plan, one man could cover a tremendous amount of distance in a short length of time, and there was no doubt in Mandell's mind that if the third Indian was not already waiting in ambush, then he soon would be.

There were only two alternatives, Mandell decided. He could stop where he was and fight it out with the two Indians behind him, or he could alter his course and hope to avoid the ambush that awaited him somewhere up ahead. The condition of his horse made the second course practically impossible. He would stand and fight.

After disappearing beyond the far side of the knoll as if to ride on, he tied his horse in a secluded spot amidst some rocks. Then he withdrew his rifle from his boot and began cautiously working his way back to the crest of the knoll. What he was doing was the simplest of ruses and the Indians behind him would surely be on the lookout for just such a move, but Mandell knew it was the best plan he had open to him.

As the two riders drew nearer, Mandell stayed low. It would be foolish, he decided, to risk disclosing where he was by peering out even for an instant to mark their progress. He would rely on his ears and his memory of the terrain. They would help him determine the precise moment to make his play. At that proper time he would pop up, get off as many quick shots as he could and hope that he could kill them both.

He heard the sound of unshod hooves faint against the stony hillside. He tensed. Then he shifted his feet around more securely beneath him. He knew he would have only one chance and that the chance would be a brief one.

In his mind he hastily began to go over the area directly beyond the large stone he was hiding behind. The trail he had been following wound its way around some boulders. Then it opened into an area about twenty yards across before ascending to the crest of the knoll. It was necessary to wait until the Indians were in the midst of the open area. Then he would cut loose with his rifle.

The Indian horses left the area of the boulders and advanced into the open. The sounds of their hooves became louder and more clearly defined. Mandell held back. He would give them a count of five, and then . . .

"Ambush!"

The word was shouted in Sioux somewhere off to Mandell's left, but he did not have time to figure the exact direction. The only choice he had was to commit himself and hope he could still pull off his plan. Leaping to his feet, he snapped off four quick shots.

But the Sioux braves had reacted equally as fast to the warning they'd been issued. The lead rider of the pair cut his mount sharply to the left, intending to ride out of the line of fire as quickly as possible, and the other rider tumbled off behind his horse and made for the boulders. One of Mandell's snap shots had embedded itself in the neck of the lead rider's horse, but the other three had traveled wild and caused no damage to human flesh.

As quickly as he had fired, Mandell ducked down out of sight. What he wanted to do was cut off to the right and lose himself in the rocks on the side of the knoll.

But he heard a click no more than thirty feet behind

282

him and knew it had been made by the action of a rifle being worked. But cover was only a few feet away. He had to go for it.

At the same time that the rifle roared, a searing pain bit into his left side just below the shoulder blade. The impact of the shot threw him off balance. Instead of darting behind the large, jagged rock, Mandell slammed headfirst into it. As he fell, he tried instinctively to spin. He figured that way he might be able to bring his rifle around and put it to work. But waves of blackness were already overwhelming him. The rifle clattered to the ground. And though Mandell's mind told him that he must fight in order to survive, his body became sluggish and unresponsive. He was only minimally aware of what was going on as the three Indians approached him. But he realized the inevitability of death. It loomed over him like an ominous black cloud as snatches of conversation streaked through to his sinking consciousness.

As he'd expected, it was Blue Eagle who had shot him. But then, as the remaining portions of his consciousness drained slowly away, he thought no more.

The jolting of the travois did as much to bring Mandell around as anything else. Each time the horse that was pulling him bounced the poles of the travois across another stone or pit in the road, a tongue of fire raced through his left side. The mud that the Indians had caked over the entrance and exit holes of the wound was nearly dry, but he knew they probably had done nothing to prevent infection. He was surprised. Apparently, Blue Eagle and his braves didn't want him to die before they could get him back to camp.

During the two-day journey, he was given occasional

sips of water. But again there were no humanitarian motives connected with such a service. He was given merely enough to survive.

After a while, the pain of his wound began to make his mind sharp and clear. Nevertheless, he chose to remain with his eyes closed and his head lolling to one side when they came around to taunt him.

He could tell they were nearing the main Sioux camp because the braves stopped for a short time to prepare themselves for the grand entrance they wished to make with their prisoner. After vividly painting their faces with war paint, they carefully brushed the accumulated salt and trail dust from their animals. This moment would be a triumph in their lives—Mandell knew that—a major coup that would exalt them in the eyes of their tribe and provide them with storytelling material for years to come.

Once they had prepared themselves, the Indians started up again, but only a short distance away from the camp, Blue Eagle halted once more. The stop confused Mandell. Then, experiencing a flash of dread, he realized the purpose for the delay. No legendary foe of the Sioux Indians would be brought into camp enjoying the luxury of a travois.

Blue Eagle cut the ropes holding Mandell on the travois and rolled him off. Then he stretched Mandell's arms above his head, tied a rope around his wrists and remounted his horse.

Mandell listened to Blue Eagle's savage whoop and felt him goad his horse into a run. If he was lucky, being dragged into camp would kill him before the Indians had their chance to murder him more methodically. But the long meadow Blue Eagle dragged him across was thickly carpeted with summer grass, so the last portion of the trip

284

into camp was only painful, not deadly. Mandell struggled to make most of the trip on his back. He wanted the worst of the abuse to be absorbed by his thick buckskin shirt and trousers, but he was unsuccessful. When the Indians stopped at last, his clothes were in tatters and the flesh beneath them was raw and bleeding.

Mandell could scarcely open his eyes or catch his breath, his face was so coated with dust and grime. But he sensed that a great number of Indians were gathering to stare at the gruesome trophy he'd become.

"Here is the treacherous White Wolf. You ordered us to catch him and return him for punishment." Blue Eagle puffed his chest out proudly as he made the announcement.

"You have done well," Mandell heard Red Cloud say, "and you deserve the praise of all the people for accomplishing your mission. From this day forward when the Sioux sit around their fires recalling the great deeds of their most famous warriors, your coup will be remembered. And now you will prepare the white man for his fate."

Blue Eagle issued a shrill cry. Prodding his horse once more, he dragged Mandell to a large open area near the center of the camp. Behind them, hundreds of Indians followed along, shouting encouragement to their hero of the day, as well as derisions to the white-faced enemy.

Eventually Mandell felt the bindings around his wrists. Then almost immediately he was dragged over and tied to a pole that was sunk in the ground in the center of the clearing.

Almost at once the spectators fell silent. Red Cloud was advancing across the clearing. Mandell struggled to open his eyes and saw him. Everyone else was watching their chief closely. Mandell thought they might be wondering, as he was, whether Red Cloud planned to commit the first act of torture himself. In a moment the chief was standing directly in front of him and Mandell found himself staring directly into the familiar depthless brown eyes.

When the chief spoke at last, his words were so faint that only Mandell could hear them, and to him it sounded as if a trace of regret lurked beneath Red Cloud's bitterness.

"When you were among us," the chief began without emotion, "you earned our respect and love for the great courage and loyalty which you showed. We took you in as one of us. In council I myself argued for your life when the Blackfoot and others wished to take it. But you paid back the Sioux with treachery. Now the hate we feel for you is stronger than our love had ever been. Once among your own, you became a scheming, white-eyed dog and you fought to take our lands from us, as all the rest have."

There would be no use, Mandell knew, in trying to explain himself. Besides, he had neither the strength nor the will to argue. The Sioux had fought bravely and this time theirs was the victory. Perhaps, Mandell conceded reluctantly, they deserved the privilege of destroying him. From their perspective, he was a traitor, and any hasty defense would sound simply like the whimperings of a condemned man.

"But I hate you most," Red Cloud went on, "for what your treachery has done to Eyes Like The She Wolf."

At the mention of his wife's name, Mandell for the first time tried to speak. But his throat was so dry and caked with dirt that the effort was beyond him.

"Because of her refusal to denounce you, she has become a scorned outcast among us. As her uncle, I begged her to declare that you were dead and to take another man as her husband and father to her children. But

286

she would not. So I, too, was forced to turn my face from her. In a time of war I could do no differently.''

"Is she . . . is she all right?" Mandell managed to ask.

"She has been stripped of all her possessions and she feeds her children on camp scraps and what she herself can kill or catch. Only her pride and the knowledge that she has nowhere to go keeps her with us. But to our people she is lower than a camp dog.''

Hearing the chief's words was more painful to Mandell than any physical suffering Blue Eagle and the others could have inflicted on him. And he was surprised. He had no idea that Eyes Like The She Wolf's love for him was so deep and would last so long.

Mandell frowned. He was puzzled. The respect of his wife's people had always been so important to her. At least when he was dead, Mandell thought begrudgingly, the people of the tribe probably would accept Eyes Like The She Wolf once again.

When he had said all he wanted to say, Red Cloud turned his back on Mandell. "Let it begin!" he proclaimed to the onlookers.

Blue Eagle stepped out from the crowd just as Red Cloud moved to take his place with those eager to witness the execution. "Great Chief Red Cloud," he boomed respectfully, "because I am the brave who hunted down this dog and returned him here, I would claim his scalp for my war belt.''

"And what of the brothers who went with you?" Red Cloud asked.

"They fought bravely and deserve the white dog's weapons and horse. But it was my bullet that brought him down.''

"Then claim your prize," the chief announced, moving away once more.

Mandell knew it was not uncommon for an Indian to scalp a prisoner before he was dead. During the recent warfare, the Sioux and Cheyenne had occasionally scalped a man and left him alive as a reminder of their savage power. In his own case, Mandell decided, it didn't matter much. If the Indians had made any mistake in deciding what to do with him, it was that they had already abused him far too much. He wouldn't last long once they went to work on him.

Blue Eagle advanced and drew his knife. But as he came closer, Mandell noticed a blur of movement to one side. A woman rushed between him and Blue Eagle.

"Get out of here, you stupid bitch," Blue Eagle snarled. "By trying to stop all this, you can only bring more shame on yourself."

"I know I can't stop you," the woman snapped back defiantly. "But I can make you kill me first!"

Even though he had not been close to her in two years, the voice of Eyes Like The She Wolf was as familiar to Mandell as if they had talked only the day before. He fought his eyes open, desperate to catch at least a glimpse of his wife before he died. But her back was to him as she faced Blue Eagle. Mandell couldn't be certain, but he thought she was brandishing a weapon and holding Blue Eagle at bay. Then he remembered the narrow, sharpened knife she often carried strapped to her lower calf.

"This is tribal business. It is no concern of yours," Blue Eagle proclaimed. "Besides, you are scarcely one of us any longer."

Mandell realized that despite Blue Eagle's words, the Indian was hesitant to advance on Eyes Like The She

Wolf. Obviously he had expected this moment to be a triumphant one. After all, he'd intended to slice Mandell's scalp free and brandish it in the air for all to see. Killing a young woman first would mar his glory.

"What you do here *is* my concern," Eyes Like The She Wolf contradicted. "This man is my husband. He is the father of my two children. You must either kill me or let me claim him as *my* prize."

Seeing the determination in the Indian woman's eyes, Blue Eagle glanced uncertainly at Red Cloud. Oddly, the chief made no move to interfere.

"Are you suggesting that we let this man live?" Blue Eagle demanded incredulously.

"Why not?" Eyes Like The She Wolf responded. "I have paid for his life with two years of suffering and abuse. And my children have paid, too, each time they cried out in hunger and no one spared them a scrap of meat to ease the gnawing in their bellies. As you say, I am no longer one with the people of my birth. But this man and I are one, and whether we both live or die, we will remain that way from this day on."

"Then you have chosen your fate!" Blue Eagle spat threateningly. As he raised his knife to strike, Eyes Like The She Wolf refused to defend herself. Instead, she lowered her hand and held her dagger to her side.

For a long moment Blue Eagle hesitated. Then his hand began to descend. But instead of plunging his blade into the breast of the defiant young woman who stood before him, he hurled his knife to the ground.

The spectators gaped in stunned silence as he stomped angrily away. Next, with steady hands, Eyes Like The She Wolf slit the ropes that bound Mandell to the post. For a moment she looked at him gently. Then tenderly she placed his arm around her shoulder to support him as they moved away.

A path parted in the circle of onlookers as they passed. Mandell blinked. And in a blur of joyous tears, he saw two young children waiting expectantly beside the horse and travois that had brought him there to die.

Seventh Powerful Novel in

THE AMERICAN EXPLORERS
Zebulon Pike

PIONEER DESTINY

by Richard Woodley

It was a trail that led ever westward, into the trackless wasteland of the Louisiana Territory. Zebulon Pike began his journey as a young man, yearning for fame and glory, too idealistic to understand the motives of his superior, General Wilkinson. Not even Clarissa Pike could convince Zebulon to turn down the challenge of a courageous mission. Dangers stalk the trail as Pike discovers a traitor among his ranks . . . a battalion of Spanish sharpshooters . . . and a Mexican general who owes a debt of gratitude to General Wilkinson and a man named Aaron Burr. Only the sensuous Juanita Alvarez can tell him the bitter truth—that he has been betrayed by those he trusted most. . . .

Please send me _____ copies of book #7 in the *AMERICAN EXPLORERS* series, *Zebulon Pike: PIONEER DESTINY*. I am enclosing $3.45 per copy (includes 50¢ postage and handling).

Please send check or money order (no cash or C.O.D.s).

Name _____
(Please Print)

Address _____ Apt._____

City _____

State_____ Zip_____

Please allow 6-8 weeks for delivery.
PA residents add 6% sales tax.
Send this coupon to:
BANBURY BOOKS, INC.
37 West Avenue, Suite 201, Wayne, PA 19087

THE SAGA OF A PROUD AND PASSIONATE PEOPLE—THEIR STRIVING FOR FREEDOM—THEIR TRIUMPHANT JOURNEY

THE JEWS

by Sharon Steeber

Fleeing from the Russian pogroms, Zavel and Marya Luminov came to a new land, America, not knowing or understanding the test that awaited them. Through hard times and bitter struggles, they planted the seeds of a family fortune. As the abandoned years of the Roaring Twenties gave way to the darkness of the Depression, Zavel, Marya and their children would learn the heartbreak of bitterness and loss as they clung to their hopes, their dreams and their unbreakable loyalties. THE JEWS is the towering novel of their achievements and heritage . . . and of the nation they helped to build with their pride.

Please send me _____ copies of *THE JEWS* by Sharon Steeber. I am enclosing $4.50 per copy (includes 55¢ postage and handling)

Please send check or money order (no cash or C.O.D.s).

Name _____
(Please Print)

Address _____ Apt._____

City _____

State _____ Zip _____

Please allow 6-8 weeks for delivery.
PA residents add 6% sales tax.
Send this coupon to:
BANBURY BOOKS, INC.
37 West Avenue, Suite 201, Wayne, PA 19087

FIRST IN *THE JAZZ AGE* series . . .

NO FUTURE, NO MEMORY
by
Richard O'Brien

**THE SAGA OF A NEW GENERATION, TOUGHENED BY WAR,
GREEDY FOR LOVE AND WEALTH . . .
AND HUNGRY FOR PLEASURE**

In the first, gripping novel of *THE JAZZ AGE* series, Richard O'Brien traces the rising fortunes of John Crain as he returns from the war and begins to search for a new life. His passionate affair with Nadine Berns, his rebellion against the family that would use its fortune to control his life . . . and his final, violent confrontation with the New York underworld . . . all are portrayed in a stirring novel that vividly re-creates the beginning of the Roaring Twenties.

■■■■■■■■■■■■■■■■■■■■■■■■■■■■■■■■■■■

Please send me _____ copies of the first book in *THE JAZZ AGE* series, *No Future, No Memory*. I am enclosing $3.75 per copy (includes 50¢ postage and handling).

Please send check or money order (no cash or C.O.D.s).

Name _____
(Please Print)

Address _____ Apt._____

City _____

State _____ Zip_____

Please allow 6-8 weeks for delivery.
PA residents add 6% sales tax.
Send this coupon to:
BANBURY BOOKS, INC.
37 West Avenue, Suite 201, Wayne, PA 19087

BOOK #3 IN *THE JAZZ AGE* series . . . .

Ballyhoo Years

by
Richard O'Brien

***MEN AND WOMEN MADE HEADLINES—
AND A CUB REPORTER CHALLENGED THEIR POWER . . .***

Joe Flaxton was the chosen man in Hearst's vast empire, a reporter with a reputation for dogging the truth and getting a jump on ballyhoo. But then a hot tip led him to the heart of the Teapot Dome Scandal . . . and to the door of a man named John Crain. As the headlines flashed across the nation—telling the story of the greatest scandal in government history—Joe Flaxton found himself playing a dangerous game, with one beautiful woman on his side. He would have sacrificed everything for her—even his career—but the pull of ballyhoo was strong. And when the moment came, Joe Flaxton would give up the woman he loved for a once-in-a-lifetime story. . . .

■■■■■■■■■■■■■■■■■■■■■■■■■■■■■■■■■■■■■■■

Please send me _____ copies of the third book in *THE JAZZ AGE* series, *Ballyhoo Years*. I am enclosing $3.75 per copy (includes 50¢ postage and handling).

Please send check or money order (no cash or C.O.D.s).

Name _____
(Please Print)

Address _____ Apt._____

City _____

State _____ Zip_____

Please allow 6-8 weeks for delivery.
PA residents add 6% sales tax.
Send this coupon to:
BANBURY BOOKS, INC.
37 West Avenue, Suite 201, Wayne, PA 19087